# The Perfect Kiss

Karen Tucci

True Heart Romance

This book is dedicated to my son, Dominic.

The funny quotes, fixations, struggles, and love of video games, Legos, and stuffies (stuffed animals) are 100% real. You make life adventurous. I love you. Your kindness and compassion is what everyone should strive for. Never lose your heart!


Love,

Mom

# Contents

# *Karen's Other Books:*

**Stand Alone Books:**

<u>When the Dust Settles: A Sweet Romance with a Navy SEAL</u>

**G & G Security Series (Coming 2025)**

(The characters from When the Dust Settles cross-over in this series)

Operation: Heal my SEAL Book 1

Operation: Find my SEAL Book 2

Operation: Keep my SEAL Book 3

Operation: Train my SEAL  Book 4

**Second Chance Series:**

KAREN TUCCI

<u>Starting Over</u>

<u>Moving On</u>


**Big L' Ranch Series**

<u>The Perfect Kiss: Book 1</u>

<u>The Perfect: Cowboy Book 2</u>

<u>The Perfect Match Book 3</u>

<u>The Perfect Christmas (Holiday Novella)</u>

<u>The Perfect Sheriff Book 5</u>


**Best Friends Series**

<u>Let Me Carry You</u>

<u>Let Me Marry You</u>


**YA Cumberland Christian Prep School Series**

The Big Score (Coming 2025)

# *Prologue*

In the dead of night, darkness loomed over Big L' Ranch. Outside, the temperature dropped to a frigid negative of ten degrees! The bare branches slapped the ground and whipped back into place, rebelling against the forceful movement. Inches of snow had assaulted the ground over the last three hours.

Despite being a hard-working, assertive, thirty-five-year-old woman, Amelia Lawrence dreaded storms. *Dad, I miss you. I can't do this without you.* Fortunately for Amelia, Jeff, the resident ranch butcher and her dad's best friend, had taken over her dad's role of protector for the last two months. He and his wife, Kathleen, stayed in a guest room at the main house this evening, anticipating Amelia's anguish with the storm.

Amelia had learned to keep herself busy to prevent panic attacks that broke through her tough walls whenever faced with a storm. Preparing for the worst, she spent her time in the barn checking on the animals. "Hi, Duncan," Amelia called out when she entered. He snorted and blew air at her. "I love you too." She sidled up to her horse's mane and rested her head while running her hand down her neck. "You doing okay, boy?"

Talking to Duncan had helped her navigate life. She had assisted her dad with Duncan's delivery on her fifteenth birthday and claimed him for herself. Fortunately, her dad had agreed. Duncan has been her best friend ever since. Amelia had lost so many loved ones; she couldn't imagine losing Duncan, too. Horses, like humans, don't last forever, though. She'd be lucky if Duncan made it another ten years. "I've got to keep moving, Boy. See you tomorrow."

Just as she finished checking on the livestock, the lights flickered. Amelia froze in fear. She hated storms. At five years old, she had witnessed a lightning bolt strike a tree in half, landing one side five inches in the ground.

Thud!

The other half had gone through her aunt and uncle's cabin on the property, killing Amelia's aunt, Sara, instantly. Since then, no matter the storm, Amelia's body constantly trembled, and her mind drifted to another place, hoping to forget about the situation causing her distress. Her dad had always compared her to the little girl in the movie *My Girl,* who would plug her ears, squeeze her eyes shut, and sing as loud as she could when panicked. Amelia needed the same thing the little girl from the movie needed—someone to shake her out of it and give her instructions to occupy her debilitating fears and thoughts.

A weather alert blared on her phone, causing her to jump. *Great, more power outages.* Leaving the barn, she caught a glimpse of the powerlines that ran from the street to the side of the main house . . . her house, now that her dad had died. They were crying under the weight of the heavy snow. *Please keep our power on, Lord. You already know this is hard for me; don't make it more challenging.* Thankfully, everyone on the property worked hard and got along for the most part.

Yesterday, many hands prepared for this storm. If the power did go out, the logical side of Amelia knew everything would be okay because they were ready—she had filled the tubs with water to flush the toilets, replenished the batteries in the flashlights, made sure the generator they used for the butcher shop and general store fired up and filled the gas cans to the brim. She was ready. Despite her preparedness, calm and rational were not Amelia's allies.

Entering through the living room, Amelia glued herself to the television. The news anchor reported that over forty thousand people had lost power and crew workers would not be dispatched until the storm ended. Fear washed over Amelia's face—that was almost the entire population of North Central Montana. Thank God she still had power, but for how long? *Help me, please. I cannot fail—this is my family's business.* Amelia wasn't ready to face her first winter storm as the sole owner of Big L' Ranch. Amelia wondered if the foreman, scheduled for an interview tomorrow, would make it through the storm. *One step at a time, Amelia. Get through tonight first.*

A loud bang outside the closest window penetrated her ears. The fierce wind howled outside the window. Sleet pelleted the window panes. A moderate amount of snow had fallen before the sleet began. Amelia leaned back against the back of the couch, pulled her legs to her chest, squeezed her eyes shut, and covered her ears. She didn't sing, but she rocked back and forth.

Her dad had always been the person to pull her back into reality. Not anymore. Sadly, two months ago, a tragic accident ripped him from his ranch. His life. And, most importantly, from her. Using a tractor on a ranch in the winter was always dangerous, but Jack Lawrence had done it for over twenty years. When he couldn't stop the tractor, and it rolled, everyone knew it was a freak accident given his expertise, but that hadn't eased the pain . . . at all.

Jeff grabbed her shoulders and gently shook her, "Amelia!" He pulled her hands away from her ears. "Amelia, you are okay!" Jeff dropped her wrists and hugged her tight. "C'mon, let's go see Katherine." Jeff pulled Amelia to her feet and walked her into the kitchen.

"What do we have here?" Katherine set her coffee cup on the hardwood kitchen table that Amelia's grandpa had handmade years ago. Amelia had helped her dad refinish it when she was five. After that first task with her dad, Amelia worked by his side and learned everything she could from him until his death.

Amelia pulled out one of the matching handmade chairs and rested her face in her hands. Amelia sighed, "Sorry. Listening to the news anchor made me panic about the storm."

"Well, there's your problem, Dear. The news will give any ol' person a panic attack; someone with your history shouldn't watch those buffoons!" Katherine rubbed Amelia's shoulder to show support.

"Thanks, Katy," Amelia roared, swiping the back of her hand over the tears straggling on her cheeks. Just about everyone on the ranch called her Katy.

The lights flickered again. Then . . .

Blackness filled the room.

Fear shook Amelia's body so violently that her teeth chattered. Arms wrapped around her shoulders. "It's okay, Amelia, everything will be fine," Katy assured her. Amelia didn't feel okay. She hadn't felt okay in a long time.

Within moments, the lights flickered twice. Everyone held their breath briefly, hoping the power would stay on for good. The bright lights helped ease some of Amelia's worry.

To control her anxiety, Amelia offered her help to Cash and Carolyn, the ranch's chefs. They were preparing the following day's dinner. Losing some sleep now would be worth it if they lost the power for good later. At least they would be able to feed everyone tomorrow. "What can I do to help you finish and get some shut-eye?" Amelia sidled between them.

Carolyn handed Amelia a bag of potatoes to start peeling. The chefs had already prepared six pounds of beef jerky, a fruit bowl, tossed salad, and two shepherd's pies in cast iron dishes. With Amelia's help, they'd get a third prepared quickly. They could use the snow outside to keep their food cold if necessary. They could bake the pies on the grill if they lost their power again, disrupting tomorrow's schedule. Amelia could avoid the need to prepare by getting another generator for the main house. That would make it easier for everyone involved, but she hadn't thought of it until right now.

Though Amelia couldn't forget about the brewing storm that shut down the power for most people in her area, she was grateful for her family. She had few blood relatives left, but no doubt about it, the people on this ranch had always been and always would be her family. "Cash, please remember you have two more mouths to feed tomorrow as long as the storm does not delay the potential foreman."

Cash tilted his head as he turned toward Amelia, "Two more? I thought you just had one interview for tomorrow."

"True story, but he has a son coming with him." Amelia explained further, "I checked with the owner from the man's last placement in Texas. He assured me that Quinton will make the best foreman I could ask for..." Amelia's words dropped off.

"What's the problem then?" Carolyn wondered as they continued to peel potatoes.

Amelia lifted her shoulders and held them there briefly before dropping them back down. "The owner mentioned some trouble on the ranch between Quinton and the other ranchers related to Quinton's son. He didn't want to share too much of the man's story, but I wonder how forthcoming this man would be if he'd made such a drastic location change. I don't want to ruin our family dynamic on the ranch."

Jeff sat in a chair beside his wife, wrapped his hand over her knuckles, and gently squeezed them. "Family is important, and you're a smart woman, Amelia. You'll know if this fella will fit here or not."

"Thanks for always encouraging me and being supportive, Jeff." Amelia turned to face him, and her entire face lit up brighter than the room a few minutes ago when the power returned. "I just wish Dad were here. He always did the right thing."

"Did you ever ask your mom that? I don't know if she would agree," Jeff chuckled.

Jeff and Katy were friends with Amelia's parents growing up. Given that it made sense when he'd become Amelia's surrogate uncle after her blood Uncle, Sean, had lost his wife in the storm thirty years ago that still paralyzed Amelia.

"Katy, do you remember when Jack thought it would be fine to take out a loan to expand the business without asking Marilyn first?"

She let out a quick breath and laughed. "Do I ever. He certainly didn't do the right thing that time." Addressing Amelia, she added, "Your mom made him drive to the bank to talk with the loan officer. She almost made him cancel the loan. Your dad had never made the mistake of leaving her out of business decisions again."

Jeff reminded Amelia of other troubles her parents had faced—a possible foreclosure during Amelia's upper elementary years. They'd also endured and recovered from the Whittakers spewing slander all over town in an attempt to force Amelia's family out of town.

Amelia smiled. "The last thing I want to do is ruin my dad's legacy." Amelia declared.

"Not possible. You've worked this ranch with your dad since you were a toddler." Jeff assured her. "He molded you to be the owner. You can push through the tough times."

At present, Amelia's insecurity seemed to be the only problem. Maybe she didn't need a foreman. She had been doing the job since her dad died and could continue.

Every generation, each heir had built upon what his ancestors had before him. Before he'd died, Jack had established partnerships with other ranchers to bring in a significant income. He'd also developed a working family group who looked out for each other — Big L' Ranch had become one unit. The employees and their families all lived on the property.

Upon her dad's death, Amelia had become the first female heir in charge of keeping the business as her dad had left it and improving it. She needed to stay calm and focused to expand the ranch. Would taking on another employee change their bottom line? Even though her dad had expanded the business into an eight-figure enterprise, he'd always warned her that it could be gone in a flash due to a lousy season or poor leadership. When thinking rationally, she had known that bringing on another employee wouldn't change their financial status. In fact, it would help Amelia build on what her dad had left behind.

"Think about how persistent you were with your dad about teaching you how to do every single chore and day-to-day operation on the ranch," Jeff gently reminded her. "You now have the opportunity to make your parents proud by extending the business and handing it down to your children one day because you can run this ranch with your eyes closed. You're lucky you have great people who work for you, so you don't have to run it alone."

Just like everything else in Amelia's life, she doubted her worth to operate or expand her father's business — now her business. Amelia knew she'd never have kids to pass the ranch onto, but maybe this new foreman would help her make the business even more successful, and she could leave it to her cousin, whom he had always considered a brother. If not, perhaps Amelia should avoid the headache and stress and hand over the business now before she ruins it like she had the rest of her life.

# Chapter 1

**Amelia**

While the moon still dimly shone through her window, Amelia stumbled out of bed. Despite only having four hours of sleep, she felt honored that Cash and Carolyn let her help them prepare meals last night. She loved them, and they were her family despite lacking similar DNA.

For the better part of fifteen years, the powerhouse couple fed everyone who showed up at the main house. When they'd first arrived looking for a job, Amelia's dad, Jack, had challenged their young age and ability to feed a ranch of this size three times a day. Not all the families had eaten all three meals together, but they could have. Jack had believed in treating everyone who worked on his ranch like family. He'd given them a trial run for one week, and before the trial ended, Amelia remembered her dad telling her that he couldn't let them leave.

Even without any formal training they'd won over everyone with their warm hearts, tender love, and delicious food. Once they'd worked for Big L' Ranch for a year, Cash had spent six months at culinary school learning fundamentals and culinary techniques to improve his cooking skills. Carolyn had risen to the challenge and single-handedly had kept everyone well-fed. Amelia and her mom, of course, had helped out, but the majority of the responsibility had fallen on Carolyn. Later on, she received formal culinary training, too, making Carolyn and Cash's work together a true art form. The entire time Carolyn had been away, the men had joked with Cash that his wife had handled herself better under pressure than he had. The camaraderie truly made Big L' Ranch — a big, loving family — just the way her dad's family had expected when they started the ranch in 1860.

It wasn't long after Amelia's mom had been diagnosed with cancer that she'd died in her home, just the way she'd wanted. Carolyn had let the grief-stricken Amelia, then a teenager, help her in the kitchen whenever she'd wanted to keep Amelia's anxiety at bay...most of the time. Amelia had learned early on if she'd kept herself busy, she could control her anxiety. Her parents and Raddix had always told her she needed to talk about her problems, and that had helped her anxiety more effectively. Amelia, however, chose, more often than not, to bury her feelings and keep on going.

Nothing had changed. Instead of dealing with her dad's loss, she'd suppressed her grief and focused on the business. After he'd died, Amelia had vowed to do her best, even if it had meant placing unrealistic expectations on herself. Amelia had worked seventeen and eighteen-hour days for the last two months, pushing her to near exhaustion. As tired as she was, Amelia knew what type of person it would take to lead this ranch. She sure hoped Quinton, from Texas, was up for the challenge. In addition to the physical workload, he'd have to love and respect everyone here as if they were his family. Her dad had shown her that was the best way to keep this business prospering. Currently, Amelia has five families working full-time and many seasonal ranch hands. After today, there would be six if Quinton struck her as the type of person who would fit in her already well-established family.

She'd received a voicemail from Quinton last night confirming the interview. Her first thought had surprised her—*I wonder if he's as handsome as his voice.* Amelia chastised herself to stay focused on the goal — securing the right foreman so she could build on her dad's legacy. She knew that even if he were handsome, Quinton wouldn't be interested in her—no man had ever been...for real. *Lord, please give me the wisdom necessary to make the hard decisions.* Amelia wondered if the storm would prevent Quinton from making his interview. Without a doubt, she wouldn't hold that against him, but she would have to move her schedule around.

Amelia knew that Mother Nature was a beast sometimes, and even the best superheroes couldn't compete, so how could a cowboy from Texas push his way through? Even though last night's storm hadn't lingered for the Lawrence family, and the roads seemed passable, she would give him grace if he was late. She wouldn't even hold it against him if he called and said he'd already turned around because he couldn't handle the northern weather.

She threw her phone on her bed and sighed. Amelia observed her dad during interviews. He'd never acted like a powerful ranch owner. He spoke to the men respectfully, allowing them to open up and tell their stories. Her dad never had a preset list of questions to ask—he let his "gut" do the talking. Amelia prayed for her dad's innate skill.

After conducting the morning meeting with the cowboys and ranch hands, Amelia would exercise, so she pulled on a pair of leggings and a dry-fit shirt. She always wore functional clothing. Trying to dress up had seemed like an occupational hazard. Amelia had never painted her nails or done anything fancy to her hair—she sported either a French braid or a ponytail. Her clothing, since she could remember, had consisted of jeans, a t-shirt, and an oversized flannel shirt. Perhaps this was another reason why men had never been interested in her. Amelia hadn't known, and until now, she hadn't really cared...well, since high school, anyway.

When Amelia entered the kitchen, Cash and Carolyn had a breakfast spread of bagels, fruit, scrambled eggs, milk, and orange juice, ready for the typical daily meeting, Amelia held with her crew.

"Good Morning." Amelia greeted the couple. "Thank you so much for breakfast."

"Of course." They responded in unison without missing a beat.

Amelia put eggs and fruit on her plate while she waited for the employees to arrive. She stayed away from bread and anything junky so that she could save room for her one weakness—ice cream. No one from this family, other than Amelia, would say a derogatory word about her for any reason, including her looks. She'd always argued that it was only because they were family.

During high school, her peers had belittled her enough for a lifetime. The worst one of all had been none other than Selena Whittaker, the vivacious blonde at the Whittaker Ranch. She'd spent her time in high school telling everyone what to do as class president. Everyone, except for her and her handful of insecure friends, had known she'd only won the popular vote...nothing more. Selena had always looked immaculate with painted fingernails and matching toenails, even in the winter. Sheesh. Amelia wondered to this day if Selena even knew the difference between a saddle and a bridle. The entire town had talked about how the prissy woman hadn't ever done any ranch work. No one had ever said that to her face, though. If they had, she'd try to have her influential family cancel the culprit, just like Selena had tried to wipe out Amelia in high school.

Against Selena's petite frame, Amelia still towered more than a foot over the girl. In fact, she'd towered over most of the girls and some of the boys in high school. By the end of her senior year, she reached five feet ten and a half inches. She'd always tried to get the doctor to keep the half-inch off, but, in retrospect, that had been silly. What did a half-inch matter in the scheme of things?

Selena had broken Amelia's spirit during high school, and despite any success that Amelia had achieved in adulthood, she never recovered emotionally. Selena had bullied Amelia excessively with taunts that she would never have a boyfriend tall enough or strong enough to do the fun things with her, like pick her up and swing her around in a full embrace before giving her a beautifully tender kiss. Selena had never called Amelia fat, probably because she never had been, but that hadn't stopped Amelia from making self-deprecating comments about her weighing too much. Selena had repeatedly taped Amazon Girl, Beanstalk, and Great Dane to her lower back or locker during their academia together. The bully had always pointed out that Amelia's shoulders were rock hard, her arm muscles bigger than most of the boys in the school. Selena had made her opinion known—Amelia Lawrence was too *big* for a man to love.

Amelia didn't know why all these self-deprecating thoughts had cropped up this morning, but they had. She emptied her remaining food in the trash just as her employees arrived for the meeting. And true to form, Amelia pushed the memories deep down somewhere within and greeted her last two blood relatives with the biggest *fake* smile. "Hi, Uncle Sean. Hi, Raddix. How's our livestock today?"

"I'm Doing great. We'll have a heap load of calves before you know it," Sean said dryly. He'd lost his cheerful personality when Aunt Sara had died. Amelia was grateful that she had her uncle on the property. She would be lost without him, especially now that her dad was gone.

Thirty years ago, when his wife had died in the thunderstorm, he'd wanted to move away. Amelia's dad hadn't wanted to operate the ranch without his brother, so he'd convinced Sean to tear down the remains of his and Sara's cabin and rebuild on another spot on the property. Fortunately, Sean had obliged. He'd spiraled into a deep, dark depression for eighteen months following that storm. Without family around him and his son, Raddix, Amelia had always wondered what would have become of them.

Selfishly, Amelia was grateful that she'd grown up with Raddix. While Amelia had talked to Duncan in the confines of her family's barn, treating her horse like a therapist, Raddix had stood up for her against anyone and everyone throughout high school. Without him protecting her and comforting her, dealing with the bullying would have been even harder.

"What's your plan for the day?" Amelia inquired.

"Dad's going into town to get more protein supplements. I will use the tractor to bring over hay to feed them." Raddix stated.

Amelia stared at her cousin. "You're not using that tractor." Her direct tone was one of worry and concern, not bossiness.

The thought of losing Raddix —her cousin, best friend, and protector— the same way she had lost her dad ripped through her heart like a chainsaw.

Raddix filled his plate with fruit, eggs, and biscuits and sat beside his dad. "I'll be careful. Dad fixed the tractor, so it's good to go."

After her dad died, they planned on getting rid of the tractor and getting a new one. Amelia couldn't handle having the monster responsible for her dad's death still on the property. "You were supposed to get rid of it, Uncle Sean."

"Didn't seem logical. Tractors are expensive. Your dad wouldn't want you to spend money on things that weren't a necessity." Sean's monotone voice revealed his years of pain. Even though Amelia knew he was right, a brief thought to override him and sell it herself came to light, but she wouldn't. Amelia trusted her uncle just as much as she'd trusted her dad and Raddix. There wasn't another man alive that she could ever trust since she'd been humiliated in high school by any boy interested in Selena, which had been all of them, or at least it had felt like it.

"You're right. Thanks for helping me avoid a bad business decision." Amelia smiled at him as she brought her empty plate to the sink. "I want to know when you get on that thing and when you're done, no exceptions."

Raddix grinned. "I promise." He held up three fingers as if he were in the Boy Scouts.

Amelia handed over a winter chore sheet for Raddix to hang on the bulletin board in the livestock barn. Raddix read it over. "Clean the pens, straighten the gates, level the dirt..." his voice cut off. "What are cut fence stays?"

"They're new supports for the barbed wire fencing. They increase the strength and rigidity of the fence while cutting our post-installation down by a third, saving us money," Amelia explained. " The salesman showed me how to install them. I can come show you how when you're ready," she offered.

The business side of the ranch had always intrigued Amelia. She said a quick prayer that Quinton would be the foreman to relieve her of that responsibility, letting her focus on what she considered the fun stuff.

Katy hollered from the enclosed porch as she slipped off her boots. "Good Morning." She entered the kitchen quickly. "Jeff will be in for some breakfast soon. He's finishing up an order of beef for the Whittaker's. Selena will stop in today or tomorrow to pick it up." Based on the partnership Amelia's dad had created with Selena's dad long ago, the Big L' Ranch traded Jeff's butchering services for an unlimited supply of fresh eggs from the Whittaker's.

"Katy, are you able to deal with Selena? I have that interview later, and frankly, I don't want to deal with her today," *or any day for that matter.* Amelia almost grumbled in her out loud voice.

"Of course, I will," Katy agreed. "Hopefully, she will come tomorrow. We need to keep Selena away from the potential employee." She started fixing a breakfast plate for herself. "If she gets wind of *new meat* within a hundred-mile radius, she'll find a way to make herself known."

Amelia sighed. "All of us should pray for this poor man. If he stays and Selena is interested, he'll probably fall for her beauty. If he's smart, though, it won't take him long to realize she's a vixen."

Raddix tsked in agreement. Unfortunately, he knew all too well that Selena Whittaker was a cold, calculating person who always got what she wanted...always. In high school, Raddix had grown instant popularity as a freshman when he'd become the lead running back for the Varsity Football team. For months, she'd deceived Raddix, telling him she loved him. Once the football season ended, her true colors showed. She had been using him to get to the quarterback. Raddix and he developed a bond, but the quarterback refused to talk to Selena even after her shenanigans.

It's funny how Selena had always deemed Amelia unworthy of a man marrying her because of her strength and height. What was her excuse? Apparently, men don't like beautiful, petite, unmarried women either—Ha! Perhaps it had nothing to do with her looks and more to do with the venom that ran through her veins, threatening to pierce her victims' flesh, leading to their ultimate demise.

"Great," Amelia addressed everyone in the room. "Once she gets her claws into him, she'll break his heart, and he'll leave. Then, I will have to hire another foreman."

Katy tossed her hand in the air, dismissing the negative thought.

"I'm going to exercise downstairs," Amelia strode out of the kitchen. It bothered Amelia that her thoughts were instantly negative whenever Selena's name was mentioned. Typically, Amelia had a positive attitude, at least when she wasn't thinking about herself, and wanted to share the light today.

Amelia's dad had custom-built this home gym at her request. Once she'd started focusing on feeling good about herself, she hadn't let the past bother her... regularly. At this point in her life, she'd accepted her destiny to be alone, working on the ranch. Some might say it sounds sad, but Amelia didn't mind. At least she hadn't, but today was one of those days. Once she released some endorphins, her mood would change drastically. She would embrace and appreciate the strong, toned shoulders she had acquired from dumbbell exercises, planks, and her work on the ranch. Lifting hay bales from forty to seventy pounds had built her muscles quickly.

Amelia warmed up on the treadmill. The proverbial, ominous cloud hovered over her head. With her dad gone, she had a crater-sized hole in her heart. She recalled how annoyed she'd gotten with her dad just before his passing. Her mind drifted back to all their late-night conversations. All too often, she'd heard her dad explaining the importance of Amelia finding a spouse. "It gets lonely operating the ranch alone," she remembered him saying. She could do it, though. Amelia had lived this long without a man; she certainly didn't need one now. Or did she? It would be nice if she found a cowboy to handle the ranch's physical aspects while maintaining the business side of things.

Had Amelia taken her dad more seriously years ago, she might have actively sought out an eligible bachelor . . . who would have ended up making a fool of her again — no thanks. By looking at Jeff, her dad, and Uncle Sean, she knew there were genuine men out there with integrity. Sadly, after years of not finding a decent man, unrelated, or already married, she'd given up the idea of her happily ever after. In fact, she convinced herself that honorable, noble men didn't exist—at least not around here.

Amelia increased her speed on the treadmill. A strong feeling washed over her — for the first time — maybe she should entertain the idea of getting married someday. That, of course, would require Amelia to venture off the ranch to find her future husband. That didn't appeal to her at all. She liked the safety of her ranch. Maybe if Quinton worked out, she would take the time to entertain the idea. *Lord, I seek your will.* One of her favorite verses in Isaiah came to mind. *Here I am, Lord, send me.*

After a quick ten-minute warm-up, Amelia had turned off the treadmill. Grabbing two twenty-pound dumbbells, she started to work her back body with bent-over rows. Something Katy had told her, for as long as she could remember, is that when the right man comes along, Amelia would know it by the way he is sweet on her and appreciative of her. Amelia smiled between sets, thinking about the possibility of finding someone to love who would return that love.

# Chapter 2

## Quinton

Quinton Richards pulled the job description from his shirt. On that, he checked the address—2457 Elk Road. He realized it'd been ten minutes since he'd seen the mailbox numbered 2455, so he expected to arrive at his destination shortly. *This place is more isolated than any ranch I've worked before.* Thankfully, his full-sized truck plowed through the snow from last night's storm. The ice was the biggest concern, causing him to drive much slower than the speed limit.

He glanced in the rearview mirror and spied his boy snuggled up to his Sonic the Hedgehog pillow. Quinton had dedicated himself to raising Emmanuel after his wife, Rose, had died in a car accident four years ago, leaving him to raise their then-four-year-old... alone. Other people didn't understand all the extra time and support Quinton had to dedicate to his son. Heck, Quinton didn't realize all the hard work Rose had done to raise their boy until he had to do it.

Despite being eight now and very successful academically, Emmanuel still struggled socially. He'd become fixated on anything that interested him and unable to let it go. One moment, he could be talking in his soft, sweet voice, and the next, he'd yell like a raging teenager. Emmanuel could make all the noise he wanted, but if anyone yelled back, his body would shake out of control. Fortunately, he didn't intentionally slam his head against walls any longer, but if he were lying on the floor or sitting in a chair when an episode occurred, he'd revert to banging his head against those surfaces. Quinton's heart broke for his little boy. If he could endure all his son's struggles, he would so his child could live a typical life.

Quinton and Emmanuel pushed through every day together. Quinton never dated after his wife—not that he hadn't necessarily wanted to, but none of the women who'd tried to capture his attention truly cared for Emmanuel. They hadn't understood him. Most of the women had used their sweet voice when Quinton had been in earshot but a snarky, impatient tone toward Emmanuel when they'd thought he hadn't been paying attention. Fortunately, he'd seen through their facade and ditched those women quickly. For the last three years, he'd focused on working hard to provide the best life for Emmanuel and himself. Women had seemed to flock in his direction, claiming how handsome he was, but Quinton had never used his appeal to land a date, so he hadn't appreciated women trying to do that to him.

Emmanuel still longed for his mom. For him, the sun rose and set on his mother. Rose had always gotten away with giving Emmanuel hugs and kisses whenever she wanted. Emmanuel had usually wiped off her kisses;

they had an agreement — she could kiss him, and he could wipe it off — that had worked for them. Whenever Emmanuel got hurt, he wanted his mother. Right after she had died, Emmanuel still needed assistance when using the bathroom, and he'd refused to let Quinton help. He'd declared, 'I'm waiting for Mom.' Tears sprang to Quinton's eyes, remembering that first time. He'd waited on the toilet for just over an hour before finally letting Quinton help him. It had taken longer than Quinton ever imagined it would for his son to get used to him as his primary caregiver.

He'd pleaded with God often—*You took her, now You need to help me. I'm failing.* He'd had a relationship with Jesus, but since his wife's death, Quinton had become less focused on allowing God's will in his life and focused more on taking care of things *himself.*

This long drive and quietness inside the cab had stolen his attention, and his mind wandered. Quinton's blood boiled as he thought about leaving the ranch in Texas. *No one will degrade my son!* Quinton felt terrible about not having remorse for knocking the foreman's teeth out. He did, however, feel kind of bad that the man's children had to see their father dismantled like that. "You have to leave Quinton." The owner's words had run deep. Clearly he hadn't respected Quinton after all these years. In fact, he should have left well before now and hadn't. He hoped moving so far away would give him and his son a fresh start.

While researching Big L' Ranch, he learned that Amelia Lawrence, daughter of the late Jack and Marilyn Lawrence, had recently acquired ownership of the ranch when her father died a few months ago. He'd never liked the idea of gaining something due to someone else's loss, but he also couldn't pass up this opportunity to become a foreman and provide for his son.

Last evening, as he and Emmanuel grabbed a sandwich at a rest stop, Quinton called Amelia Lawrence to confirm his interview for eight o'clock in the morning. Though he had to leave a message, he thought it showed his professionalism to call and confirm, assuming it gave him a leg up on other potential candidates. He hoped the weather wouldn't interfere with the early morning interview. He'd gone slow and drove through the night to make sure he wouldn't get stranded anywhere.

Despite the slow going due to the weather, he felt close. *Where is this place?* Quinton hadn't realized how isolated he would be from everything if he got offered this job. He hadn't thought of anything other than getting to work, specifically as a foreman. He'd prepared for this position all his life. Maybe being very far removed from everything in Texas would be precisely what they needed.

*Finally!* Turning onto a long gravel road, Quinton couldn't wait to relieve his swollen legs, ankles, hips, back, and backside. Hopefully, the trek north would be worth it. Now, he had to convince Ms. Lawrence that he could oversee her entire enterprise — one hundred twenty-five thousand acres. As he put the truck in park, he sat still for a moment, letting the mountains in the backdrop draw him into the serenity of this place.

Hopping out of the truck, the winter air smacked him in the face . . . hard. Perhaps he'd given himself too much credit thinking he could embrace such a drastic change of environment. Emmanuel's groggy eyes peeled open at the bang of the driver's side door. A rush of bitterly cold air filled the cab's backseat when Quinton opened his son's door. He wrapped the blanket around him, "I'll carry you, Buddy. Come here." Despite being eighty-five pounds and tall for his age, Emmanuel needed his dad to carry him whenever he faced a new situation. As soon as he felt comfortable,

Emmanuel would be a nonstop chatterbox about his own fixations and interests.

"Wait."

Startled, Quinton looked around his immediate surroundings, thinking something scary needed his undivided attention. Nope.

Emmanuel's little voice could get really loud when he needed it to. "I need my stuffies and headphones."

Quinton had given up on trying to reason with or persuade Emmanuel to do something different as long as it didn't cause him or anyone else harm or grief. Setting Emmanuel back on the seat, Quinton reached for the noise-canceling headphones while Emmanuel searched through the back, trying to decide which stuffed animals to bring. The entire cast of Winnie the Pooh and the characters from his favorite video game — Mario Brothers — were inside his backpack. By the time Emmanuel had Pooh, Rabbit, Piglet, Tigger, Roo, Eeyore, Luigi, Mario, and Yoshi in his arms, Quinton realized that holding Emmanuel would prove to be a challenge with all of his buddies.

"EJ, can you just choose one or two special friends to bring with you right now."

"Don't call me that."

"Sorry." Quinton enjoyed calling his son EJ because it was quicker to get out and he just liked combining his first and middle names Emmanuel Joseph together, but Emmanuel didn't allow any nicknames...ever.

"No, they are all my friends and want to see this place too, Dad!"

Quinton inhaled a deep breath and squeezed his eyes shut. He'd thought only girls gave sass, but obviously, he hadn't a clue. His eight-year-old son gave sass...often.

"Why don't you put them back in the bag; we'll bring them all with us," Quinton suggested, bracing himself for the reason why it wouldn't work. Though they hadn't even argued once in this moment, Quinton felt like his life was a constant negotiation resulting in him being habitually exhausted.

For a nanosecond, the corners of Emmanuel's mouth quickly lifted and dropped back down again. "Thank you, Daddy." Emmanuel's now sweet voice sounded even younger than his numeric age.

Emmanuel put on his headphones, raised his arms, ready to go, and grunted. Before picking up his son, Quinton coached him. "Say, pick me up, please."

"Up, please." Quinton lifted him off the seat for saying the main points of the request. Emmanuel always showed impeccable manners—as long as he regulated his feelings and body.

The father and son sauntered up to the door, observing the vast farmland that surrounded them. There were five more minutes until his scheduled interview. Fortunately, last night's storm hadn't held him up.

"Look at the horses, Daddy. Maybe you'll let me ride these."

"We'll see." Quinton's trademark response. He'd rarely given a definitive answer because with Emmanuel, the slightest disruption or deviation to his day made for misery...for everyone in the vicinity.

"Let's see if I can get the job first, then we'll see about riding horses." Quinton turned toward the wraparound porch, ascended the three steps toward the door, and knocked.

"You'll get this, Daddy. You're the best cowboy in...where are we?"

"Montana."

"You're the best cowboy in Montana." Emmanuel fist-pumped his dad's knuckles.

"Thanks, son. You are so sweet." He ruffled his son's hair right as the door opened.

"Hi, you must be Quinton. I'm Amelia. Come on in." She moved to the side and fully extended the door, leaving him room to enter. *Wow!* Quinton's heart skipped a beat. He was definitely going to like Montana.

# Chapter 3

**Quinton**

Quinton crossed the threshold, still staring in awe. Amelia was only seven or eight inches shorter than him, which he was not used to. His late wife had just barely reached his chest. Amelia's light brown hair ran halfway down her back with swirls of blond. The strand that weaved through her French braid caught his eye. She wore a purple fitted v-neck shirt that showed off her toned shoulders and developed chest. It sunk in nicely at her waist and flared slightly over her curvy hips. Quinton sucked in a quick deep breath, preventing him from being able to speak.

He wondered if Amelia noticed his instant attraction or could hear the insane thoughts barreling through his mind because she grabbed a teal sweatshirt off the rack on the wall and threw it over her head.

Quinton appreciated the help. He needed to focus on acquiring this job, not drooling over his new boss...potential new boss. He might have succeeded in focusing on the task at hand until his eyes traveled over her black leggings, which showed off her beautifully toned legs. His eyes made their way back to her sparkling tropical ocean-colored eyes.

"H-Hi, it's nice to meet you," Quinton finally spit out. *Yup. I've made a fool of myself in the first five seconds.*

"I'm really sorry. With the storm last night, I am running a little behind this morning, and I just finished my workout. I'll show you to the office and then go change."

Quinton stared just a little too long, pushing the situation past awkward. "N-no, you're fine. Don't change on my account," he finally sputtered out.

Emmanuel lifted his head off his dad's chest. "Dad, your heart is fast. It's going faster than Luigi in Mario-Kart." Quinton laughed, embarrassed, and gently bounced his son in his arms. *EJ, you're giving your dad away.*

Heat ran up Quinton's neck as he met Amelia's eyes again. She tried to hide a smile. Quinton hoped she wouldn't hold any of this against him. He needed to work, and now, seeing his new boss, he *really* wanted to work here.

"And, what's your name, little guy?" Amelia asked the boy in Quinton's arms. She reached out to touch his back and the boy literally crawled up his dad's shoulder and repositioned himself on Quinton's back just to avoid being touched. Amelia drew her hand back as fast as someone who touched a hot stove would. "I'm sorry."

"No worries. That's Emmanuel. He doesn't like to be touched by anyone unless he initiates it." Quinton gave her a sympathetic look when he noticed something in her eyes—sympathy, concern, or maybe rejection—but he couldn't identify it.

Amelia pointed past her guests, indicating an office space through the mudroom. "Shall we head into the office?"

Quinton stepped back toward the door, trying not to squish Emmanuel, but wanted Amelia to lead. Amelia accidentally brushed his chest with her shoulder as she squeezed between the bulky winter coats on the opposite wall and him. Heat sizzled throughout his pectoral muscles upon contact. His body had never reacted this way when meeting a woman for the first time, not even his late wife.

Inside the office, Amelia motioned for Quinton to sit down. Grabbing his son's hands, he helped Emmanuel hop off his back. Quinton's body jolted when Emmanuel wrapped his arms around his dad's waist. He looked at Amelia with unsure eyes. "I can just stand if you don't mind."

"Of course not. Whatever makes Emmanuel comfortable is fine by me," Amelia assured him.

Quinton smiled. *Does she really mean that? We'll see.* He'd heard all the compassionate words before, but no one had ever meant them.

"Tell me, Quinton, what prompted such a radical transition at this point in your life?" Amelia rested her hands on the top of the desk.

He chuckled. "At this point in my life?" He rested his hand on the back of the chair. "How old do you think I am?"

"I'm sorry." Amelia brought her hand to her chest. "I didn't mean to imply you were old."

Her pink cheeks caught Quinton's attention. "I'm kidding, but you like to start with the tough questions, huh?"

Standing on his tiptoes, Emmanuel took one step forward and then back repeatedly. He began conversing with his stuffed animals as if he were alone in the room. Quinton rubbed the back of his neck with one hand while the other rubbed his son's back. Emmanuel sidestepped, and Quinton's hand dropped. "Four years ago, my wife, Rose, lost her life when some young punk, high out of his mind, crossed the center line and killed her. She left me to raise this handsome little man." Quinton quickly squeezed his son to show him love and steal some strength before Emmanuel once again stepped away from his dad.

"I am so sorry. That must have been a painful ordeal....for everyone." Amelia's eyes showed compassion, not pity, which Quinton appreciated. *Maybe* she's different. He had started to wonder if all women were cold and calculating. His heart skipped a beat as he studied her ocean-colored eyes.

Quinton flashed Amelia a quick smile, "Thank you." He took a deep breath as he sat down. "At two years old, Emmanuel was diagnosed with Autism. He paused. Quinton studied Amelia's expression. Again, he saw compassion. Quinton had never imagined getting this type of reaction from an employer or a woman in general, let alone one he'd had an instant attraction to. He sucked in a deep breath and let it out slowly, and then he shared most of the situation that happened in Texas. He spoke quickly and then waited for her response. He wasn't a rambler; in fact, he preferred silence, which was safer that way.

She seemed to share this belief. He felt like a specimen under a microscope as she studied him, contemplating what to say next. Quinton's heartbeat and the ticking of the wall clock were in sync. The longer Amelia stayed quiet, the more nervous Quinton got.

Amelia moved out from behind her desk. Quinton's pulse raced. Was she going to comfort him? Crossing in front of him, she knelt close to his side. In doing so, she almost lost her balance and grabbed onto Quinton's bicep. She quickly stabilized herself and pulled her hand away. He couldn't read the expression on her face. Perhaps she felt terrible for grabbing him. Other than the zingers that flew through his arm when she made direct contact with him, it hadn't hurt. In fact, he liked her touch; he only wished it had been longer.

Before trying to make eye contact with Emmanuel, she mouthed, *sorry*. Then she spoke soft and sweet, but not like a baby. "That must have been very hard for you, huh, Emmanuel?" He turned his head in the other direction, avoiding her presence.

He liked this woman already. Her outward beauty captivated him, and her kind-heartedness made her even more beautiful. She really seemed to care about people's feelings, especially Emmanuel's. Quinton started to have his son turn back around to acknowledge her, but Amelia stopped him. Instead, she continued with her questioning: "Emmanuel, do you like to play with kids your own age?" He shook his head and shrugged his shoulders.

Still wearing his noise-canceling headphones, Emmanuel yelled loudly to respond. "Sometimes, but I like to play with big people. They are nicer to me. I can talk about more things. Like, did you know that the leader of France could have stopped World War II before it happened?" He turned to face her, but he didn't make eye contact. Instead, as he spoke, his pupils were fixed in the corner of his eyes.

Amelia smiled in Emmanuel's direction and then at Quinton. "WWII buff, huh? I'll have to read up on it so we can talk about it. Does that sound good, Emmanuel?" He nodded his head but didn't say a word.

"Emmanuel's grandfather served in WWII, so a lot of his knowledge comes from their conversations. He died last year. Now that he's eight, he thinks I should remove the parental controls on his iPad so he can search anything he wants on Google." Quinton shook his head. "Not going to happen."

While Amelia stood and walked back toward her desk, Emmanuel kept regurgitating facts about World War II. He moved his fingers wildly and shifted from tiptoe to tiptoe before Quinton rested his hand on the young boy, "Why don't you teach Amelia about World War II later?"

"Later when?" Emmanuel's tone remained flat, though Quinton's excitement soared over the thought of getting this job.

"We'll see."

"Thank you for being honest with me, Quinton; I appreciate that. In return, I will be completely transparent with you." Quinton liked how Amelia focused on his eyes, bringing them back to the purpose of this meeting.

Quinton shifted in his chair, wondering if he'd have to spend hours searching and then driving to another ranch for a job. He hoped not.

"As a teenager, I made my dad teach me every aspect of how this business operates. So, I understand the back-breaking, grueling work that everyone who works for me goes through. I knew that when I ran this ranch one day, I wanted to be the type of boss who understood what every employee would have to endure daily to complete their day's work. More importantly, I needed to be able to help. There isn't a day that goes by when I will not be helping someone complete essential work. We are a true ranch family. How does that make you feel?"

The corner of Quinton's mouth curved upward slightly. He wondered if he could trust the other adults here, or the kids for that matter. How long would it be before someone mistreated Emmanuel and they would have to leave here? "I like that, but I've seen some families that are quite nasty to each other, so I just would like some clarification…"

Amelia chuckled at his apprehension. "True story. Some families are downright brutal to one another; we are not. With as many men as there are on this ranch, tempers flare occasionally, for sure. The women also have their fair share of disagreements, but we get over them quickly."

She began to whisper for dramatic effect. "Run the other direction if you are anywhere near the married couples during their arguments," Amelia chuckled. "But at the end of the day, we love each other here. I believe there's always room for forgiveness and starting over." Amelia locked eyes with him. He pulled on his shirt to cool himself down. Was it hot because he was in an interview, or did the sparkle in Amelia's eyes push him to elevated levels? "As long as we don't knock each other's teeth out…"

*Touché.*

Now, a fire blazed through Quinton's chest, neck, face, and ears. *Of course, she knew what had happened.* Maybe he shouldn't have left out the effect of the fight he'd told her about initially. He was still distracted by the most beautiful teal eyes he had ever seen. They were not blue or green, but some bright spots in the middle. The way wisps of her light brown hair with even lighter highlights fell loose from her braid and framed her face choked Quinton's gut. He let his eyes gravitate to her leggings again. Big mistake. They hugged her curves in all the right places, causing Quinton's heart to beat erratically. Quinton yearned to return to the below-zero temperatures outside to cool himself off.

"I'd like to hire you today for a one-month trial run. That will give everyone time to adjust to the new norm. Instead of everyone reporting to me, they'll report to you, and you'll take care of the situations unless you feel something needs my attention. Then we'll take care of them together. With as many loving people on this ranch, we can all help with Emmanuel, too, if you'll let us."

*Together?* "I am thrilled that you are willing to give me a shot, but I have to ask one thing. Why doesn't anyone here want the foreman job?" Quinton gave Amelia a quizzical look.

With a stone face, Amelia shared her belief, "Probably no one wants to deal with me. I can be a bear." A deafening silence fell upon the room.

Quinton's eyes widened, and mouth dropped into a frown. If her own family, whom she said was wonderful, didn't want to have her looking over her shoulder every day, she must be way too challenging to deal with. "T-That seems—"

"Just kidding!" Amelia laughed.

Quinton shifted in his seat and now held on to Emmanuel again. Quinton didn't expect Amelia to be a jokester. The bosses he'd had before who ran a successful ranch this size had never laughed about anything. Also, he'd never worked for anyone this attractive or delightful before, either.

She explained the truth. "There are too many family members here, so it gets awkward when the kids order their parents around. As an only child, I took on the role when my dad died. But the foreman puts in just as much, if not more, manual labor than the rest of the crew. My dad didn't want that put on me. He believed the men should do the heavy lifting and I should operate the business side of things."

"That makes sense."

"Really, how come?" Amelia crossed her arms over her chest and compressed her lips. At that moment, his eyes drifted to her mouth. He wondered what her lips would taste like if given the opportunity to kiss her. Given her height, he wouldn't even get a stiff neck. Quinton shook his head. *Focus. Kissing is not the purpose of this meeting.*

Heat filled Quinton's cheeks for the second time in this interview. Had he put his foot in his mouth again? "Because a dad's relationship with his daughter is different, I've heard. They want to protect them from being hurt as much as they can emotionally and physically."

"So you don't think I could emotionally or physically handle the job of working on the ranch?" Amelia pushed.

This woman was feisty and twisting his words. Quinton couldn't tell if she was still joking, but he didn't think so. "I'm saying you shouldn't have to handle those pressures, which is very different from being unable to. Any father or husband wouldn't want to put his girl through that." *Girl, yeah, right. Amelia is all woman.* Quinton grinned at his thoughts.

"I don't have either of those anymore, so it looks like *I'll* have to determine how much *I* can handle." Her arms relaxed by her side.

Flashing a sympathetic smile, he said, "I heard about your dad when I researched the job. I'm very sorry." He wondered if she'd had a husband before, too. He'd never seen a woman this beautiful who was not attached to a man.

Amelia forced a smile, handed Quinton a clipboard with paperwork to complete, and then broke eye contact. Kneeling in front of Emmanuel, she gave him her undivided attention. "Are you excited to live here, Emmanuel?"

"Yeah, sure." Quinton winced at his son's straightforward, dry answer.

By addressing Emmanuel directly, Quinton saw that Amelia would treat his son like an eight-year-old, not a baby or an invalid. *I think I'm going to like it here.* He smiled at Amelia. Her full smile, in return, set off a flame deep in his chest.

Emmanuel flapped his hands and bounced on his tiptoes. "Can I ride the horses?"

Amelia smiled. "That will be up to your daddy."

Quinton saw this as a step in the right direction for him and his son; he just hoped he wouldn't get too caught up with his new boss.

# Chapter 4

**Amelia**

There hadn't been enough space for her and the larger-than-life Quinton Richards. Would Amelia truly be able to let this man work here? His deep, husky voice captivated her thoughts, while his dreamy chocolate eyes, strong jawline, and broad shoulders enthralled her entire being. Amelia took too many glances at the cowboy's full lips during the interview, which produced an impulsive idea to kiss him. Funny. This was the first time since she'd vowed to avoid men that her mind entertained the idea of kissing one.

She also caught him stealing glances at her, which took her breath away. As if he could hear her thoughts, his deep-as-night eyes were upon her again.

*Please let me focus on the job at hand, Lord.* Amelia sent up a quick prayer, hoping she could anchor her thoughts on training Quinton as the foreman instead of having Quinton train her. Amelia hadn't ever kissed a man. After being the subject of Selena and her cronies' bullying in high school, Amelia hadn't trusted anyone. Figuring people were conspiring with Selena, Amelia had ostracized herself from anyone and anything except the day-to-day ranch operations. There is no way on God's green earth that the way this hunk of a man was looking at her meant anything. All she knew was that she didn't need this distraction right now.

Amelia refused to let the past or the present deter her from her goal of expanding the ranch. She wouldn't think about the cruel words from the most popular guy in school, nor would she think about the way Quinton interacted with his son, igniting a small fire within her abdomen. Nor would she focus on how she'd caught him gazing at her when he didn't think she was looking, having her pulse skyrocket. She accepted her destiny of being an old maid, to steal her mother's words, may she rest in peace. Amelia hated that phrase. Everyone knew what it meant—the girl never grew into anything beautiful, and every man passed right by her.

Yup, and Yup.

"Are you okay?" The side of Quinton's lip rose slightly. He seemed amused that he'd caught her daydreaming.

*I'm not trusting you either, buddy, so stop with that alluring smile and just do the job I hired you to do.* Amelia gave him a half smile and kept her snarky thoughts to herself before she proved that she really was a bear . . . and injured one at that.

At this moment, her focus needed to be on running the ranch and ensuring her dad's legacy continued for another two hundred years, God willing. She couldn't let herself get smitten with a man the instant he arrived for a job. *That's right, he's here for a job, not you.*

Amelia liked Emmanuel, but her heart broke when he instantly wanted to be in Quinton's arms again when she mentioned meeting the crew. Trying to help ease the situation, Amelia stepped a little too close to Quinton. His musk cologne filled her lungs, making it hard to take a full breath. It should be against the law for a man to smell this good.

"I think there are warm chocolate chip cookies in the kitchen. Maybe your dad will let you have one while he fills out some paperwork."

"No, thank you." Emmanuel didn't even flinch.

Amelia beamed. "He's so polite."

"He sure is. I get the same response when I ask him to brush his teeth or do anything else he doesn't want to do," Quinton explained. "He thinks if he's nice about it, then he won't have to follow the request."

"We can leave that here, and you can fill it out later if that's easier." Amelia offered with a warm smile.

Emmanuel slid out of his dad's arms without indicating anything verbally but remained connected to his side. Quinton dropped his hand and rested it on his son's shoulder.

"Does that mean you want those cookies?" Amelia clapped her hands together. She made eye contact with the youngster, but he buried his face in his dad's hip and shook his head. Amelia flung open the door and left the room, "C'mon on boys."

*Boys. Really?* How embarrassing. Quinton was far from a boy. How his shirt pulled on his broad shoulders and sculpted chest made Amelia's throat dry. His robust and stiff jaw, oh, how she wanted to run her fingers down the two-day-old scruff that made him all the more appealing. If Quinton's dark chocolate eyes held her gaze anymore, Amelia would melt into a puddle instantly. She'd only ever read about a man this wonderful in her books and seen them in her movies. They don't exist in real life, do they?

Amelia heard a thunderstorm of words coming from the kitchen, which grew louder as they approached the ranch's central hub. Everyone gathered here for at least one meal or conversation every day.

When Amelia entered the room with Quinton and Emmanuel, an abrupt hush startled her. Five sets of eyes peered back at the trio. Speaking to the crowd, "This is Quinton. He's accepted the foreman position, and this handsome guy is his son, Emmanuel." Amelia ruffled Emmanuel's hair. To her surprise, he didn't even flinch, but his head had resumed the buried position from earlier. Pointing at each person, she introduced them, "Quinton, Emmanuel, this is Cash, and that is Carolyn. They cook for us, so be extra nice to them." She saw Emmanuel's little eyes peeking around his dad's waist at the couple. Amelia winked at Quinton.

*Why did I just wink at him? Traitorous eye!* Amelia's cheeks grew hot. She hoped Quinton wouldn't notice that he made her nervous.

Carolyn smiled knowingly at Amelia and then moved toward the new hire and his son. "Oh goody, another child on the ranch." She shook Quinton's hand. "Great to have you here." Then she knelt down, smiling. "Do you like to be called Manny?"

Emmanuel shook his head. "Emmanuel," he said matter of factly.

"Would you like to help me with the cookies and be the first to get one?" Carolyn asked.

Emmanuel looked up at his dad, who encouraged him. "Go ahead. I would if I could. They smell delicious."

As they walked to the counter, Emmanuel asked, "Did you know that Patrick G. Emmanuel fought in the Battle of the Bulge in World War II?"

Silence. Quinton leaned in close and whispered into Amelia's ear, "I'm sorry. Please don't let my son's obsession with that war get him ostracized from another ranch. I have a good feeling about this place."

The way his eyes smiled at her sent her heart thumping like the sound of Duncan in a full gallop. "I know a thing or two about being ostracized, and I won't let that happen to Emmanuel." Amelia flinched, wondering why she revealed so much.

Carolyn tightened her lips into a thin line, "I am sorry, Emmanuel. I did not know that." Straightening her posture, she slid the sheet of cooled cookies toward Emmanuel and handed him a spatula. When he finished transferring the cookies to the plate, she handed Emmanuel a cookie, who smiled and thanked her.

Renee appeared in the kitchen with the kids dressed and ready to play in the snow. She stopped beside Amelia and whispered loudly, "Who's the hunk?" She pointed toward Quinton.

Amelia swatted at her friend as she spied the side of his lip curl slightly. How embarrassing.

"Renee, this is Quinton, the new foreman, and that is Emmanuel." She pointed toward the little boy devouring the cookie. "Quinton, this is Renee. She homeschools all the kids that live on the ranch."

Quinton extended his arm toward Renee. "Nice to meet you. Many people just refer to me as 'the hunk,' but Quinton works too." He winked at Amelia, and her already racing heart skipped a beat.

Renee ushered the kids outside. "Emmanuel is welcome to join us." Renee addressed Quinton but didn't wait for a response. As she left the kitchen, she spoke to Carolyn. "We'll be back in for cookies after we play." The baker smiled and nodded.

Getting back to introductions, Amelia directed her attention to Damon, the one in charge of all the horses and their needs, including breaking them and running the therapy program for special needs children. All the children had made great gains. She wondered if Quinton would let Emmanuel participate.

Sean, her uncle, and Raddix, her cousin, were next. They both handled the livestock. Since his wife's death, Sean had become quieter than the typical cowboy. Raddix, the same age as Amelia, had turned into a broody cowboy three years ago when his longtime girlfriend decided the ranch life wasn't for her and left him. He definitely didn't have good luck with women. At least he wasn't interested in Selena anymore.

Damon shook Quinton's hand, but the other two men nodded toward Quinton, who lifted his chin in return.

Raddix approached Amelia from behind. He got real close to her ear and loudly whispered, "Don't slip on your drool when you leave."

Amelia swatted at him, but he ducked out of the way to put his glass in the sink. Quinton's unwavering gaze made her face flush. She ducked her head and elbowed Raddix in the gut as he passed by her again. There wasn't anything worse than being embarrassed in front of a group of people.

Raddix grunted, holding his stomach. He straightened and gave her a side hug, whispering, "All joking aside, be careful."

Had she been staring at Quinton? Raddix could always see things about herself that she could not. He was the brother she never had. With only five months between them, that also meant he protected her with the fierceness of an older brother.

Quinton handed Amelia the clipboard with his completed paperwork. "Do you want to go out and play with the kids, Emmanuel?"

"I don't have any of that stuff. It's my first time, right, Dad?" The little boy squeezed his four fingers together using his other hand and then quickly repeated the action, letting each hand take a turn, crushing the other hand's fingers. Amelia's empathy for Emmanuel's struggles pulled at her heart.

Quinton stiffened. Amelia could see the angst in Quinton's eyes. She wondered if the interaction with kids and adults on his last ranch would be difficult for them to overcome.

Emmanuel started chewing on his hair. Amelia liked how it hung to his shoulders, but the ends were all curly. "Are you nervous, Emmanuel?" Amelia knelt in front of him.

He shook his head. "I don't know them, right?" Emmanuel pushed onto his tiptoes and clapped his hands wildly together. "I talk about war. But wait, Daddy said people don't want to hear about it anymore...something about the war being over." Everyone laughed, so Emmanuel laughed too, but Amelia could tell he didn't understand why that was funny.

A few minutes passed while Emmanuel thought about what he wanted to do. Cash asked Quinton if he or Emmanuel had any food allergies he needed to be aware of and shared the meal times with him. Amelia noticed the ranch hands she hadn't had a chance to introduce to Quinton had started welcoming him on their own.

"Can I go play in the snow now?" Emmanuel tugged on his dad's shirt.

As Amelia rummaged through a hall closet to find Emmanuel some ski pants and gloves, she heard Carolyn say, "That little boy is great. They'll fit right in here."

Amelia smiled at Quinton, knowing he must have heard the same comment. "Let's hope so," he pushed out a light laugh.

That laugh hit her deep within. Matched with his dark-as-night hair and dark caramel eyes, she wondered why this man was still single.

Once Amelia got herself and Emmanuel ready, the rest of the adults had finished their break, too. They all ushered the little guy out where the kids were having a snowball fight.

"I don't know what you have planned for Emmanuel regarding school, but all of the kids who live on the ranch are homeschooled, so that's an option to consider." Quinton held the door for Amelia to walk through. The brittle air would have caused her body temperature to drop instantly, but Quinton remained close to her, and even through the jacket, she felt a burst of heat run through her shoulder when they accidentally bumped into each other.

A cease-fire lasted for about one full minute — long enough for Amelia to introduce Emmanuel to the eight children ranging in ages from seven to eleven.

After a long while and much intervention from Quinton and Amelia, Emmanuel finally grabbed a handful of snow and tried to make a snowball. When he couldn't quite get it, he just threw it at the child closest to him. At different times, both Dean and Dominic tried to show Emmanuel how to make a snowball, to no avail. At eight and nine, respectively, they were a perfect match for Emmanuel's first day at his new home.

Renee's husband Rocco came rushing out of the barn and blasted his wife with snowball after snowball until she couldn't breathe from laughing so hard. They'd moved to the ranch six years ago when Rocco became the head veterinarian for the ranch. With as many animals as her dad had had, he'd wanted a full-time vet on the ranch, and Rocco fit right in. His wife, Renee, a school teacher, hadn't wanted to send her kids to public school, so they'd created the homeschool space in the main house's basement. Amelia wondered what Quinton would choose.

Amelia watched as the rest of the staff joined in on the snowball fight. She caught the glimmer in Raddix's eyes and knew what he was conjuring up...an initiation.

Gathering a clump of snow, Amelia shoved it down Quinton's back. He grunted. "Oh, is that how we're going to play?" She hadn't flirted with a guy, maybe ever, but something about the new foreman stirred up giddy feelings that one would expect from a teenager.

Quinton chuckled but never took his eyes off Amelia. Her body shuddered. Each calculated step reminded her of a strong, sleek, very muscular jaguar going after its prey. The intense yet playful look in his eyes revealed to Amelia that she was his prey. She stumbled on a thick piece of ice. He grabbed her around the waist before she could fall. Then, he tossed her into a spot the kids dug out and ordered, "Bury her!" He and all the kids started tossing snow on her.

Fortunately, her crew came to her rescue. They pelted Quinton with snowballs and snorted out a laugh, "Bury him!" The kids began throwing snow at Quinton.

"The winner buys dinner." Amelia challenged, getting up and brushing the snow off her pants.

"Not fair. You'll just make Carolyn and Cash cook." Raddix complained. "How about the winner decides what he or she wants from the loser." he countered, and the adults agreed.

"Come here, Emmanuel." Dominic waved his hands and patted the snow next to him. The kids sat in the snow to judge the battle. "It's like a game of dodgeball, but with snow instead of a ball, and they can go anywhere." He explained.

Rocco and Renee eliminated each other quickly. Raddix spent his time trying to get Quinton out, but he moved quickly for a big guy.

"Ouch! Amelia, you traitor!" Raddix grunted.

She shrugged her shoulders. "All's fair in love and war."

After a relatively quick battle, Quinton and Amelia remained. They circled each other like they were getting ready for a shootout, and they were, just with snowballs, not bullets. Quinton threw his ball, and it whizzed by Amelia's face. It was so close that one had to pay attention to see if she got hit.

"Foul. That was ice. I think I'm bleeding." Amelia turned away from her assailant and cried into her hands, covering her face.

Quinton started to move toward Amelia. "Don't fall for it, Man. She's ruthless." Raddix shook his head as he warned the new guy. Quinton kept moving toward her. "It didn't hit her. You'll be sorry."

He grabbed Amelia's shoulders and whipped her around so she was facing him. The warmth of his hands almost made her rethink her next steps. He pulled her hands away from her face, and she smiled at him. "You should have listened to Raddix. She pulled a little snowball from her sleeve to tag him, but in one quick swoop, he ducked out of the way, grabbed a handful of snow, and hit her in the shoulder before she could get him.

Raddix erupted into delightful laughter. "Yes, someone finally beat her."

Amelia glared and shoved Raddix, pushing him closer toward the barn. He curled his arm up under his chin. "That hurt."

She rolled her eyes, "C'mon, a big burly cowboy like you, and you're whining about a little shove."

Raddix straightened back up, "You're little shove isn't anything to squawk at; you have guns...for a girl."

"Watch out for that one, she's tough." Raddix stopped next to Quinton. Shoulder to shoulder, he threw his thumb backward toward Amelia.

Emmanuel appeared at his dad's side again. He tugged on Quinton's shirt, pulling him down, and the little guy not so quietly whispered, "Can I stay here and do whatever they're doing?"

"Is that okay?" Quinton sounded hesitant.

Amelia and Renee smiled in unison. "It's perfectly fine.

Renee asked, "Does he have any specific strategies that will make the transition easier for him?"

"Talk sweet, even if you are angry, talk sweet…trust me." Quinton forced a smile.

Amelia smirked, feeling bad that he obviously hadn't talked sweet at some point and had learned his lesson. "You won't have to worry about that. Renee is the best."

A snowball fight at her age was super silly. Ridiculous. She'd felt like a teenager again, except this time around, contentment rushed through her body. Her only worry was figuring out what Quinton would want for winning. Amelia needed to keep her distance from Quinton Richards before she forgot to keep her vow to stay away from men, and this one hurt her, too.

# Chapter 5

**Quinton**

Quinton dug his heels into Rocky's sides, pushing the stallion to his galloping limits. Guilt ate away at Quinton like a stomach parasite. Quinton's dad had compared him to their stallions throughout his childhood and teenage years, highlighting his thick, muscular frame and easy-fighting tendencies. Stallions are also known for their vast interest in the many mares around them — that's not Quinton.

Truth be told, Quinton's dad had been the womanizer, more like a stallion in that manner than his son. On the ride to the northwest side of the ranch, he'd tried to process his instant attraction to Amelia. He hadn't felt such quick, immense feelings for any woman since Rose, and he wasn't sure how to handle them.

Just like Rose, Amelia's beauty had pulled Quinton in the second she opened the door, but his gravitational pull toward his new boss was driven by more than her looks. The loving way she interacted with Emmanuel reminded him of Rose, making Quinton's heart flutter with joy.

Pulling on Rocky's reins, he slowed the stallion to a canter to breathe in his surroundings. Amelia hadn't been kidding about the vast amount of undeveloped land. It'd been so long since he'd rode for fun. Appreciating God's beautiful earth. He'd been so lost since Rose had died that he hadn't noticed the beauty of his surroundings; only the mundane daily tasks.

Over the past week, his tasks had been anything but tedious. In fact, he found excitement in his work again. He pulled Rocky to a halt. Resting his forearms over the saddle horn, a smile spread across his face as he thought about Amelia interacting with the other staff and the kids. Her authentic concern for and desire to help others intrigued him even more with his boss. Even Emmanuel seemed comfortable with Amelia — he shared stories about her from school every night at dinner. Yesterday, when Emmanuel finished school for the day, Amelia brought him to the barn so he could meet Duncan. Quinton had been replacing the hay and refilling the water buckets, all the while gawking at his beautiful boss. She'd caught him several times, blushing increasingly with each occurrence. The soft-spoken, gentle manner she'd used with Emmanuel had warmed his heart.

"I'm sorry, Rose," Quinton spoke into the vast open space as snow started falling. "I'll always love you. Right now, I feel like I did after meeting you. You intrigued me, breathed life into my lonely soul..." He hung his head and sat in silence for a heartbeat. "We always said we'd date again if anything happened to the other. That sounds fine when your spouse is alive and well. Right now, I feel like it's wrong." He shook his head. "Falling for Amelia wasn't my plan, but it's happening." Quinton smiled, remembering when he told Rose he'd fallen for her. What would Amelia say if he told her about his feelings? *You're crazy!*

The snowflakes grew in intensity and size, but the silence of winter gave Quinton peace. He remained still, and then the answer was crystal clear. Quinton looked upward and said, "Thanks, Rose. Amelia is great with Emmanuel. I'd never let anyone in who wasn't."

Clicking his tongue, Quinton signaled Rocky to trot back to the barn. For the next twenty minutes, while he rode back to the barn, peace washed over him, leaving a permanent grin on his face. So far, he'd unhooked Rocky's saddle and filled his water bucket. Rocky neighed and nudged his head toward Quinton as he brushed the animal's back. "Sorry for the quick grooming today, buddy. I have to shovel the sidewalk. See you later."

"Hey," Amelia waved. "Do you want some help?"

Quinton tossed a shovel full of snow off the walkway. It only took him a week of shoveling for too long for springtime. He stood swiftly, "Hey, yourself." Locking eyes with Amelia's, her teal eyes captured and twisted his heart. His eyes trailed over the baggy sweatshirt that hung to her mid-thigh. The tight leggings revealed her perfectly shaped legs, making his heart beat erratically. Quinton rubbed the back of his neck, silently praying for pure thoughts.

Amelia gave him a half smile. Could she read his thoughts? He certainly hoped not. "I just left Emmanuel with Renee, and he wanted me to tell you he's good."

"Thanks." It pleased Quinton that Emmanuel transitioned nicely into school on the ranch. With Emmanuel, though, everything is relative. Now, Quinton just needed to ensure his transition went as smoothly as he hoped.

Grabbing another shovel, Amelia tossed a scoop over her shoulder.

"I thought the purpose of hiring me was so you could handle the business side of things while I took care of the labor." It wasn't a question, but he wanted to hear her response.

"You're right, but old habits are hard to break."

"I'm not complaining about you being around. . . not at all. . ." Shock, or maybe distress, appeared in her eyes; he wasn't sure. Perhaps that look had something to do with her feeling ostracized. Maybe she'll share that story with him sometime soon. ". . . but I didn't expect to see you helping Raddix with feeding the horses, replacing hay, sweeping the barn aisles, and refilling water buckets. Do you feel like I can't do what you hired me for?"

Amelia blew out a breath that floated through the air. "You are more than capable. I apologize. Those are important skills that even our youngest cowboys and girls can do. So, when Emmanuel's excitement soared, I showed him how to complete the chores. I can back off."

Quinton could tell he'd unintentionally made Amelia feel bad. Stepping closer to his boss, but hopefully far enough away that she felt comfortable, he captured her eyes since she'd been looking everywhere except at Quinton and softly assured her, "This is your ranch; you don't need to back off."

She grinned. Quinton wondered what it would take to make her eyes light up when she smiled. "No, you're completely right. I hired and trust you to do your job; I just like to move and help."

"I like you being around to help, too." Quinton winked at her before he returned to shoveling.

"You won't mind if I continue showing Emmanuel how to brush down the horses and feed them, do you?"

Her simple question made him even more twitterpated with Amelia. Even after calling her out, Amelia's first concern was helping his son.

"No. Thanks for showing Emmanuel everything about the horses. He's never been interested in anything resembling work, but you had him sweeping, getting feed and water to the horses, and brushing them. He's been begging me to let him ride Duncan." Quinton didn't know if he should come out and ask her directly or if the passive statement was enough, so he went back to shoveling. Based on past events from the past week, Amelia would either walk away or let 'em have it."

"He can ride Duncan anytime you're *both* ready."

*She gets me. Emmanuel might be ready, but am I?* "Do you have any hobbies, Amelia?"

Amelia chuckled. "That was out of the blue?" The slight lift of his eyebrows and shoulder simultaneously brought out her wide smile, sending rockets off in his gut. "I've secluded myself to the ranch for years."

"Why?"

She ignored his question. "If I'm not working, I'm off with Duncan, reading a book, or stargazing. How about you?"

He loved how the blue shade of her sweatshirt produced the fiercest ice blue in her eyes. "I don't have much spare time between the ranch and Emmanuel. I like to work out and watch movies." Amelia was studying him intently.

"Let me guess. You're a die-hard Jason Statham fan. Watching him take people down in seconds makes you smile."

Quinton released a belly laugh that echoed off the nearby structures. "You think you have me all figured out, don't you?"

"Maybe not *all* figured out, but you're a guy, the basic traits are universal." Amelia's confidence impressed Quinton, even if she was sort of wrong.

"I do like Statham's movies, but I watch a wide variety of movies. For the last four years, the bulk of my movies have been either rated G or PG." Quinton moved closer with every word. Now, standing face to face with Amelia, electricity sizzled through the dry Montana air.

"I'm sorry you've lost both your parents." Quinton pulled off his hat, ran his other hand through his hair, and stepped back.

"Thanks, but everyone goes through it." Amelia returned with a one-sided shoulder shrug.

Her Uncle Sean still hadn't recovered from his wife's death. Since then, he'd lost his sister-in-law and his brother. The other ranch hands had filled

Quinton in on a lot of the history, so it would help him understand Sean's actions.

"Are your parents still living?"

"No. They died ten years ago—both within six months of each other." He'd always hated having older parents growing up. He thought losing his parents at twenty-five was young. Then he found out that Amelia lost her mom when she was a teenager, and Emmanuel had lost his mom when he was four.

Placing her gloved hand on his forearm, Amelia apologized for his loss. Quinton looked down at her hand, which at the moment produced a ring of fire even through his long-sleeved flannel. His eyes fell to where her hand rested and then back up to study her almond-shaped eyes and high cheekbones. He paused on her soft, full lips.

Feeling brave after talking to Rose in Heaven, Quinton decided to pursue Amelia. He licked his lips as he took a step closer to her. He placed his hand over hers. "Amelia, I hope I am not overstepping my—"

"—Quinton, stop flirting with Amelia and come here." Raddix ran back into the barn.

Amelia stepped away quickly, with heat visible in her cheeks. She bit on the inside of her lip, "Don't listen to Raddix. For all intents and purposes, he is my older brother, not a cousin. He teases me like a brother and protects me like a brother, but he's a good guy." She shifted from side to side. "Besides, you're just doing your job, not flirting. As the new guy, he'll raz you for a while."

"It's obvious he cares a lot about you." Quinton imagined he and Raddix would have words at some point if Raddix was anything like Quinton, who interrogated his sister's dates. If it came down to it, though, Quinton knew he could win a fight against Raddix. At six foot four inches, Quinton stood at least three inches taller than Raddix and had about ten pounds of muscle on the guy, too. He'd definitely fight for Amelia. *Whoa. Back up, Cowboy. Why would there be fighting? Amelia all but warned him that everyone here is family. Just focus on doing your job!*

As Quinton and Amelia strolled over to Sean and Raddix in the barn, their hands brushed against each other. What Quinton wouldn't give to lace his fingers through Amelia's. *Not right now.* Quinton silently chastised himself.

Before Amelia could open the barn door, Quinton stretched out his arm to place his hand above the handle, keeping it closed. His pulse quickened, and they were close enough that he knew Amelia could see it throbbing in his neck if she looked. Quinton liked that he captured her eyes instantly. "You were wrong. I was flirting with you back there." His words came out more breathy than he anticipated but couldn't control. A slow grin spread across his face when he heard her suck in a breath that took his heart prisoner.

"Amelia," Raddix yelled from inside the barn.

Quinton swung the door open and gestured to a speechless Amelia to enter. He either started the process of getting to know Amelia on a personal level, or he wrote his own pink slip.

"This never gets old, does it, Son?" Sean slapped Raddix on the shoulder as they stood in awe of the baby calf they had just helped bring into the world.  As Sean strolled toward the barn doors, he looked Quinton square in the eyes, "Have you ever delivered a calf before?"

"Yes, sir, many times. You're right; it never gets old." Quinton half-smiled, realizing that Sean seemed to be sizing him up and not looking for confirmation of his comment. The older gentleman lifted his chin toward Quinton and left the barn without another word.

Addressing Raddix, Amelia asked, "Do you know where the other snowmobile is? I only saw one out there."

"Dad said that it's not running right. I will look at it right after I get washed up."

Amelia sighed slightly, "I need to take Quinton around the property."

"Well, you have two choices: walk or get really cozy on the one sled out there." Raddix waggled his eyebrows at both of them. Amelia immediately turned red. "Even in below-zero weather, I can embarrass you until your face is red hot, and you can't blame it on the weather because you haven't been out here long enough." Raddix chuckled.

Riding close on a snowmobile with Amelia caused his gut to erupt like Mount St. Helens did decades ago—after a string of earthquakes built up the activity, it just exploded. Quinton got hot all over thinking of his week of restless nights. He'd imagined holding her hand and hugging her; last night, he'd dreamt of kissing her. He just might explode if any of that activity came to fruition.

"Which do you prefer?" Amelia waited for his answer, but he hadn't heard the question.

Quinton had to admit to being distracted. Would she send him packing right now if she knew his thoughts?

"Do you want to ride double on the snowmobile? You can also walk the property, but I won't be able to show you everything today."

Raddix chuckled again. "From what I imagine he's thinking…" he strutted toward the exit, "you may want to walk to burn off some pent-up energy."

Fortunately, over the last week, Quinton spent a lot of time getting to know Raddix, so he didn't hesitate to throw the feed scoop at him. He knew it wasn't much and wouldn't hurt him, but he didn't expect him to laugh even harder. Quinton caught Amelia's surprised look when Raddix opened the door and looked back at them. "Enjoy your tour."

"Bye, Raddix." Amelia avoided looking at Quinton as she headed toward the exit herself.

Maybe Raddix was right, but Quinton didn't care. "Let's take the snowmobile."

"Alrighty." If Amelia had been affected by Raddix's comments and insinuations, she wouldn't have shown it. Did that mean she wasn't interested? He reached the barn door first and held it open for her. His Mama instilled in him the importance of being a gentleman. Amelia walked past Quinton, and her shoulder gently brushed against his chest. He squeezed his eyes shut as her coconut scent swarmed through his senses. Quinton fought the urge to reach for her hand, pull her into his chest, and steal a hug. Even a quick one just to see how she felt against his body. He needed to get a hold of himself and find out what she thought of him first.

"Do you want to drive, and I can give you directions, or would you like me to drive?"

Yup, definitely a bad idea to be that close to this woman. Either way, his brain wouldn't be able to function normally. If he held onto her, her scent would tantalize his entire body. Not to mention, he'd have to hold onto her waist, and the combination could be detrimental for him. On the other hand, if he drove, she'd hold on to him, which would be just as much of a distraction. He didn't need to wreck the boss's snowmobile in the first week of employment. At least his hands would have to be on the handles.

"I'll drive, as long as you don't mind. I've got to get used to it sooner or later, right?" Who could argue with his logic?

Amelia didn't seem to care who drove. She's probably ridden on the back of a snowmobile before holding on to other ranch hands. That thought sent a pang of jealousy through his chest. That might seem ridiculous to others because he hadn't known her for long, but just like he knew within a week that he loved Rose, he'd fallen for Amelia just as quickly.

"True story. Have you ever driven a snowmobile? Texas certainly isn't known for its snow." Her light chuckle vibrated through his chest.

With a deep, huskier tone than intended, he squared right up to her and said, "No, but I'm sure you're the best teacher around. A quick tutorial will get us on our way."

Yup. He'd pushed too hard. Amelia turned a shade of red he had never seen before— even brighter than they'd been with Raddix— and she took a step back to focus on the snowmobile.

"Does my flirting bother you, Amelia?"

She took what seemed like a lifetime to answer. "I'm not sure yet." She raised her brows. "Why are you doing it?"

That seemed like an odd question. *I think you are exquisite, and I'm crushing on you.* He learned from his experience with Rose that he shouldn't share all his thoughts right out of the gate. "I find you attractive."

"For real?"

"Are you doubting my opinion? Did you recently have a rough breakup?" Quinton queried.

Amelia winced. "Something like that."

Not sure which question she was answering, or both, but Quinton let it rest...for now. She'd seemed so confident. Maybe she was a good actress.

After taking the time to show Quinton the basics of the machine, she had him start it, and they loaded onto it. Quinton felt every muscle in his body stiffen. Even through her jacket, he could feel the softness of her curves resting on his back. He hoped he didn't run into a tree.

Desperate, he did something he hadn't done in a long time — prayed. *Dear God, please help me figure Amelia out. Thank you for this job. Don't let me blow it by scaring her away.*

Slowly, he guided them along a well-worn snow trail to the first location. She had him stop at a large orchard that he imagined would be blooming with flowers in a few months. Soon after, they'd be rewarded with fresh fruit. Amelia reached around Quinton and hit the kill switch. He stiffened as her body pressed against his back. When she hopped off, he instantly felt the frigid air on his shoulders and missed her warmth. "Axel, Jeff's son, and Allie, his wife, are in charge of produce on the ranch."

Standing close to Amelia, he placed his hand on the small of her back to turn her slightly. Acting like an electric probe, his hand tingled, sending currents up his arm. "Are those greenhouses over there?" Quinton pointed to his left.

Amelia nodded. "After preparing everything for the winter, Axel and Allie left to visit her mother. They'll be back by the end of February or the beginning of March to get ready for spring and summer. And then, of course, they'll need lots of help during harvest. Will that be okay with you if I help, or will you give me a hard time about that, too?"

Her grin let Quinton know she was teasing him. "Ah, you are capable of teasing. Good to know."

Without warning, his pulse picked up speed again. Quinton still hadn't taken his hand off her back, and Amelia hadn't moved away either. He considered that a win. "Who takes care of things for them now?"

"Me. Hence, why I needed you."

*Needed me?* Quinton smiled at her bold statement, but he knew she meant just as a foreman. *Maybe she'll need me for more than that if I give her some time.* He definitely needed her...yeah, like a hole in the head. What he really needed was to find out who hurt his beautiful boss, making her doubt her attractiveness.

Amelia muttered, "Let's move on." Quinton's hand dropped to his side as they walked shoulder to shoulder back to the snowmobile.

Quinton started the snowmobile and sat on the seat. Amelia placed her hand on his shoulder to keep her balance as she swung her leg over the back. As she settled into her seat, she gently wrapped her hands around his waist. "Head north for about three miles; you'll see a warning sign we put up. Stop about ten feet before the warning sign." He felt her breathing on his neck as she spoke inches from him.

"What's the warning for?"

"The river," Amelia stated.

Quinton wanted Amelia to hold him tighter, so he hammered the throttle harder than before, and instinctively, she tightened her grip on his waist. For the next three miles, Quinton tried to focus. When Amelia had rested her head on his back, he'd almost lost it. He told himself that she was just trying to block the wind from whipping her in the face, but he hoped there was more to her action.

He let out a low growl of desire, and Amelia lifted her head off his back. Even though he'd rather have her head on his back, he realized it was probably better to go slow until he found out Amelia's story.

Following her instructions, Quinton slapped the red kill switch when he reached their destination. His shoulders embraced the warmth of her hands again as she gracefully leaped off the machine.

"This is my favorite place on the entire ranch, regardless of the season." Amelia shivered. "I don't usually come here when it's this cold, but it's still beautiful to me."

Quinton unzipped his heavy Carhartt jacket and wrapped it around her shoulders. "No, no. It's literally freezing out here. Take this back."

Without letting her remove the jacket, he wrapped his arms on either side of her shoulders and rubbed his hands up and down the length of her arms to warm her up. "Nonsense. I'll take it back when we start driving again. I'm fine for now."

Amelia smiled. *Finally, some reaction.* Even though it was quick, Quinton hadn't missed her lips turning up slightly or rosy cheeks.

"At least three times a week during all the seasons except winter, you need to check to make sure the irrigation system is working properly." Amelia showed him where the piping started. "The fall is the most important because leaves will get trapped in there and block everything up, making springtime a struggle."

Quinton stared back at the land they'd just traveled. "How many paddocks do you have on the ranch?"

Turning to share the view, Amelia's shoulder bumped into him, causing him to take a side step. "Raddix was right; you are tough." She didn't really cause him to move; he just wanted to flirt more with her and see what happened.

Amelia rolled her eyes, "I barely touched you." She continued before he could say anything else, "We have fifteen paddocks that we use for rotational grazing. Sean and Raddix have it down to every two or three days. They rotate the cows and sheep. They often need a hand or two convincing the herd to move on, so you'll probably find yourself working with those guys often."

Quinton didn't mind getting the cattle to move, but he wondered if working closely with Raddix would be bad. Raddix had already seen right through Quinton's teasing of Amelia, which explained his warning from the beginning of the week that he'd never allowed anyone to hurt Amelia and wouldn't start now.

"We have a couple of young, ornery cows who'll keep you busy fixing fence lines regardless of the season."

Quinton gently bounced his shoulder off hers, "I can see why you wanted a foreman. I hope I live up to your expectations." If Quinton was honest with himself, he wasn't just talking professionally. What would it take to date Amelia Lawrence, and why hasn't anyone snatched her up yet?

Amelia smiled reassuringly, "I'm sure you'll do just fine, cowboy." She gently bounced off his shoulder.

Quinton over exaggerated even more when she tapped him, but he truly lost his balance in the snow. Amelia reached out for his arm, but it was all in vain. There wasn't any way she could prevent him from going down. Instead, he pulled her along with him, and she landed right on top of him with a thud.

"I'm so sorry. Amelia quickly put her gloved hands in the snow on either side of his shoulders to hold her own weight. Quinton's hands wrapped around her waist.

She tried to wiggle off, but he held her in place. "You have nothing to be sorry for. I was fooling around with you. I'm not sorry." His gaze locked with hers. Amelia's ocean-colored eyes looked bright green today. "Do your eyes change color?"

Amelia planted her feet underneath herself. He released his grip on her, and she stood erect. Reaching her hand out to help Quinton up was a sweet gesture, but she couldn't actually lift him on her own. Quinton enjoyed enveloping her gloved hand, which fit nicely inside his large, calloused hand.

"Yes, depending on my background and what I'm wearing, my eye color will alter." She pulled her hand back from his, looking sheepishly at her now free hand. Quinton wondered what that look meant. Did she get sparks like he did?

He lifted her chin with his thumb and forefinger. "You are beautiful." He didn't wait for a response. Instead, he moved in for the kiss he'd dreamt of last night. Their breath mixed just inches apart. Quinton smiled as he tightened his one-arm grip around her waist, but she pulled back before he could land the kiss.

"We should get back so you can change. I don't want you freezing and quitting on me." Amelia chuckled. It sounded like a nervous laugh. That left Quinton hopeful that Amelia would be open to a kiss but just needed more time.

*Quit. Never!* Quinton knew he'd stay here as long as Amelia would allow. "I rode down that trail earlier this morning. You really do have a lot of land to develop. Any plans for the land?"

"Dad had plans for it, but he instilled in me not to build up the ranch too quickly regardless of how prosperous they were," Amelia explained as she returned his jacket.

"It sounds like your dad was a sage man." Quinton heard the pang of sadness in her voice whenever she mentioned her dad.

She shook her head and smiled but changed the subject. "If you follow the trail around, we'll end up right in front of your cabin."

Quinton hadn't expected to live on the ranch, but Amelia said her dad believed the foreman should. There were things he'd have to take care of after hours, and living on the property would be easier. If he was being honest, it was challenging living so close yet so far from Amelia that his heart cried.

They arrived at his cabin. "May I use your bathroom?" Amelia disembarked from the machine.

Quinton rushed to open the door for her. "You know the way." The inside of the cabin still mesmerized Quinton every time he opened the door. This wasn't a cabin. This was a beautiful log home. A full kitchen with stainless steel appliances that looked brand new opened up to a dining area with a rectangular, possibly handmade table, two benches on the sides, and a chair at the top and bottom. A large bathroom off to the left provided easy access for guests. A thick wooden ladder led up to Emmanuel's loft bedroom. He would set his stuffies between the balusters to watch Quinton make dinner.

At that moment, Emmanuel burst through the door. "Dad, look what I made in school?" He held up a heart cut-out craft with jagged edges and extra-large print, which took up more space than he thought the craft intended.

"That's awesome, buddy. I'm going to hang it on the refrigerator." Quinton moved toward the fridge.

Emmanuel followed, tugging on Quinton's forearm. "Actually, Dad, I made this for Amelia. I think I love her as much as you do."

For two reasons, his heart fell into his boots. First, he didn't expect his son to express emotion like that for Amelia—he'd only ever told his mom that he loved her. Second, Amelia walked out of the bathroom at that exact moment, and her jaw hinged open like the rattlesnakes he used to decimate in Texas.

Quinton slowly met her gaze and involuntarily grinned at her, then his eyes shifted back to Emmanuel. The little boy shrugged his shoulders, wrinkled his nose, and lifted his hands, palms up toward the ceiling. "Oops!"

# Chapter 6

**Quinton**

The alarm blared on Quinton's phone and he threw the covers over his head. One might think he was exhausted from the manual labor it takes to run a ranch this size—he was. One might assume he spent the night tossing and turning not able to get a certain female owner off his mind—he did. But the groan and lack of desire to face the day had nothing to do with either of those things.

He needed to prepare for a bigger battle. A battle that would challenge his brain way too early in the morning. A battle that would most likely end with him feeling intellectually stilted. A battle that even Hitler would have waved the white flag after five minutes. That battle didn't have a cool name like the Battle of the Bulge, the Battle of Normandy, or the Battle of Iwo Jima. This one word battle was kind, friendly, and very empathetic seventy-five percent of the day. The other twenty-five percent of the day, Quinton coined the time: Emmanuel's Battles.

Battles. Plural.

What the battle began about was usually not what it ended about. Before his feet hit the floor, Quinton prayed. *Mornin' Lord. Emmanuel—God is with us— I need you with me right now. Emmanuel couldn't get up for school at eight in Texas; five is asking a lot even though he went to bed at seven. Thank you that the bedtime battle didn't last as long as usual. He gets tuckered out easily here. Please give me the wisdom not to fall into his traps. Help me to acknowledge him and show him that he is loved and safe here. Thank you for this opportunity to raise your child. Help me to lead by example.*

With a big sigh, Quinton tossed the covers off his legs and dragged himself out of bed. He pulled a pair of work jeans on and secured his belt. He pulled a dri-fit shirt on first. Then a t-shirt, A long-sleeved shirt covered both layers. He grabbed a pair of socks and put them on the counter prior to climbing the ladder to Emmanuel's loft.

"Hey buddy. Time to get up." Quinton turned on the overhead light.

Emmanuel shot up like a jack-in-the-box. "I don't want to go to school."

"We're not starting this way. You like school." Quinton started toward the boys closet. "Am I picking your clothes, or are you?"

"Dad, you're not listening to me. I don't like school today."

"I heard you—you don't want to go to school. I don't think you have listened to me because I've said for the last, I don't know how many days, that's not an option. When you get to school, you're fine." Quinton scrolled through the shirts in his son's closet. "You can either go to school with Miss Renee and the kids who live here on the ranch, who, to my knowledge, have been really kind to you, or you can go to the big school about five miles down the road with a lot more kids from who knows where."

Emmanuel slapped his hand on his still-covered legs. "I...don't...want...to...go...to...school."

"Looks like I'm picking the clothes today." Quinton pulled a shirt free from the hanger.

"No, thank you. I...don't... want to wear that."

Dang it. How could he be upset with his boy during the difficult times, when he's being so kind about it?

"Dad, you know you're wrong."

"Oh, yeah. Do tell."

Emmanuel steepled his fingers and then started to move them around rapidly at the tips. "Miss Amelia has been the one teaching me, not Miss Renee..."

The mention of his boss's name made his hollow stomach nervous. Right after overhearing Emmanuel's declarations, she bid them both adieu and he hadn't had any alone time with her since. Maybe this morning he'd get an opportunity. Raddix hadn't been any help either. Like a middle school boy he teased Quinton.

Every. Single. Day.

The teasing wasn't the problem. That was what he enjoyed about working on a ranch—the camaraderie. The issue was that he didn't know how Amelia felt about him, so he was. . . stuck. At one point he thought he'd seen her eyes soften and show interest during one of their morning meetings, but then something snapped and her unreadable persona returned.

"...isn't that right, Dad?" Emmanuel broke into Quinton's thoughts.

"Huh?"

"Nothing."

By this point, fifteen minutes had passed and Quinton's patience was all but gone. "I'm going to start the coffee. I need to drop you off for breakfast and get started with my work, so if you don't want to wear what I picked out, don't..." frustration leaked into his semi-rising voice and Emmanuel covered his ears. "Sorry, Bud, I'll lower my voice." He took a breath and continued. "Feel free to pick out whatever you want to wear. Please be downstairs in three minutes."

"But Dad...Let me talk!" Emmanuel's loud voice irked Quinton. His muscles tensed half-expecting steam to come out of his head like the Tin Man's hat.

Quinton waited. "I don't want to go to school."

"I can't do this." Storming out of the loft and down the ladder Quinton started his coffee.

Almost instantly, Emmanuel started screaming. "Daddy. No. I want Daddy."

Quinton remembered how much worse it was when he'd yell for his mommy. Rose was the strongest person he knew because it would go on for hours.

Not today.

"I'm down here. If you want me—"

"—I want Daddy." Emmanuel didn't mind interrupting others, but heaven forbid interrupt him.

Quinton started to feel sick. His muscles were tense. If Emmanuel could express himself more specifically, things wouldn't be as big of a battle. Quinton gripped the counter top and hung his head, broken-hearted that his son struggled and frustrated with not knowing how to fix it. Sure he could say Emmanuel didn't have to go to school, but that didn't fix anything. Who knew if that was even the true problem. He tried another approach.

Flipping through things in the 'catch-all' drawer, he found a whiteboard and marker. Renee had given him on the first day of school. He scribbled a message on the whiteboard for Emmanuel:

*I am not happy with this battle. I need you to:*

*Get dressed*

*Brushed your teeth*

*Get out the door*

That was as clear as he could be. Hopefully he didn't forget anything on that list, or it would become the next battle.

Emmanuel asked Quinton to pass him the board and the marker. Quinton climbed a couple of rungs, stretched out and handed his son the items.

Then beautiful silence.

Two minutes later. Yes, only two minutes later, Emmanuel jumped off the third ladder rung, fully dressed. He wore a new, clear pair of pajamas. Quinton didn't care, he stopped battling that long ago. Emmanuel said the pajamas were softer and didn't have any tags. Running water in the bathroom and his electric Mario toothbrush signaled one more battle being crossed off the list.

"Where's the brush or comb?"

"No, No, Please." Emmanuel put his hands over the rat's nest that protruded from the back of his head. "It's not on the list!"

"Sorry, Buddy. Can I please just try to get these knots out?"

"Please, just use your fingers. Here, let me see." While Quinton slowly tried to unmangle some of the snarls, Emmanuel ran his face up and down the soft shirt covering Quinton's arms.

A mess still existed at the back of his head, but Emmanuel said that he couldn't take anymore, so Quinton stopped. He grabbed Emmanuel's socks off the counter as Emmanuel opened the door to leave. That's when Quinton noticed his son's footwear...crocs. "You need to put on your socks and boots."

Emmanuel squeezed his eyes shut and started to shake. His fingers were working faster than any manufacturing machine—his fingers twisted and pulled at the bottom of his shirt, while he stuffed who knows how much of the collar in his mouth and his jaw chewed like a motor. Quinton wrapped his son in a bear hug and squeezed him. "Are sock too much, Buddy."

"YES!"

"I'll just bring them for you." Quinton assured his son. A few seconds of pressure is usually what Emmanuel needed. Quinton felt his son's body relax. "Are you better?"

"Yup, let's go."

Happy as a clam he tiptoed his way toward the main house, while Quinton dragged himself. . . completely, and utterly...

Exhausted.

"We're playing on the playground today." Emmanuel shared with his dad on the walk over.

At that moment, Quinton noticed the playground off behind the ranch. It seemed promising and terrifying at the same time. Emmanuel needed to be around kids his own age, but some kids are just so mean. It broke Quinton's heart a little more than Emmanuel's at times because Quinton fully grasped the situation, whereas Emmanuel didn't—always.

Heat rose in Quinton's neck as he recalled Emmanuel's time at a playground right before they'd left Texas. Instead of asking the unknown kids to play, Emmanuel had chased after them. One of the kids had called Emmanuel 'creepy'. Emmanuel had hung his head and had walked toward Quinton solemnly. Unable to find the parents, he'd gotten relatively close to the kids and gave them a piece of his mind.

"He's not creepy. He's just trying to play. It's a playground that's what kids do here. In fact, kids who don't let other kids play and make them feel bad because they are different, they're the creepy, mean ones."

Those kids had run away. Quinton hadn't felt bad for them. He'd felt mad that they made his boy feel bad. Quinton didn't have a temper, unless someone messed with Emmanuel.

Inside the main house, Renee and Amelia were at the table with the other kids. He locked eyes with Amelia. He must have looked like he'd been through the ringer because Amelia's eyes softened and she gave him a sympathetic smile.

"Hi, Amelia. What's for breakfast?" Emmanuel sat right next to her.

*Seriously, how could Emmanuel warm up to Amelia and give her the sweet, non-argumentative side of him when not only two minutes ago, socks sent him over the edge?*

"How was the morning?" Renee asked.

Still watching his son with Amelia, Quinton lightly sighed. "It's improving. He wouldn't put socks on for his boots, but maybe Amelia can get him to put some on." He pulled the pair from his back pocket and handed them to her.

Renee gave Quinton a reassuring smile as Emmanuel plowed into him for a long hug. "Have fun, Buddy. Remember, when school's done, you get the rest of the day..."

"With Amelia." Emmanuel finished. "Amelia and Renee are letting us play on the playground!" He pumped his fists in the air with excitement.

With one last look at Amelia before leaving, his heart fluttered. Trying to tease her, he wagged a finger at Amelia. "Don't let him do anything I wouldn't.

Her smile dropped instantly. "We kinda have to..." She shrugged her shoulders. "You want him to have fun, don't you?" Her smile returned and her light laugh filled the room.

*Yes, she's flirting!* Astonished, Quinton pointed at her with his own grin. "Later we'll see how funny you think that is." That made her smile bigger. "The cabin's open if Emmanuel needs anything. Thank you, ladies." His eyes remained on Amelia until he shut the door.

# Chapter 7

**Quinton**

"How ya doin' there?" Jeff asked Quinton when the foreman entered the butcher shop.

Quinton threw an apron on. "I saw the light and wanted to help you out before the morning meeting."

Jeff waved his hand in dismissal. "Nah. I'm good. How are Raddix and Sean holding up? It's so much harder in the winter than any other time to care for all the cattle and horses."

"They're good. I just checked in with them." Being Raddix's target this early in the morning wasn't anything Quinton was interested in.

Jeff placed a large piece of some animal on the counter. Quinton wanted to ask where it came from but didn't. "Where do you want me?" Quinton queried.

"You're not a hacker are you?"

"Hacker?"

"You know, someone really bad at cutting meat."

Quinton smirked. "I guess we'll find out."

"Give me a break." Jeff shook his head. "Where's Amelia today?"

"With Renee. Why?"

"When I get backed up, that ol' princess comes to my rescue." Quinton didn't miss Jeff's proud smile. Jeff fixed a penetrating gaze on the new foreman. "You interested, Son?"

Quinton was well aware of what Jeff meant with that glint in his eye, but chose to ignore it. "Grab me a knife, I'm ready to go."

Jeff let out a loud chuckle. "You do have it as bad as Raddix said."

Quinton cocked an eyebrow. "Excuse me?"

Wiping his hands on his apron, Jeff looked apologetic. "Amelia's like a daughter to me. She's probably not going to date you, so from one man to another I wanted to give you the heads up."

"Oh." Quinton's heart plummeted into his chest. *Not date me. What happened to her?*

"Look, Son, my Katy and I have seen the looks passing between you too. It doesn't have anything to do with you. Katy's convinced if Amelia can. . . well Katy's convinced you'd have a chance based on the chemistry between you two."

Quinton tried his best to follow Jeff's instructions, but thinking of him and Amelia having a connection filled his mind. Amelia's face flashed into his mind. *Who hurt her?* Quinton remembered Amelia's few looks of desire. Weird. Determination filled his body. His mission to find out what happened to break Amelia emotionally intensified.

For sure, no one would hire him as a butcher. Things moved quicker when Jeff focused on the cutting and trimming, while Quinton did the heavy lifting. He'd take moving herds into a new paddock any day over the heavy lifting of different carcasses for hours.

The bell above the shop door alerted them. Moments later Amelia appeared in the doorway between the store and the butcher shop. "Hey Jeff, are you ready for a break?"

"Ah, Amelia. Please teach him how to cut."

"Oh no, we have a hacker, huh?" Amelia teased.

Heat and hope filled Quinton's chest at the thought of Amelia being close enough to teaching him how to cut. *Hopefully I don't lose a finger.* "Well, if you can do it so much better come show me." Quinton smirked and set the knife down as a challenge to Amelia.

"I'll be back in an hour. You two play nice, now ya hear?" Jeff shared a look with Quinton that said *ask her.* Quinton mock saluted him as he left the shop.

"Ah, pork belly. Making bacon, I see. First time?" Her soft expression melted his heart.

"Yup, but I'm ready for you to teach me." He gestured to the pork belly on the table. *See I'm a quick learner—that's pork belly.*

Time slowed as Amelia sauntered closer to him. Tingles penetrated his arm when her hand gently turned his body in toward the table. "I'll show you how Jeff taught me."

She stood behind Quinton, placing her left hand on his upper back while she placed the knife in his right hand. "How do you know I'm right handed?" He turned his head.

"I. . . I'm a good observer." He loved the way her cheeks blushed. Closing his eyes, Quinton inhaled her pina coladá scent. "You might want to watch what you're doing to make sure you keep all your fingers."

"Point taken." Surprised by his own husky voice and pleased with her shy smile he decided to lay it all on the line. He dropped the knife on the counter. Turning to face her, he breathed, "Amelia, I want to know you better." He paused for her reaction, but she didn't have one. *This woman is difficult.*

Unable to resist, he trailed his fingers down her shoulder, bicep and fore-arm. He laced his fingers with hers. "How about I take you to dinner tonight?"

She took so long to answer that Quinton wondered if she would. "That sounds. . . nice, but I enjoy eating dinner with everyone here." Amelia pulled her arm free and took a step back.

*Strike one.* Instead of guiding instructions, she showed him how to make the cuts then released him to complete the task on his own. It took multiple times for him to get the cuts right, but after many, many tries, he finally got it. By the time Jeff came back, he finished the last cut.

"Well done, Son. Looks like Amelia is a better teacher than me, or our boy had more incentive to pay attention to you." Jeff slapped him on the back.

Amelia scoffed, "Yeah, right." Quinton thought he heard her mumble, *maybe there's a first time for everything.* What did that mean? He'd only find out if he could be alone with her.

"Thanks for your help, Amelia." Quinton's voice filled with appreciation.

Her quick wave and slight smile were a win in his book.

"Didn't go so well, huh?" Jeff inquired.

Quinton continued to stare at the door Amelia had just walked out of. "Tomorrow's another day. I'll break through her walls. Mark my words."

# Chapter 8

**Amelia**

The sun had almost peeked over the horizon by the time Amelia returned to the ranch with Duncan. Leaving him in the pasture, she turned out the rest of the horses, so she could clean their water buckets. "Where's the scrub brush?" She asked to the empty barn.

"We need new ones; I forgot to tell you."

Amelia jumped and let out a big breath. "Quinton! You scared me."

Quinton chuckled and put his palms up. "Sorry, I was just trying to figure out why you're doing my job...again."

Amelia carried a handful of hay and Duncan's water bucket to the spigot outside the barn; Quinton followed with more buckets and some hay.

So many thoughts zoomed through Amelia's mind. Quinton looked so handsome in his fleece lined flannel, at least two days of stubble, and a musky scent mixed with hay making her pulse race.

"You haven't talked to me in days. Are you secretly looking for a replacement for me and going to let me go when the four weeks is up?"

She dropped her hand, clenching the hay for control. "Never. You're a great foreman. I'm lucky to have you."

"Gotcha. I'm just not boyfriend material." The words came out sharper than he intended.

Gulp.

Biting the side of her lip, her nerves took over. "It's not you, It's—"

"Don't finish that sentence, please." Quinton pulled his glove off and let his thumb gently pull her lip free from her teeth. "I know someone hurt you, and when you're ready to share, I'm a good listener."

Amelia examined his eyes, seeing if she could read his thoughts, or if his real feelings would be revealed. *Would she ever be ready?*

"I have strong feelings for you." He caressed his fingertips down her cheek.

"Oh, no you don't." Amelia stepped back and Quinton's arm dropped to his side.

Grinning, "Oh, yes, I do."' Stepping forward to close the gap rubbing his hands up and down her arms, Quinton gazed into her eyes.

Amelia pushed at his chest to create space, but he didn't move.

"What happened to you, Amelia?"

Her heart raced. *Sure I'll just tell you how much of a loser I am. No, thanks.* "My parents died, remember." She didn't mean for it to come out so snappy.

"Why aren't you married, or at least dating?"

*Going for the jugular, I see.* "The ranch is my family and that's all I need." Amelia focused her attention back on the water bucket and scrubbed it vigorously.

"Perfect. I'm part of the ranch now, so it looks like I'm family." A slow grin matched his alluring eyes. "Let's see, Raddix plays the part of the overprotective brother, Jeff and Katy play the surrogate parents. Fittingly, Sean's your uncle and the others are your brothers and sisters. Looks like I'll pick up the role of an overprotective boyfriend."

Amelia's eyes widened. "Not likely, Cowboy."

"Why?" he countered.

Amelia tried to escape, like she'd been doing for a long time when things got tough, but Quinton put his solid, taut body in her path.

Softening his eyes and voice, and gently caressing her arms, he captured Amelia's eyes—she couldn't pull her gaze away if she wanted. "Why?"

Amelia squeezed her lips tight into a straight line. *Tell him. No, thank you, Lord. Next request. Tell him.* The same request came from within. *Huh, politeness works for Emmanuel.*

"Amelia, you can trust me. I'd never do anything to hurt you—not only because Raddix threatened me within an inch of my life if I did, but because I have real feelings for you."

Could she really trust Quinton? *Real feelings for me? Yeah, right.* Amelia retreated to the barn, set the bucket with clean water in its place. Still ignoring Quinton's question, half hoping he'd leave, and half hoping he'd ask again.

"I'm not above begging for things I want." Quinton stopped behind her—way too close, her heart slammed against her rib cage.

"I don't date." Quinton gently grabbed her elbow trying to spin her toward him, but she tightened everyone of her muscles to prevent it. "Don't. I can't face you, or I'll never tell you. He rubbed his large hands up her arms like the day he'd given her his jacket. That movement had made her feel cared for.

"Whatever makes you comfortable."

"It started off so subtle. Selena Whittaker called me names when we were kids. Our dad's traded with one another. As I grew taller and stronger than her she started giving me backhanded compliments about how great my muscles and height were. Since I wasn't attractive enough to get a man, I'd be able to take care of all my needs." Amelia froze. She didn't want to relive this.

Quinton squeezed her hand for strength to continue. "She started to recruit others and they too called me names, left giraffe figurines taped to my locker, or tape names to my back, and refused to partner with me for school assignments, to list just the tip of the iceberg. The short story, that

Selena convinced Ethan Hawkins to pretend he wanted to date me then he and his cronies humiliated me in front of everyone at the pizza shop in town."

"People are mean, Amelia, but you can't put me with the likes of Ethan Hawkins before giving me a chance." A valid point, but Amelia never claimed her feelings were rational.

Amelia ignored Quinton, so she could finish the story. "I left the pizza shop and refused to date anymore, figuring every male was under Selena's spell and they'd call me Amazon girl, or whatever they felt like at the moment. Selena, a true she-devil, had promised Ethan that she'd go out with him, if he embarrassed me. Of course the most popular boy in class would do anything Selena asked and in the end, I realized I had been stupid to believe that *the Ethan Hawkins* would have been interested in me. At least Raddix took care of Ethan and there weren't any more guys who teamed up with Selena." Silence. *Say something, Quinton.* The quietness suffocated her like a weighted blanket.

Tears pooled in her eyes during the entire story. Now they threatened to spill over. She'd never allowed herself to be this vulnerable since that night. How could she have let her guard down? What did that mean? She wasn't blind, Quinton's fabulous features sucked her in, but could her heart handle another trick? A letdown. No. It could not.

Amelia wouldn't let Quinton turn her toward him, so he shifted in front of her. Putting his index finger under her chin to lift it up. Amelia saw exactly what she'd feared—pity. *I'm such a loser.*

"Why would you deny yourself all this..." Quinton stepped back and spread his arms wide then pointed toward himself to erase the tension between them. "…just because of some losers in high school?" His joking tone made Amelia chuckle.

"It's nice to see how humble you are."

"What are you laughing at? Quinton's voice shook as he bent his head closer to her resting his palm at the nape of her neck pulling her closer to him.

*He's going to kiss me. Oh, dear God, please no.* Amelia stopped, what would either be the most magical moment in her life, or the biggest train wreck. She imagined banging teeth, noses, or bad breath ruining the moment. *I wouldn't care so much if I wasn't interested. Who said that?* Amelia put her hands on Quinton's chest to stop him. "I can't. . . I have to go. See you at the morning meeting."

# Chapter 9

**Amelia**

Quinton conducted the meeting all the while shooting her teasing and alluring looks that made Amelia's head spin. Fortunately, he needed to help Raddix in the barn, while she covered Katy in the store. They were the last two out of the meeting. He sidled up to her and spoke into her neck allowing his fragrance to envelop her. "Thank you for telling me who hurt you. I promise, I won't hurt you. " His breath tickled her neck. "Please give me a chance. I think you could fall in love with me too."

*Too. Did that mean he loves me? Not likely. It's definitely another trick.*

In the store, Amelia looked through the orders for pick up. "Of course, she'd be here today." Amelia grumped aloud.

As if on cue, Selena Whittaker pranced her petite ol' self into Amelia's store, making every one of Amelia's muscles tighten.

"Hi Amelia, love." Amelia rolled her eyes at the sound of her high pitched irritating voice, but plastered on a smile and turned to face the pretentious woman. "I've heard that you hired yourself a new foreman, yet I haven't even got a glimpse of him yet. That must make it a little easier on you, though I'm not sure what you do with your time if you're not doing all this work," she waved her hand through the air.

Flabbergasted by her appearance a few beats passed before Amelia could find her voice. Selena stuffed herself in a skin tight bodysuit that zippered up the front, except she didn't zip up the suit entirely. Instead, she let most of her very expensive chest remain exposed. She knew it was the middle of winter, right?

Ignoring her appearance and everything Selena had just said, Amelia asked, "Selena, what can I do for you?"

"I'm here to pick up an order and a few things Mother needs for dinner. Then, I hope to finally meet your new foreman." Selena put six eggs in a basket on the counter for Amelia to ring up with her meat order.

As she finished the sale, Amelia informed Selena where she couldn't find Quinton, "Last I knew Quinton and Raddix were in the barn, so you might want to meet him another time."

"If I didn't know better, Amelia, you were trying to keep this new cowboy for yourself."

Amelia chuckled, "Actually, I'm trying to keep you far away from Raddix."

"Pish posh that was high school, he doesn't even remember high school. But that's good to know that you're not harboring your cowboy because I'd hate to see you get hurt again, I can only imagine how that feels."

*I bet*. Amelia imagined breaking every one of Selena's eggs over her head.

As if reading Amelia's thoughts, Selena picked up her basket of eggs and swaggered on her way. That obnoxious vixen reminded Amelia of Sharpay from *High School Musical*, but worse.

Amelia would give her a minute and then help the guys out. Once Selena opened and shut the barn door, Amelia bolted across the property and through the entryway. She quietly opened the door, but stayed out of sight. Why did she care to see Quinton's initial reaction to Selena? She'd seen the way he'd looked at her over the last few weeks. Plus, he'd just declared his intent and desire to date Amelia.

"Woo hoo, gentleman are you in here?" Selena took two short, calculated strides across the barn floor like it might turn into an abyss and swallow her whole. Amelia didn't think anyone would mind that turn of events.

Amelia felt bad for Raddix and Quinton, as they didn't realize they were Selena's prey. Well, Raddix did and she hoped the villainess didn't affect him any longer.

"Hi, I'm Selena." She stuck her hand out to Quinton. Amelia wondered if the look he made toward Raddix was a look of fear or wonderment. Ameila held her breath awaiting their next moves. Quinton shook her hand and smiled his studly smile right at her. Amelia's lunch threatened to make a second appearance when Selena giggled.

Amelia felt like she'd been sucker punched. *He lied. How could I have fallen for another trick?* With Selena around she'd never have a chance.

Was Selena doing this to torture Raddix, Amelia or both of them? Selena would stomp all over Quinton and spit him out, just like she'd done to Raddix. She'd dated him for almost a year before she dumped him for a chance with his friend and quarterback of the high school football team. Amelia didn't think he had ever gotten over the break up, but Selena's name didn't come up very often unless they were in a foul mood.

Things got quiet, so Amelia couldn't quite hear them anymore, but she definitely got the picture when Selena pressed her body up against Quinton's and squeezed his biceps." Amelia took in a deep breath to control herself from ripping every piece of hair and probably extension from Selena's head.

Amelia could never compete with the Barbie doll currently seducing Quinton. Anger bubbled in her gut. Warm bile rose to her throat. She couldn't watch this any longer. How could she have let her guard down? This was the perfect reminder of why she shouldn't have told Quinton anything or let herself be attracted to him.

She didn't see the need to torture herself any longer. Amelia returned to the store full of sorrow. Only a few hours ago Quinton had asked her to take a chance on love with him, yet he let her arch enemy press up against him. Maybe she missed her chance.

"Amelia, what's wrong dear?" Katy arrived to finish off the day.

After explaining the things Quinton said and the interaction with Selena, Katy's eyes sparkled. "You need to take the first step—admit you're interested."

Of course Amelia had already branded Quinton's physical features to her brain. His arms housed muscles everywhere. His biceps bulged, his triceps popped every time he straightened his arm and his forearm muscles emerged every time he clenched his hands. The most dangerous thing on the man was his eyes. He conveyed looks toward Amelia that stopped her breathing.

"You know how the vulture works. She'll mess with Quinton. Is that what you want?

"No."

"Then take a chance. Things aren't always as they seem."

"He's been married. I haven't even kissed a guy before." No guy had ever wanted to kiss her, so why would Quinton?

"Don't try to rationalize things or think for him. You can't help who you fall in love with."

Love, seriously? It's been what, a little over three weeks, there's no way they loved each other.

"None of us here will think any differently of you or Quinton if you date each other—you deserve to be happy."

Raddix joined them in the store. "Can I hide out here?" The ladies nodded their heads. "Whatcha gossiping about?"

Katy laughed. "Not what, who—Quinton likes Amelia and I'm trying to get her to take a chance.

"Please, tell me something I don't know." Raddix scoffed. "He's a good enough guy; I enjoy working with him and all, but I don't trust him." Raddix grunted out.

Both Katy and Amelia lifted their eyebrows, "Why?"

"He's shown interest in Amelia since the day he arrived. That just seems too convenient for me. What if he's trying to woo her and take the ranch from her?" Raddix never held back his thoughts.

Amelia's lack of confidence cropped up again. Amelia let her attraction for Quinton build, as he tried to pursue her and she shouldn't have. "He's right, no one as good as Quinton would like me for real."

"That's not what I mean though," Raddix tried to explain himself. "Don't get down on yourself again. You've worked so hard to build yourself up and you are the strongest, most beautiful woman my age on this ranch." The trio laughed knowing that she was the only *single* woman his age on the ranch he dare say is beautiful.

Katy added, "Jeff has had a few conversations with the young man and he believes Quinton is authentic and has legitimate feelings for you." Katy gave Amelia a hug. "Raddix is just being overprotective of you."

Amelia loved that Raddix looked out for her, but maybe he was right. The end result would lead, most likely, to her heart being crushed into a million little pieces, but what if it didn't? Could God have sent Quinton here for her. Maybe Amelia needed to put on her big girl panties and take a chance.

# Chapter 10

**Amelia**

Emmanuel skipped from the main house to his cabin with Amelia trailing behind texting Quinton.

**AMELIA:** HEY, QUINTON. EMMANUEL IS STRUGGLING A LOT TODAY. WE'RE HEADING BACK TO THE CABIN.

**QUINTON:** OKAY. THANK YOU. SORRY FOR ANY TROUBLE.

**AMELIA:** NO TROUBLE.

Quinton gave her a thumbs up reaction that made her smile.

"Amelia, where ya'll goin'?" Damon rested his forearms on the fence in the front corral.

Both Amelia and Emmanuel joined Damon at the fence. "He needs a break, so we're heading to the house. He wants to show me his legos and maybe teach me how to play a video game, or two.

"Good luck, kid."

"Hey!" Amelia swatted his forearm.

Emmanuel moved from tiptoe to tiptoe while staring at the horse trotting in the penned area. His little fingers rapidly bounced off each other.

"Would you like to ride a horse, Emmanuel?" Amelia asked quietly.

"Yes!"

Damon shrugged his shoulders, "Give me twenty minutes and I'll get Duncan ready."

While they waited, Emmanuel showed Amelia 'Lego City'—a short table with drawers on both sides of an opening where Emmanuel kept his big lego creations. The drawers were filled with legos. Emmanuel had them sorted by shapes. All his one by one and two by two legos were organized in small buckets in one drawer. He had a slew of different colors for each of those designs. The rest of the drawers mimicked the same set up, just with different sized legos.

On top of Lego City, Emmanuel showed her the DeLorean from *Back to the Future* and the Millennium Falcon from *Star Wars* that he and his dad had put together 'from a box'. "I built this one with my brain." Emmanuel pointed at and explained King Kong and the World Trade Center. This little boy continued to amaze her. He could be on Lego Masters.

Moving around to the other side of 'Lego City', Amelia stood too quickly and banged her head off the slanted ceiling. "Ow." She rubbed her head quickly to take the sting out.

"You're tall like Daddy. He can't stand in here either."

Emmanuel pointed out the obvious—his speciality. It triggered something deep within Amelia though. Instantly, Amelia pictured her mom, Marilynn, in her mind, pre cancer, of course. They could have been twins despite the age difference. Both of Amelia's parents were tall. She took turns blaming each of them for the inherited gene. Before Amelia's mom became bedridden, Amelia still needed to look up, at least two inches, to meet her mom's gaze. Amelia had obviously grown since her teen years when her mother died. Who knows, she might have been taller than her mom at this point. It really didn't matter. Amelia still found her appearance a nuisance and not a blessing.

Her mom had always told her that she had found the most wonderful man when she married Jack, Amelia's dad, so there was hope for Amelia, right? Amelia's mom reminded her of a professional basketball player, tall and fit, but Amelia couldn't see that in herself despite admitting their resemblance. Her dad had always said he loved Marlynn's height because he could kiss her for hours without getting a kink in his neck. As a teenager, she'd winced at listening to her parents be sweet on each other. Now, she worked hard to bury any sweet thoughts in an attempt to keep herself from yearning for what her parents had had.

Amelia thought of Quinton. When they stood next to each other, he'd still have to bend to kiss her, or she'd have to go on her tiptoes—he must be six or seven inches taller than her. Drifting off, Amelia imagined flicking Quinton's hat to the ground, running her fingers through his short hair.

"I'm talking to you." Emmanuel threw a lego at Amelia bringing her back to the present. "Has it been twenty minutes yet?"

"Sorry, buddy, I was lost in my thoughts. Next time tap me on the shoulder instead of throwing something at me. Is it hot in here?" Amelia tugged at her shirt, pulling it back and forth quickly for air to cool her down.

"No. Dad keeps the heat low, so it's cold." Emmanuel put his legos down meticulously in his "Lego City." What's that mean? Lost in whatever."

"It means my brain was thinking of something so strongly I didn't pay attention to life right in front of me."

"Oh. Has it been twenty minutes?"

"Let's go see if Damon's ready?" Amelia stated, as she made her way to the ladder.

Guilt shot through Amelia, as she let Emmanuel work with Damon. She should have at least texted Quinton. Watching Emmanuel interact with Duncan made her heart melt. Everything worked out perfectly. Emmanuel only had about thirty minutes, but Amelia wanted to get him back in the cabin and explain to Quinton what she'd done instead of him catching Emmanuel on top of Duncan.

"Thanks, D." Emmanuel tiptoed back to Lego City with ten minutes to spare before Quinton entered the house..

"Emmanuel, are you here?" Quinton's voice carried upstairs.

"Yup." Emmanuel responded.

Descending the ladder first, Emmanuel jumped into his dad's arms. "Dad, I did it. Duncan galloped today. Damon says I'm a natural."

Quinton scowled and looked confused, as he placed Emmanuel on the floor. "Huh?"

"I dug my heels and moved the way Damon told me too, and Duncan went with me." Emmanuel's loud voice and fast moving hands were the only indicators of his excitement.

Amelia cringed. "Damon taught Emmanuel how to ride Duncan. You're not mad at me are you? Damon offered. By the time I thought to text you, he was already on the horse and if you said no . . . well. I'm sorry, if you're mad." She felt herself talking really quickly and with her hands too—indicators that she was really nervous.

"I really appreciate your thoughtfulness, just talk to me first, please." Quinton then smiled at, and gave his son a high five.

"Are you happy?" Emmanuel asked his dad?

"Yes, Emmanuel. I am happy for you. I'm also proud of you." Quinton's eyes softened, as he answered his son.

"Phew!" Emmanuel let out a breath. His shoulders fell simultaneously with his tiptoes. "Can I do it again?

"I'll talk to Damon." Quinton's intense eyes softened. His gaze settled on Amelia making butterflies glide around her belly in random motion, permeating excitement in the air.

"I see he roped you into building Legos, too."

Amelia waved it off. "I love building Legos, so he didn't have to rope me into anything. I didn't actually get to build anything because you interrupted us…" She winked at Quinton to let him know she was playing. "…there'll be time another day to build Legos."

*Don't wink. What are you doing? Control yourself, would ya?* Amelia could admonish herself all she wanted, but her brain was acting on its own volition.

She pointed at the creations that could barely be made out through the balusters in the loft area. "He created those in like twenty minutes.

Quinton's face reddened slightly. "Emmanuel doesn't really even need the instructions, he puts the pieces together without them. "I feel so stupid sometimes working with him." They laughed knowingly with each other.

Amelia said bye to Emmanuel and strolled toward Quinton. She placed her hand on his strong arm. Her fingers instantly lit up with pleasure. "You don't have anything to feel stupid about, except maybe siding with the enemy.

Emmanuel climbed back upstairs to keep building.

"What do you mean?" Quinton shoved his hands in his pockets. Was he nervous, or was that just her imagination?

"I saw Selena pressing her extremely expensive body up against you the other day. She's my nemesis, who partnered with Ethan Hawkins, the dirtbag from high school."

Quinton reached for Amelia's hand. "You're jealous." A smirk filled his face.

*Really, that's your first thought. How arrogant.* "Perhaps confused, or sad would be a better word." Amelia pulled her hand free and crossed her arms over her chest. "It wasn't even ten minutes after I shared that story with you before you were in the barn giving her the smile of a lifetime when she was...you know." Amelia's eyes stung. *Oh no. Do not cry!*

Amelia saw sympathy all over Quinton's face. "Ask Raddix, I put space between us quickly. She is not my type. I promise." *Great so your type isn't the hot blonde. Am I to believe it's the tall freak with too much muscle. Yeah, right.* Quinton pulled her in for a hug; she kept her arms crossed. "Please don't cry. I have feelings for you, not her."

"When's dinner?" Emmanuel hollered from above.

"Soon," Quinton replied frantically.

"Do you really think I would tell you how interested I was in you and minutes later be flirting with another woman?"

*Yes. No. Maybe.* "I don't know. I'm going to head out." Amelia stepped away. "Remember, you both are welcome to join everyone for dinner. Every night at least one person asks when you guys will join us." Amelia had her hand on the door knob.

Quinton leaned his strong shoulder against the adjacent wall and crossed his buff arms across his chest. Amelia instantly recalled the satisfaction she had placing her hand on that same shoulder moments ago. She let out a quick little breath. Each of his muscles in his forearm popped when he clenched his fist and released. Quinton smirked. *Great, stop ogling him.* Amelia lectured herself again. "This conversation isn't over by a long shot."

Amelia felt the sexy, demanding way he said that from the top of her spine down to her toes.

Thankfully Emmanuel interrupted the moment when he appeared at the top of the railing. "Can Amelia have dinner with us?"

"Of course she can, Bud. However, I imagine she'd want to eat Carolyn and Cash's well prepared meal instead of whatever I am about to throw together."

Quinton and Emmanuel had eaten dinner in their own cabin thus far. He needed an electronic device while he ate and that just wouldn't fly in the main house with all the other kids not getting that same option.

"Do you want to join us at the main house tonight?" Amelia offered.

Emmanuel brought his fingers to his lips and shook his head. "Too many people."

Amelia's heart broke for the little boy. She knew how difficult it was for her to move on from the pain she suffered as a teen. This cute, little boy was born struggling to be around people who genuinely like him.

"Please stay." Emmanuel's sweet voice made her smile, but filled her soul with sorrow.

"I'll be right back." Looking right at Quinton she said, "Don't start cooking anything."

# Chapter 11

**Quinton**

Quinton loved Amelia's spontaneity. He could only imagine what she ran out of his house to go do, but based on what he'd seen so far, it would be something thoughtful to benefit someone else.

After a long day's work he stunk. Who knew one could break a sweat in this close to arctic weather? Amelia didn't say how long she'd be gone, but Quinton rushed to his bathroom and took a quick shower after he'd told Emmanuel to let Amelia back in if she returned before he finished.

Ten minutes later, Quinton returned to the kitchen smelling clean and fresh. He also dabbed on his rosewood cologne, hoping it grabbed Amelia's attention.

Quinton looked out the window. There, he caught a glimpse of Amelia leaving her house with her arms filled. Quinton rushed outside to help. "What's all this?"

"Dinner." He took the box out of her left arm and the two bags from her right hand. She looked like she might've protested him carrying everything, but before she could, he took off toward his house.

"Could you get the door for me please?" Quinton asked.

As they entered the kitchen, Quinton set the items on the table. "Emmanuel, come down for dinner."

'Be right there." Emmanuel yelled down.

Quinton's heart swelled as he and Amelia emptied out the different containers of food that Carolyn and Cash packed up for them. *Amelia knew how difficult eating at the main house was for Emmanuel, so she brought dinner to us.* He couldn't think of anything more thoughtful.

Emmanuel finally joined them. "Should we say grace?" Amelia asked.

"Yes, will you please do the honors," Quinton requested.

Amelia asked for God to bless the food, every hand that got the food to their table, and prayed that everyone would have something to eat that evening. She thanked God for adding Quinton and Emmanuel to the ranch family.

"Amen," the trio spoke in unison.

"What are we having?" Emmanuel scrunched up his nose looking at the different containers.

Amelia smiled. "Green beans, rice, and chicken."

"Chicken? I hate chicken. Dad, you know I hate chicken. No, No, NO! I can't do it." Emmanuel's little hands started moving together rapidly. He threw himself on the floor on the verge of hyperventilating, "I...can't...eat...chicken."

Quinton's face turned bright red. Sadly, this wasn't anything new for Quinton, or Emmanuel, but it still wore on him. Amelia would think he couldn't control his son, which wouldn't be a wrong assessment. He couldn't.

To his surprise Amelia sat on the floor next to Emmanuel. "I hate chicken too."

He tried to stop his tears. "I don't care...You do?"

"Most definitely, but I do eat this particular chicken. Cash makes mine a little different than everyone else's. He flattens really thin, so I don't have to taste too much chicken then he puts the coating on it. The coating is really crunchy and sweet at the same time." Emmanuel sat up. "Would you like to trade? You can have mine and I'll eat yours.

"It feels weird. I don't like it," he stammered out in between sobs.

Amelia looked up at Quinton. She mouthed, *cereal* and shrugged her shoulders. Could this woman get any better? Most people would have thought he let his son control him, but not Amelia. He appreciated the help—this was the first time in four years, it wasn't all on him. He nodded his head letting Amelia to roll with it.

"Emmanuel, if you try one bite of my chicken and eat your veggies, you can have some cereal if you don't like the chicken."

Wiping his eyes, Emmanuel said, "Thanks, guys." Amelia offered her hand to Emmanuel and he took it. She helped him stand up. Excitement rushed through Quinton. Emmanuel was making more progress.

After dinner Quinton was convinced that Amelia wasn't pretending to like Emmanuel. They were building a relationship that would be so great for Emmanuel. Now he just needed his own relationship with the woman. Geez, he was getting shown up by an eight-year-old.

Emmanuel and Amelia agreed to build up Lego City the next time she came over.

Quinton walked Amelia to her door. He wished it was more than twenty-five feet away, but he'd take any time with Amelia that he could. "Thank you for dinner tonight. I love... your thoughtfulness." *Good catch. Raddix said she'd run scared if I told her I'd fallin' for her so quickly.*

Once they reached the door, Amelia turned to face Quinton. "So, the month is almost up. Are you planning on staying?"

"Do you want me to?" *Please say yes.* Quinton silently begged.

Amelia smiled. "You've been a great addition, so I'm hoping you'll stay."

*Yes!* Quinton's smile reached his ears. "Is that the only reason you want me to stay?"

Rolling her eyes, Amelia turned toward the door, but Quinton gently captured her arm. "I'd like an answer." His heart raced faster than any horse he'd ever ridden. "I don't know if it's smart of me to tell you this..." he loved the way she held onto his every word. Right now she looked like she really cared what he was going to say.

Amelia curled up the corner of her lips and teased and her teal eyes gazed directly into his. "Are you afraid that you would never find another boss like me and wouldn't be able to function for the rest of your life?"

Her tone and the glimmer in her eyes said she was teasing, but Amelia Lawrence was the perfect person for him. He brushed his knuckles down her jawline and cupped her cheek. He wished she would have leaned into his hand, but she remained stiff. "Yeah, something like that." He smirked. "Amelia, I told you how I felt. What I need to know is how you feel."

Her eyes widened and her mouth dropped open slightly. "I was joking. There are a lot of great ranch owners out there who would be happy to have you and you'd function just fine."

"I'm not joking Amelia. I wouldn't want to work for anyone else. You are an amazing boss, but I enjoy being around you, like tonight when you're not my boss."

Silence. In the distance the sound of a coyote howling was music to his ears. He didn't want to press his luck, but he wanted to feel her lips dancing with his.

He wrapped his other hand around her waist and closed the gap between them. When he pulled Amelia against his chest, she let out a little moan. His breathing turned into quick pants. He pulled Amelia's head closer to his as he bent slightly toward her lips. She grabbed onto his flannel shirt at either side of his abdomen. Even through his shirt, the touch of her fingers made sparks ignite in his stomach. He let out a slight moan of his own and their hot breath intermingled, "Amelia, can I please kiss you?"

"I—"

At that moment his front door swung open, "Dad! Come on, what's taking you so long?"

Amelia jumped back from his embrace and the moment disappeared, leaving Quinton feeling deflated. "I love that kid, but his timing is terrible."

"I should go, Quinton."

He watched her run up the stairs and rush in the house. *Maybe tomorrow.* Without a doubt, he knew Amelia felt something for him. Elation soared through his body as he traveled back to his cabin. She didn't have to admit her feelings; she had shown them and that was good enough...for now.

# Chapter 12

## Amelia

Amelia couldn't sleep at all Friday night. She's kept imagining Quinton getting ready to lean in and kiss her. At the last second he'd stop, laugh in her face and say that she'd kissed like a newb. The thought wasn't wrong, she hadn't kissed a man before, but the idea of Quinton laughing at her for being a horrible kisser was more than she could handle. Her chest constricted, like a snake coiled around her heart and squeezed it to smithereens.

Saturday morning Amelia barely met Quinton's gaze during the employee meeting. Fortunately he had transitioned into his role smoothly and Amelia only interjected when she could help or contribute to the daily events. Thankfully, Quinton had everything planned and set for the day, so she hid away in her office doing payroll and working on a few deals to acquire more livestock and a few mares. Everything had taken her longer than it should have. Quinton filled her mind continuously throughout the day.

By dinner time when he and Emmanuel hadn't shown up again, Amelia's stomach tore in two. Her brain had told her to keep her distance, but a nagging voice within told her to pack up dinner and bring it to the newest members of the ranch family who'd taken up residence not only in one of the cabins, but in her mind and heart as well.

*I can do this.* Amelia coached as she walked across the yard and knocked on his door. Seeing Quinton in joggers and a t-shirt that accentuated his muscles made her mouth go dry. "Here's some lasagna for you and Emmanuel."

"Care to join us?" She felt Quinton's deep voice throughout her body. She was too conflicted to spend time with him this evening. What if another moment to kiss presented itself and she embarassed herself?

"I wish I could, but I can't tonight. I hope you guys enjoy it." Amelia all but ran back to her house. Needless to say, she suffered another night of restless sleep.

On Sunday, the other kids on the ranch really wanted Emmanuel to go with them to church, so Amelia knocked on Quinton's door. She almost walked away waiting for him to answer, but when the door swung open, she lost her voice.

Standing in front of her stood over six feet of pure manliness, and without a shirt every muscle popped. Amelia couldn't think straight. She sucked in a deep breath and stared hopelessly at his bare chest that tapered into a V forming his impressive six pack abs. Her eyes finally made their way to his eyes and the humorous smirk on his face confirmed that he was fully aware of the effect he has on her. Quinton pulled a t-shirt over his head and slid it down his abs. Covering up did only a little to help Amelia focus because the previous image had been branded into her brain.

"T..the kids would like Emmanuel to go to church with them. Is that something you're interested in?" Quinton's smile disappeared. Amelia couldn't quite figure out what that meant, but she didn't want to make this anymore awkward, "It's okay if you don't do church—"

"—Let me see what I can do and I'll text you."

Amelia smiled, "Okay." She didn't want to push her luck, but figured it couldn't hurt. "We also want you guys to have Sunday lunch with us when we return. I know how much Emmanuel depends on his electronics, but he does okay without them at school. Maybe you guys can try it."

"We'll see." Quinton watched her walk off his porch, but before she walked too far away he called out, "It's okay you were ogling me. I didn't mind." His mischievous grin caused her cheeks to rise in color, warming her from the inside out.

*Urg. The cocky cowboy caught me.* Amelia realized that it might be hard for her to deny an attraction at this point, but she still needed to keep her distance to avoid embarrassing herself due to her lack of experience. Quinton had been married and had a child...she'd never even kissed a man, this could never work. "In your dreams, Cowboy!"

"Every night," he hollered back with a deep, flirty voice.

"Amelia!" Emmanuel raced up to her in the church parking lot and grabbed her hand sandwiching himself between Amelia and Quinton. For a split second, Amelia imagined the three of them a real family heading into church. Sadness ripped at her chest knowing that a husband and child were not in her future.

Amelia's stomach did a backflip when Quinton smiled at her. She let out a soft nervous laugh and wrapped her free hand around her stomach, a calming technique that usually worked for her, but not now.

Quinton's muscles filled out a crisp, white, button up shirt that he combined with a pair of dark blue jeans that fit him like freshly washed jeans. Regardless of what he wore, Amelia had a difficult time taking her eyes off him.

"Did you guys go to church regularly in Texas?" Amelia tried to distract herself and get more information out of this duo.

Emmanuel shook his head, "Not anymore. I used to take my ipad with me and be just fine, but then dad wouldn't let me bring it anymore, so we stopped going."

That broke Amelia's heart. "Well, I'm glad you're here now...both of you."

Their motley looking crew took up three full pews until the children left for Sunday School. Damon offered to take all the kids downstairs. Emmanuel had only met Damon once, so it made sense when he sunk down into the pew to avoid going with him.

"Do you want me to walk you down," Amelia asked.

Emmanuel shook his head. Very early on Amelia experienced Emmanuel's lack of flexibility. Once he had his mind up, he struggled to see other possibilities. Quinton told him it was fine, but he had to stay quiet and listen to the sermon.

Amelia sat back against the pew. At the same time, Quinton put his arm behind his son to rest it on the back of the pew. His fingers brushed Amelia's arm. A jolt of electricity ran down her arm, clouding her ability to focus on Pastor Myles's message.

A few moments later two of Damon's children, Dean and Darlene, appeared. They knelt down at the end of our pew and asked Emmanuel if he wanted to go have fun with them. Emmanuel looked at his dad. "Sure."

Quinton leaned in close to Amelia's ear and whispered, "Where do I go with him?

Amelia couldn't have stopped the shiver that ran down her spine if she wanted to. "Down the stairs; first door on the right."

"I'll be right back." The instant Quinton's hot breath slapped her neck, and his musky cologne tantalized her senses, she had goosebumps down her arms and legs. Quinton reached for Emmanuel's hand as he exited the pew.

She involuntarily smiled as she'd replayed their almost kiss on Friday night in her head. When would she break the news to him that she'd never kissed a man and she never planned to. Maybe that would prevent him from trying to kiss her again, or maybe it would make him see her as a challenge and he'd pursue her more claiming he could teach her what a sensational kiss entailed.

Raddix nudged her with his shoulder, "What's the smile for?" He whispered.

Shaking her head free of thoughts that she probably shouldn't have had at all, she straightened her back and focused herself. "Nothing." He smirked at her like he could read her mind, too. What was it with the men around her? Could they truly read her mind, or did they just enjoy teasing her?

"Be careful. I'd hate to wreck your new foreman for hurting you." Raddix smiled, but Amelia knew he wasn't joking.

Without Quinton's close presence and Raddix's silence , Amelia focused on the message. Pastor Myles truly loved the people of this congregation. He wanted every single one of them to enter the kingdom of Heaven when their time came.

"Our hearts are liars." Amelia started silently singing the song, *Devil is a Liar* by one of her favorite artists. Then, she asked God to help her focus. She was interested in where the Pastor was headed with this message.

A long while later Quinton returned and Amelia noticed that he sat much closer to her leaving space at the end of the pew. Immediately her pulse skyrocketed. She feared he could hear the loud thumping of her heart in the silent church.

Amelia leaned over and whispered in his ear, "Is Emmanuel okay?"

Quinton slowly turned his head toward Amelia and nodded. "Yeah, he's good."

Amelia got lost in the intensity of Quinton's eyes. *Did you send me Quinton, Lord? Am I supposed to give him a chance?* At that moment Quinton flipped his hand over, palm up. Amelia hesitated. His eyes encouraged her to take his hand. As she fused their fingers together, her stomach dipped.

She turned her head back toward the pulpit. "Jeremiah seventeen nine tells us, 'The heart is deceitful above all things and desperately wicked: who can know it?' I interpret that to mean that our feelings are unreliable. Remember our feelings are thoughts of our hearts, so if your thoughts are telling you to do sinful things, your feelings are unreliable." Pastor Myles spoke enthusiastically.

Quinton placed their interlaced hands on his muscular thigh as he crossed that leg to rest his ankle on his other knee. White heat rippled through her arm. *Focus!* Amelia ordered herself.

"Don't let your feelings confuse you into thinking you are doing what God told you. We have an astronomically high divorce rate where people listen to their feelings and not what God has told them. Obviously, there are some circumstances that warrant divorce, those circumstances are spelled out for us, just like everything else is right here." Pastor Myles lifted the Bible he had been reading from moments ago to make his point.

Quinton turned his head, catching Amelia's attention. She saw a keen hunger radiating from his eyes. If only they weren't in church, she longed to hear his thoughts.

"One last thing..." Pastor Myles' favorite line, that he used at least twice a sermon, brought Amelia's attention back to the pulpit. Amelia smiled appreciating all of his wisdom. "...life is life. Things are going to happen that you never expected. Pray, get your answers from God. Some of the best things in life are the unplanned situations."

*Thank you, Lord. I'll take that as my answer. I won't ignore this blessing. Well, I'll try. Please help me let go of my doubts and fears that are holding me back.*

Church ended and Quinton escaped downstairs to get Emmanuel. Her hand turned cold the moment he left. She felt like a teenager having a boyfriend to hold hands with at church. The only problem was that Quinton wasn't hers. But whose fault was that?

When Quinton returned with Emmanuel, the little guy tapped on Amelia's leg, She sat back down to be closer to Emmanuel. "What's for lunch? My dad said you asked us to come."

"Yes, the kids really want to eat lunch with you. " Amelia confirmed. "I believe we're having a smorgasbord."

"What's a smug-ish-bored?" Emmanuel asked with a high pitched voice.

Amelia laughed. She glimpsed at Jeff and Quinton who were having a conversation and shaking hands. "A smorgasbord is a lot of different food, like a buffet." On Sundays, we usually have the leftovers from the week and Carolyn makes a special dessert."

"Is there going to be more of that lasagna that you dropped off? I really liked that." Emmanuel slurped and licked his lips multiple times producing a laugh from everyone who heard.

"I'm not sure, but if there is, we'll make sure you get some."

Quinton arrived at our pew and Emmanuel looked at his dad. "You're in luck, Dad, I want to go to lunch."

When Quinton gave him a quizzical look Emmanuel continued, his face lacked emotion. "Yeah, remember you said that you really wanted to eat lunch with Amelia." He stood. "You told me to get with the program."

The idea of teasing him to expound on that statement energized Amelia, but she couldn't formulate her words quick enough and the moment sped by.

Amelia thought it was adorable the way a slight tinge of pink rose from Quinton's neck into his cheeks. She could only imagine what Quinton would say if she called him adorable.

Quinton rubbed his palm over one side of his face. "Out of the mouth of babes."

"What's that mean?" Emmanuel wondered aloud.

Quinton held out his hand and led his son out of the pew, "It means that you say things you shouldn't." Everyone within earshot laughed. Quinton's eyes captured Amelia's. She quickly looked away feeling nervous herself.

Raddix sat next to her in the pew. "Be careful. I know that look," he warned.

"What look?"

"Both yours and Quinton's." He hugged her and left.

Despite definitely being interested in her foreman, it made her more nervous and self conscious. Amelia also questioned if he was truly interested. Perhaps he was just a good flirt, or maybe he was a dirtbag like Ethan Hawkins. She didn't know him well enough yet.  She created many plausible stories in her head because there was just no way that someone of Quinton's caliber would ever be interested in her.

Quinton held out his other hand to Amelia. Confusion flooded her face. "Jeff asked me to take you home. He and Katy are staying for a meeting about the upcoming carnival."

Amelia looked at Jeff who sent her a big *go get em'* grin. Without wasting any more time, she placed her hand in Quinton's and upon his touch an instant smile bloomed across her face and her pulse quickened. "See everyone back at the ranch." She all but ran out of the church, so she didn't draw any more attention to herself.

# Chapter 13

**Amelia**

During the ride back, Emmanuel monopolized the conversation. Per usual, he really didn't even want either Quinton or Amelia to say anything of value. As long as they gave him one word or short phrases as acknowledgement he rattled on nonstop.

"He's completely comfortable now. We'll never get a word in."

"Can I talk, Dad?" Emmanuel expressed his dislike for his Dad whispering during his story.

Quinton raised his hand between the seats, so his son could see it from the back, "Sorry, keep going." When he dropped his hand back on the console, Quinton bumped Amelia's hand that had been resting there since she had turned to give her undivided attention to Emmanuel. It also made it easier to sneak glances at Quinton without him knowing. He laced his fingers with hers. Immediately, her pulse flew into overdrive.

Watching Quinton's jaw tense and release gave her heart palpitations. How could something so simple send her body into desire mode so quickly. *Don't trust your feelings. Calm down. Focus.*

"Right, Amelia?" Emmanuel asked her to verify something that she didn't have a clue about. Quinton's sly smirk revealed he knew that she hadn't been paying attention. At least he didn't know what she'd been thinking. If he did, he'd probably be repulsed to know that an inexperienced, tall freak clearly developed the hots for him. *Maybe that's part of his plan to trick me.*

"Sure, Buddy."

Quinton snapped his head toward her at the same time Emmanuel said, "Really?" with all the confusion or maybe excitement of the world, she couldn't quite tell.

Trying to backtrack, "Well, I should discuss it with your dad first and let you know."

"Aw, okay." Emmanuel sounded deflated. She'd have to ask Quinton later what she promised the little guy.

When they arrived at the ranch, Emmanuel hopped out of his booster seat from the back at the same time Quinton hopped out of the driver's side. Emmanuel whipped open Amelia's door as Quinton rounded the front of the truck. "Dad says men have to open the door for beautiful women."

"That wasn't exactly how I put it, but it certainly applies in this case."

Amelia's breath caught at the sound of Quinton's deep, low voice, but she played it safe and focused on Emmanuel instead. She smiled down at him and rubbed his skater hair. "Keep following your daddy's advice and you'll be a heartbreaker when you grow up. Do you know what that means?" Quinton waited for Amelia to take another step forward and he shut the door.

"No. What?" Emmanuel asked.

"It means you'll have all the girls wanting to be around you."

With a stone straight face, Emmanuel stated, "I'll call the police on them."

Emmanuel's face still didn't show any emotion despite the ear-splitting sound of laughter exploding from Amelia and Quinton. Emmanuel asked, "Why's that funny?"

"Come on, Buddy, I'll explain it to you." Quinton wrapped his arm around his son's shoulders and Emmanuel twisted his shoulder for his dad's arm to fall.

"I'm going to change. Whenever you guys are ready, come on over. Lunch should be in about an hour."

After the kids finished eating, they geared up and shuffled out in the snow to play while the adults finished up. Quinton's leg bumped into Amelia's leg under the table and he never moved it. *Get a grip.*

*He's flirting with you. Enjoy it and flirt back.* Katy's words of wisdom, so she calls them, rushed to the front of Amelia's mind. Fear stabbed her in the heart. What if he's just trying to better himself and using Amelia for her business? What if he was trying to make her look like a fool? She'd been the butt of jokes before, but her fifteen million dollar ranch hadn't been on the line before. If she didn't guard her heart against Quinton's flirting, she could lose everything. *But didn't you feel like God was telling you to take a chance and accept His blessings?* She reminded her inner-self. In church Amelia felt The Spirit tell her that Quinton was a blessing that she should appreciate.

"Let's play charades while the kids are still outside," Damon suggested, pulling Amelia from her distress.

Amelia loved that everyone, with the exception of Uncle Sean, Jeff, and Katy were all around the same age. It made for some fun times together.

"I'll get the game." Amelia announced then joined everyone in the living room.

Carolyn and Cash, Raddix, Damon, Rocco and Renee sat on the oversized couch leaving only the love seat available where Quinton had made himself comfortable. He stretched his arms round the back of the seat. When Amelia realized that was the only seat available, besides wooden rocking chairs, she slowly descended toward the cushion.

"Perfect four and four. I'll be with Damon, Quinton and Amelia." Raddix split the groups and grabbed a card. "You two better get this." Amelia and Quinton shared a confused look.

Damon revealed the category: song titles. Renee flipped the timer and Raddix started pointing at Renee. Amelia got overzealous and competitive, per usual, during games and she yelled Renee's name a little forcefully.

When Raddix used his hands in a circular motion indicating for her to expand, Amelia yelled, "Teacher." Raddix put his finger to his nose.

Then Raddix started moving his sweatshirt back and forth like he needed air flow. When neither of them said anything, Raddix pointed at Quinton and started pulling on his sweatshirt again and wiping his brow. Amelia yelled, "Quinton's sweaty. Quinton's hot." She immediately buried her face in her hands feeling the heat rise to her face," while everyone laughed. "Hot for teacher," Amelia's head flew up just before the timer went off.

"Yes," Raddix pumped his fist in the air.

"Seriously? You two cheated." Amelia's mouth dropped at Rocco's accusation. "There's no way you should have got that."

Leaning forward and resting his palm on Amelia's back, causing a spot of origin for the fire brewing on her skin, Quinton teased, "Apparently someone's hot for Quinton."

His hot breath on her neck gave her goosebumps. Listening to him refer to himself in the third person sent more shivers through her body. Why? Who the heck knows. Amelia blushed profusely as she gazed into his eyes, but didn't deny his statement. The more time she spent with him, the more he intrigued her.

"Dream on. It's just a game," Amelia retorted with a sassy tone and involuntarily winked at him. She looked away quickly, embarrassed for giving him such an affectionate gesture, again.

The couples continued with the game. Many times Quinton and Amelia arrived at the answer together and they high-fived. Every time their hands connected she thought Quinton looked at her with alluring eyes. A couple of times she pulled her shirt away from her body quickly giving herself a much needed cool down. Quinton's sly smile revealed that he knew that his nearness and touch prompted the action.

As the sun drifted off to sleep, the kids stormed through the door ready to eat, again. Carolyn and Cash immediately rose from their positions to make sandwiches for the kids. "Anyone else want a sandwich?" The men cheered for more food. "I guess that means the game is over." Cash declared.

Thank goodness. Amelia needed proximity from one specific teammate. She put the game back in the closet.

When she turned around, Quinton was closer than she expected and her hands landed on his chest. She sucked in a deep breath, her eyes closed, and her body instantly tensed. Slowly opening her eyes, they drifted up to his liquid brown beauties.

Amelia breathed, "Hey."

"Hey," Quinton replied very close.

He wrapped one arm around her waist and dipped his head slowly toward hers. "Amelia," he drawled, pushing her heart beat to an alarming level. He brushed a loose strand of her blonde highlighted hair from her ponytail off her shoulder that initiated goosebumps across her entire arm. Within an inch of her mouth, he murmured, "Your beauty is remarkable."

*For real?* Amelia knew for sure that he was lying to her now. No one, except her family, had ever said anything remotely close to that. *Your beauty is remarkable. Ha!* He must have been looking in a mirror.

"Dad," Emmanuel pulled on his shirt so hard that Quinton's arms dropped from her waist. "Can I have a cookie with my sandwich?"

Quinton's eyes filled with what Amelia thought was disappointment for the interruption, yet he knelt down toward Emmanuel and gave him his undivided attention. "Yes, but just one." Watching that interaction between the two of them warmed Amelia's heart.

He watched his son skip a little awkwardly back to the kitchen. "He's still working on his coordination. We also need to have another conversation about timing and situational awareness; it apparently hasn't stuck." Quinton's grin did funny things to Amelia's stomach.

Amelia giggled.

"You're precious," Quinton whispered close to her ear. "Will you take a walk with me? I definitely need some *cold* air."

Maybe the moment could be recreated. Did she want it to be, or should she just give some excuse to go to bed early, though she'd never sleep at this point? That's exactly what her mind said to do. When she opened her mouth to excuse herself she giggled again, "I'd love to." *I don't giggle.* Now she had done it twice in a matter of seconds.

He rewarded her with a big smile. He stepped aside motioning with his hand for her to lead the way. He gently placed his hand on her lower back and instantly the skin underneath his large palm scorched.

Amelia shared her plans with Carolyn. "Will you text me when Emmanuel is done eating, so we can come back?"

Carolyn squeezed Amelia's hand, "Have fun and I want to hear all about it."

Quinton met Amelia in the foyer after letting Emmanuel know he was going for a walk. As Quinton helped Amelia with her coat, they heard Emmanuel in the kitchen, "Yeah, he wants Amelia to be his girlfriend. Gross!"

Quinton's head dropped as Amelia chuckled, "What are you worried about? Apparently, I'm the gross one," she joked.

"Hardly. Remember this is the same boy who's going to call the police on any girl who shows interest in him." They shared a light laugh that felt normal, so why did Amelia have a pit burning at the bottom of her stomach?

In the still of the approaching night, Quinton stuffed his hands in his pockets, "When does it get warmer here?" Quinton wondered aloud.

"April and May are the cool, spring months, but we won't hit eighties until the end of June."

Quinton gave her a flirty, sideways stare, "I guess I'll have to find another way to keep myself warm." He took his hand closest to Amelia out of his pocket and laced his fingers with hers. Amelia's gloved hand warmed even more. The big smile Quinton produced led Amelia to believe that he enjoyed the feel of her hand in his. Unless of course he's a great actor. Amelia still wondered about that.

"Tell me about your wife." Quinton stiffened, making Amelia feel self-conscious for asking. "Nevermind. That was out of the blue. You don't have to answer that."

"I don't mind. What do you want to know?" Quinton's muscles relaxed.

"Just the basics. How'd you meet? How long were you married?"

Quinton swung their attached arms, as he started to answer. "Rose was a traveling nurse. I had an accident with the branding tool one day and she was called in to fix up my leg. We were married six months later and had Emmanuel a year after our wedding."

"How'd you know you wanted to marry her so quickly?" Amelia's voice was full of astonishment.

Quinton shrugged. "I was really close with God at one point. Losing Rose put a strain on that relationship, but I've always felt that God spoke to me in such a clear way. I can't explain it, I just know it's Him...Just like He's speaking to me now."

Amelia dismissed his last statement when she noticed a light on in the store. "Let's go see why the lights are on." She pulled along with her. "Hello," Amelia called when she opened the door. Nothing. The connecting door leading to the butcher room was locked. Amelia assumed that Katy probably forgot to turn off the light.

"Oh, yeah,..." Amelia continued to check around the store to make sure nothing was out of place. "...will you tell me what I agreed to in the truck when we came back from church? I don't want to disappoint Emmanuel by not coming through with my promise."

Quinton chortled and rubbed the back of his neck, "Well, you agreed to become his mom someday."

The blood drained from Amelia's face and her jaw dropped to the floor. "I didn't."

"At least you did save yourself by saying you had to check with me. I was relieved to have a say in the situation." Quinton winked at her, but his words made Amelia feel sick to her stomach.

Of course he was relieved. He looked mortified in the truck right after she'd opened her mouth and inserted both of her feet. And now he made it clear that he wanted a say in the situation, which obviously makes sense, but to Amelia, all she heard was *Phew, I don't want to marry you.* Amelia turned her back to Quinton embarrassed and upset. She'd done it again—let her guard down. Amelia had absolutely no one to blame except for herself, it was not like she hadn't been in this same situation before.

Amelia could feel Quinton's presence, but she didn't realize he was *that* close. Quinton wrapped an arm around her waist and trailed his fingers up her neck and down her jawline. Amelia's attraction for Quinton had reached its boiling point. She found him utterly irresistible, but between his own comments, Raddix's warnings, and her own insecurities Amelia couldn't shake the doubt from her head. This will fall apart eventually, so no point in waiting.

*This tough, fit to be a model, man is not really attracted to me.* Amelia needed to get out of here and clear her head. She's stayed in control of her emotions since high school. She refused to let her new employee throw all her caution to the wind and have her heart land in a million broken pieces when he finished.

Leaning close to her ear, Quinton whispered, "I know we haven't known each other long and I know it might be weird because you're my boss, but I find you exquisite."

Amelia sucked in a deep breath. If she stayed around Quinton any longer, she just might pass out due to lack of oxygen.

He gently turned Amelia around to face him. "Every time I learn something new about you, I fall even deeper for you. If you want me to leave, I'll find a job at another ranch."

Amelia shot her eyes up to meet him, "Why would I want you to do that? You've been a great addition to our ranch family; you and Emmanuel."

Caressing her cheek with his knuckles he explained, "I don't want to leave. If you are uncomfortable with our current employment situation, I'll leave because I can't help how I feel about you."

Amelia appreciated the sentiment, but at the same time, she felt he was being really selfish. It was only by the grace of God that Emmanuel adapted as easily as he did. Despite the many meltdowns he'd had when he first arrived, he'd used his self-regulation strategies with the kids, adults, weather, everything...for the most part—he'd always have struggles. Amelia couldn't imagine disrupting his life.

She also felt like he didn't realize how hard it was to find a good foreman to run a ranch of this size. If he just up and left her, that didn't bode well with her either.

Amelia shifted around Quinton and sauntered closer toward the door to get some much needed space before stopping and turning back toward him. "Quinton, there is no denying the attraction between the two of us...I think... but..." Amelia looked away from him when she explained her concerns to him. "I am really off kilter when you're around. I question a lot of things, like how genuine your statements are; that's all on me—there's nothing you can do about that. You know my past and it's hard for me to trust what you say."

Taking a deep breath, she asked, "Have you dated since your wife died? How will Emmanuel feel about this?

Quinton ran his hand through his hair and started to pace back and forth. Amelia had never seen him disheveled and felt guilty because she had done this.

"Everything came out all wrong if you're upset. I haven't dated since Rose died. I haven't been interested in a woman; you're the first. I didn't mean to imply that I don't want to be here because that is the farthest thing from the truth. I love it here." Taking a small step in her direction, but still not touching her, "I will admit, I can't wait for it to be warmer, but everything else is perfect, especially you."

Quinton lifted his arms and then dropped them back to his sides. "Emmanuel means everything to me and you're right; he's adapted well since coming here; Emmanuel needs to be here; he needs you as much as he needs me," Quinton claimed.

"We want you here to, but—"

*BRRRING, BRRRING!* Amelia jumped and quickly retrieved her phone from her pocket. "Hello." Amelia noticed that Quinton didn't take his eyes off her. "Okay. We'll be right back."

"Emmanuel is done eating. I should let you get to his bedtime routine."

Amelia spun toward the door and Quinton gently grabbed her upper arm. She instantly felt the heat from his hand, but also a pang of hurt in her heart, "Where are we leaving this?" he asked with an ache in his voice.

"We need to take this much slower and get to know each other better. I don't want either of us, or especially Emmanuel, getting hurt." Amelia needed to figure things out for herself. Could she tear down her walls and allow Quinton in? "Sadly, I don't see myself trusting or believing for a long while."

"This conversation isn't over, Amelia."

"It is for now. Goodnight, Quinton."

# Chapter 14

**Quinton**

A week had crawled by since Quinton had talked to Amelia about anything other than the ranch or Emmanuel's schooling during their nightly check in.

Quinton had knocked on Amelia's office door at the end of a particularly draining day. It was fair to say he didn't have any energy left. In fact, he almost texted her the updates, but his desire to see her had overridden his sensible thinking.

"Come in."

"Hey." He didn't mean to sound as sultry as he did, but it probably goes without saying that the second he saw her tone shoulders in her fit t-shirt, he had a burst of energy. Oh, how he'd longed to brush her hair off her shoulder and drop gentle kisses on the spot where her collarbone protruded. He'd tried not to even think about her full, pouty lips that he just wanted to feel against his, but that was no use. They'd called his name the instant he crossed the threshold. The missed opportunities to brand her lips with his had burned his brain.

"Why are you rubbing your wrist? How'd your day go?" Amelia shuffled a few papers on her desk.

Quinton sat in the chair directly across from Amelia's desk and let out the breath. One could view it as exhaustion, but Quinton knew it had everything to do with the alluring teal eyes staring at him and her scent overpowering this office.

He realized it'd been over a month since he sat in this seat for his interview, which meant it'd been thirty days since he'd found the woman he intended to grow old with. Now, he just needed to convince her of that. "Nothing out of the ordinary. Rocco gave Duncan his annual shots, so don't try to ride him tonight or tomorrow morning." Keeping his eyes glued on hers he continued, "I tackled a particularly ornery calf during its immunizations and twisted my wrist."

"You should put ice on it. Anything else?" Amelia rested her chin in the palm of her hand, as her fingers rested on her lips.

"Not work related." Quinton braved as his belly burned with warm sensations as he imagined what it would feel like to touch Amelia's lips.

Quinton had been eating at his cabin because his sad, sappy face would just ruin everyone's meal. Amelia and the kids convinced Emmanuel to start eating with them in the main house and he'd enjoyed it. Emmanuel never adapted this easily to others. Quinton knew that meant something. He didn't want to take that away from his son's growth, nor did he want to make Amelia feel uncomfortable, so he suffered alone.

"Why don't you join everyone for dinner?" Amelia set her pen down.

When Amelia told him that everyone was family. He never imagined her words to ring so true. He hadn't had the best relationship with his own dad, but he'd learn to deal with it. Talking with Jeff every morning filled the hole in his heart that he'd never realized was there. "Give her time. She'll learn to love herself." Quinton hated that Amelia couldn't see herself through his eyes.

Even though Amelia was clearly stressed trying to work through her own things, Quinton realized that she was still worried about him, that had to mean something. "I don't think so. Raddix and I need all the space we can get. Plus, I don't know where we stand. Frankly, it's just too hard to be around you a lot."

Quinton recalled a conversation he'd had with Rocco. The man had just turned thirty-four. Three years younger than Quinton, he seemed just as wise, if not wiser than Quinton. Of course he was when it came to the technical doctoring of the ranch animals, but also when it came to Amelia.

*"Women have way too much power over us, Rocco." Quinton tried to smile, but only one side of his upper lip lifted before he let out and exasperated, "Tsk." He ran his fingers through his dark brown hair that had grown out on the top in the past month he'd been at the ranch.*

*Rocco roared as he stood from his knelt position on the hay checking out another new calf. "The right woman does," he agreed. "All Renee has to do is give me that exquisite look she has just for me, and I'm a goner."*

*Turning toward Quinton he slapped him on the arm, "I heard you were married before. I am sorry about your wife. That must have been hard, Man."*

*"Thanks," Quinton appreciated his condolences.*

*Rocco smirked and nodded in agreement. "When she's the right one, love alters your mind, body and soul. I think you'd be good for her, but that's my opinion and if Amelia corners me I'll deny this conversation ever took place." He laughed and slapped Quinton on the back.*

*Love? Could Rocco really see that? Quinton didn't say anything about love. Though he knew he felt it, he kept it to himself. Very few people fell in love quickly and those people denied it could happen so quickly. He wasn't in the mood to have others tell him how he felt.*

*"I was referring to when Amelia brushes by me I'm a goner, like you were saying before." Quinton paced back and forth for a second. "I'm sorry. I'm not sure why I shared that."*

*Rocco laughed, "Have you been talking to Jeff lately? He's a sap. He gets all of us talking at some point." Rocco cleaned himself up. "I've got more animals to check on, but I have something for you to think about." Rocco placed his strong hand on Quinton's shoulder despite the four or five inches Quinton had over Rocco. "You clearly are affecting her. Renee said that she's never seen Amelia so deflated."*

"Quinton..." Amelia broke through his thoughts.

'I'm sorry. Look, Amelia. I've let this…" He waved his hand between them "…linger. I've put all my energy into work, but nothing has helped." His heart skipped a beat as he tried to read Amelia's eyes. This woman owned his head space. He didn't even have a clue what she just said.

"…are you prepared for the storm?" her words registering this time.

Quinton inhaled big and let it out. "Jeff and I discussed it today, but why don't you share your expectations with me." He'd talk about anything just to get more time with her.

Amelia's mouth started moving. Quinton heard every word, but his focus split its time between her eyes and lips. His eyes moved subtly between the two like a ball during a slow moving tennis game.

"Everyone will gather tomorrow morning after breakfast. You'll run through the regular jobs they need to complete for the day. Then, you'll assign the storm jobs that are outside of their daily expectations, but necessary." She handed him a sheet of paper with 'Storm Jobs' written at the top.

"Thank you." He intentionally brushed her fingers, as he took the paper.

"I'm sure someone will run into town for everyone's supplies. Make sure it's early enough. If you need help, let me know and I'll go."

This was a nightmare. Having Amelia so close, yet so emotionally distant wreaked havoc on his stomach. As he sat mere feet away from her, he prayed that his lunch didn't make another appearance today. Quinton looked at her quizzically. "Supplies?"

"You know, I'm sure Cash and Carolyn will need things, Rocco usually needs medical supplies, things like that, so you'll need to figure out who should take that trip. You might have to do it to make sure everyone else gets their jobs done."

Quinton nodded, "Sure whatever needs to be done. Maybe you would ride along with me...since it's my first trip in town. I want to be as efficient as possible and return before the storm begins." Having that extra time with Amelia is exactly what Quinton wanted.

Amelia's eyes finally lifted toward him and he saw sadness oozing from them. "We'll see." She leaned back in her chair and let out a breath that sounded more like a sigh. "I usually keep to myself on storm days."

*We'll see.* That was Quinton's famous answer for Emmanuel when he didn't want to deal with making a decision at the moment and hoped his son forgot about the request. It wouldn't work on him. He'd never forget about the possibility of being alone with Amelia. He didn't care if it meant driving over an hour into town, being an errand boy, and driving back. If Amelia drove with him, he'd be the happiest man alive. *Why would she seclude herself when her ranch needed attention during a storm?* Undoubtedly, Amelia is like an onion—many layers to peel back. Sadly, Quinton was still on the first layer, maybe the second.

Silence dragged on a few more beats. Then, thankfully Amelia filled him in on what to expect during his first Montana storm. "The storm is calling for twenty-four to thirty-six inches of snow. This is known as calf killing weather," Amelia began. "Rocco put the calves and mothers together in the barn with the heifers close to the end of their gestation period. You'll want to work with Sean and Raddix to move the herds around, finding them the best protection."

"Should I use the tractor to bring more hay from the back barns?" Quinton asked.

Amelia barked, "No. A tractor in this weather is too dangerous. Isn't there enough hay in the barns?"

Quinton didn't understand what upset Amelia about the tractor or the hay, but something definitely bothered her.

"You'll also need to get the windbreak panels in place. The project forecast is calling for wind coming from the northeast and half way through it will switch to northwest. You'll want to use Bill and the other available ranch hands to get those up at day break since they didn't get put up today. Sorry, I should have come to help you with that."

"That's all right. Anything else I need to know?" Quinton noticed that Amelia stated all this on the job sheet. Her organization impressed him.

Amelia shook her head.

Standing, Quinton moved closer to Amelia's desk, and wiped his palm over the front of his face. "Will you tell me what I did wrong? The last thing I ever want to do is hurt you." Quinton watched Amelia's face and she appeared to be contemplating his answers. *Why can't women act just let men and blurt things out then explain what it meant. Does she really need to think this long?* The hum of the ceiling fan running above his head produced the only noise in the room and then finally she gave Quinton something.

"Technically, you didn't do anything wrong. I have my own stuff to work through. I'm sorry you thought you did anything wrong."

Quinton stood and took a step closer to her desk, leaning his thighs up against the mahogany wood. "I'd like to help you work through them...if you'd let me."

"Being around you makes things harder for me." Amelia admitted.

*Be careful what you wish for buddy. Amelia clearly doesn't have a problem being direct.* Quinton didn't even know how to respond to that. He'd never had a woman be so honest with him before, yet not tell him anything. He usually welcomed silence, but one thing he couldn't take at this moment was the stillness. He wanted to help Amelia through whatever she has going on, so they can move forward. If she'd only let him. How could he convince her to let him help?

"My invitation to be here for you is always open, Amelia. Before I go, can I tell you a secret?"

"Um. If you want to." Amelia leaned back in her chair. His chest ached, wanting to hold her the more she studied his face with those longing eyes. He couldn't remember Rose ever looking at him like that.

With a groan, Quinton ran his fingers through his hair. "I was always scared I'd grow up to be like my dad." Quinton rested the palms of his hands on the top of her desk and leaned forward. "He considered himself a real Casanova—broke my mom's heart. Then, I realized I'd never turn out like him if I didn't let myself, so I didn't." He stood up straight. "I tell you this because you don't have to end up alone like the people in high school said you would. You may not have had boyfriends in the past, but you have the opportunity to change that now, if you choose to. The question is: are you going to stand in the way of your own potential happiness, or are you going to take a risk? Quinton forced his feet to move once his final words left his mouth. When his hand reached the door knob, Amelia spoke again leaving him caught in his tracks.

"Emmanuel tells me you're eating in your cabin because you're being a baby."

Quinton turned to face her and noticed the half smirk on her lips. He wanted to pull her out of her chair, press her against his chest and capture her mouth with his. "It hurts too much to be so close to you." Maybe his own honesty would get her to talk.

Quinton wasn't trying to be difficult using her words as his own, but it was the truth. "Tell me about it. Like I said, the issue isn't you. I'm sorry your dad was a womanizer, but it never crossed my mind that you would be one." Her words touched his heart, making him grow even more fond of Ms. Amelia Lawrence.

Quinton had never been so honest with anyone about his feelings. Jeff was rubbing off on him. He'd given Quinton the key to a blissful relationship—*complete honesty*. Jeff had told him he used to get so mad when Katy hurt his feelings. He'd do and say stupid things, putting a wedge between them. Once he'd started sharing his pain, or begging for her forgiveness; 'Let's just say we made up quickly' he'd told Quinton with a smile. Then their relationship settled into a simulation of what the Bible expected: the husband loves his wife like Christ loved the church and the wife respected and honored her husband.

"I'll see you tomorrow," Quinton choked out and then shut the door without looking back. He went to his cabin to eat dinner. Alone.

After dinner Jeff walked Emmanuel home. Quinton thanked the man he had come to reverie like a dad for bringing his son home.Quinton sent his son in to wash up.

"I'm not one to intervene when I'm not asked, but I'm going to anyway." Quinton tried to stifle a chuckle knowing that Jeff liked to help everyone and intervened whenever he could. "Like I just told Amelia, if you two think you're fooling anyone, you're dead wrong. It is obvious there is something between you two. Whether it's longlasting, only you two can determine that." Jeff ran a hand through his hair. He had grown pretty close with and knew that Quinton wouldn't mind this advice. "Limiting your time together to the point where you are not even eating with your son is not going to bring you any closer to seeing if there is something between you too."

Jeff gave Quinton that fatherly smile he'd grown to love. "For what it's worth, If Jack were here, I think he'd approve." Quinton thought about Amelia's dad. Despite never meeting the man, he'd felt like he knew him better than his own dad through Jeff's stories. As Jeff turned to walk away, he gave his approval too. "I believe you're authentic. I don't believe you're just using Amelia to secure a ranch for yourself."

"What!? Is that what she thinks?" Quinton's heart dropped. How could she think that?

Jeff shrugged, "Someone may have planted that idea in her head, but I think I plucked that weed for you."

"Thanks, man! I appreciate it."

After washing up and reading a book to Emmanuel, his son told him how he wanted Quinton to eat dinner with Amelia and him. "Have you talked to Damon about me riding Duncan more?"

"Not yet, sorry buddy."

"Can Amelia ask him? She gets things done fast."

*Slam.* "I'll ask, Son. Very soon."

Quinton tossed and turned all night trying to figure out a way he can get Amelia to see herself through his eyes. He didn't care about her ranch. If he could just kiss her, she would know.

# Chapter 15

**Quinton**

The next morning at breakfast, everyone discussed their role in the preparation for the upcoming blizzard. Sean and Raddix welcomed Quinton's help with situating the herds. The ranch hands had already started placing the windbreaks. Quinton offered to help them finish up once the meeting ended. Clearly, they didn't need his help, but Quinton wanted to learn.

"This won't be too bad. At least it's not April, that would really destroy springtime on the ranch. Spring is Amelia's favorite time." Sean shared, his eyes trying to tell Quinton something, he thought. He wasn't sure what though because Amelia's uncle didn't talk much and was hard to read in general. "Everything comes to life and brings excitement during the spring. Perhaps something like a budding relationship."

As if she heard her name, Amelia entered the room and he locked eyes with her. She seemed tired. Quinton lifted his chin toward her, hoping she found his manly nod irresistible before he forced himself to look away.

She smiled in response, which caused his pulse to race. He appreciated Amelia's uncle and Jeff's support. *Who could have steered Amelia away from me?*

His eyes scanned everyone in the room. They landed on Raddix. He was the only one who showed any distaste for Quinton. As the meeting wrapped up and everyone finished eating, Quinton approached Raddix. "Can we have a word outside?" Silence filled the room and all eyes froze on the two men. Amelia looked concerned. Katy patted her arm trying to calm her nerves.

Neither of the men grabbed a jacket. Quinton didn't expect this to take long. "I am not sure, but since your own dad and Jeff have encouraged me to pursue a relationship with Amelia, I have to assume, you're the one who brainwashed her into thinking that I am using her for her ranch."

Raddix smirked. Quinton returned a smirk. *I'm going to hit him.*

"Look man, from my perspective, when you first arrived it was all too convenient. You didn't know anything about her, yet you're going after her like a dog in heat."

Quinton didn't appreciate the comparison, though Raddix wasn't wrong about Amelia appealing to him from the moment he saw her. Amelia turned his insides on fire and he definitely enjoyed being close to her. The idea of kissing her set him ablaze even more, but it didn't interfere with his work, and it certainly had nothing to do with wanting to steal from her.

"I obviously don't know her like all of you, but I am trying to." Quinton hoped he looked genuine.

Raddix nodded. "I believe you. I mean I made that statement shortly after you arrived." You've been here a month and other than the tension between you and Amelia right now, it seems like you've been here forever. Raddix shoved his hands toward Quinton to shake. He accepted the guy's hand. "Noone, not even my dad or Jeff know Amelia like I do. All of her fears, insecurities and dreams. I make it my life's mission to watch out for her."

A pang of jealousy hit Quinton in the gut. He wanted to be the one watching out for Amelia. "That role will serve you well in a marriage someday, Raddix, but you can't prevent Amelia from finding a husband to protect her." Quinton slapped the man on the top of his shoulder as he walked by, "I may not win that role, but it won't be for a lack of trying. I'd appreciate it if you didn't stand in my way."

"Noted." Raddix held out his hand for Quinton to shake again. "I just want to make it clear that if you hurt her, I'll thrash you."

"Not before I thrash myself. I don't ever intend on hurting her." Quinton assured him.

The men returned to the kitchen as Renee took the kids down to school. Cash and Carolyn finished clearing the breakfast table. Jeff and Sean were conversing at the far end of the table. Quinton kept making eye contact with Amelia and it stirred more feelings in him. Her eyes seemed to reveal that she was just as invested in him. Quinton anguished over the missed opportunities to kiss Amelia. He needed to find an excuse to be alone with her.

"Amelia, can you do that?" Whipping her head toward Jeff who asked the question. Quinton knew that look. She pleaded with her eyes for Jeff to ask the question again. *What had captured her attention?*

"Can you ride with Quinton into town before the storm to buy the supplies we need?" Jeff reasked.

Her gaze shifted back to Quinton, who flashed her an eager smile. "Of course."

"While you're gone, Em, I'll check the generator to make sure it's running right in case we lose the power." Raddix offered his help once he finished work with his dad.

"Thanks."

The few who remained left to make sure they got their work done in time to beat the storm. Amelia started to approach Quinton, but Rocco got to him first and added a few more veterinarian supplies to the list. Then before she could see if Quinton was ready to go, Raddix grabbed Quinton's attention. "You better treat her right. She has a difficult time during storms. Tonight, you'll get your chance to prove you can protect her."

"She'll never be in better hands than mine." Quinton slapped Raddix on the back with his free hand and he winked at Amelia.

It only took fifteen minutes to help Billy secure the windbreaks. Then, Quinton returned to the main house to pick up Amelia for their trip to town.

Amelia followed Quinton to his truck. He placed his hand on the small of her back while he opened the door for her. The heat he once felt when he touched her returned instantly. Once she settled in the cab of the truck, Quinton swiftly made it to his seat and threw the truck in gear.

She had a scent that filled the cab of the truck. It reminded him of coconut suntan lotion. Nonetheless, it increased his desire to be by her side. "What are you wearing?"

Embarrassed, she ducked her head. "It's called 'at the beach'. I've always wanted to go to the beach, but haven't, so I figured I could smell like it."

"It compliments you nicely."

"Thank you." Amelia rubbed the palms of her hands on her jeans.

After mapping out their five stops, Quinton didn't waste any time rectifying their situation. "Em, I really like you and I don't want to play any more games."

Amelia looked at him slightly offended, "I didn't know we were playing games."

"You asked me to take things slow and it transpired from slow to barely even acknowledging that I was in the room." Before she could say anything Quinton continued on, "I know you wondered if I was just trying to take your ranch. That is the furthest thing from my mind."

"Since high school I haven't trusted any man except the men on the ranch."

Trying to lighten tension in the cab Quinton wiped the back of his palm over his forehead, "Phew, I'm glad I'm a man on your ranch. You can trust me."

Amelia shot him a playful, yet serious look. "I should have worded that a little differently. Sorry to give you false hope." When he shot a glance at her, she winked, hopefully showing him that she can play too.

"I'm sorry that Ethan did that to you, but you're missing out on something great with me because you're scared that I'm like him...which I'm not."

Amelia took a breath, but continued to stare out the windshield unable to make eye contact with Quinton. Amelia braved a quick glance at Quinton. "Cowboys definitely don't have any issues with self-esteem."

Quinton smiled and shrugged his shoulders. "We know what we know."

"I'm sorry if you thought I was playing games, I'm just trying to figure out how to protect myself and not fall any harder for you."

Quinton's eyebrows shot up. *Fall for me? She only said she was attracted to me.* He released his right hand from the steering wheel and reached for Amelia's hand. She set it in his palm willingly. Quinton laced their fingers together, "I am sorry about your past. If you'll give me a chance, we could take this one step at a time, together.

Amelia smiled, "I'd like that, but I am really nervous."

"Really?" Quinton squeezed her hand before he brought it up to his lips and kissed her knuckles. The cold, dry air produced static electricity that literally snapped his lip upon contact. "Did you hear that? You are electrifying."

They both laughed and relaxed for the remainder of the ride. Amelia seemed like she was going to tell him something else, but the moment had passed.

They'd made record time gathering all the supplies they needed at various stores. At Quinton's request, Amelia opened up on the way home. She'd shared her trouble with storms since her aunt's death and how her parents had passed.

"That's why you didn't want me on the tractor. That makes sense. I'm sorry. I didn't know." Warmth filled his chest realizing that Amelia did care. "Did your mom suffer long?"

"Nah. The doctor diagnosed her with liver cancer in March and she was gone by the end of September."

"Keeping and building my dad's legacy is of the utmost importance to me". Quinton held her hand and encouraged her, "From what I've seen, Em, you have nothing to worry about."

"I love when you call me that." Amelia admitted.

Just as if it were completely natural and had happened for years Quinton asked, "Call you what?"

"Em. Raddix and Jeff are the only people who call me that, but it just sounds so different coming from you."

Why did he have to be driving now? What he'd give to run his fingers slowly up her arms and back down. Then he'd pull her tight to his chest and let his hands wrap around her waist and kiss her like she'd never been kissed before. For now he'd have to settle with resting their laced fingers on his thigh.

He wished Amelia would unbuckle and slide over close to him, but that seemed unrealistic and only done in the movies or books. It was probably for the best that she didn't. He didn't want to wreck his truck by being distracted by her flawless, smooth skin, perfectly portioned nose, and sparkly teal eyes.

He knew Amelia was feeling vulnerable. Quinton felt like a lowly offender, as his mind fixated on capturing her amazing lips. He'd respect her wishes. Moving too fast would surely push her farther away.

"You know what Emmanuel's been telling me?"

Amelia chuckled, "Oh goodness. He is brutally honest, so I can only imagine."

"He adores you." Quinton never thought any woman other than Rose would impress Emmanuel.

"What's not to adore?" Amelia waved her hand in the air from her head to her toward her feet. He knew the smile she plastered on her face was fake, but some day he'd make her believe those words.

Quinton tilted his head back for a brief moment and laughed.

"What do they say, fake it until you make it?" Amelia admitted.

'Oh you've made it." Quinton sent her a smoldering gaze. He heard Amelia suck in deep breath.

Quinton had more fire and power swirling in his body than the approaching storm. With about ten miles to go until they reached the ranch, snow started to fall. Thankfully they would get back, unload the supplies and wait out the storm. While she had a good reason for hating storms, Quinton wouldn't let Amelia isolate herself tonight. Instead he planned to hold her close, keep her safe, and help her get through the raging blizzard together. Some time after that he would deal with the raging storm brewing in him.

# Chapter 16

**Amelia**

That night Amelia had trouble sleeping. She couldn't decisively pinpoint why. It could have been the swirling sound of the wind outside her window as the storm slowly increased its intensity. Perhaps it was the way Quinton stared at her with seductive eyes, making her feel all tingly inside. It could also be the internal battle that raged within her—he truly loves me, he loves me not. She hadn't picked a daisy and done that 'game' since she was eight. Perhaps, it was the way her body lit up when they were together in the same room.

She wasn't sure when she'd started to notice those feelings, but Quinton was having an effect on her. The only question was could she get over her own insecurities to see if this was for real?

*Get with it. You agreed to try this, so try it. Go slow, but move!* Those words were not hers, but her parents. Without a doubt her mother and father were coaching her from their heavenly spots.

Since she couldn't sleep anyway, Amelia ripped herself out of bed. The clock revealed it was only eight-thirty—*it's going to be a long night.* She threw on a pair of shorts and a dry-fit shirt and covered that with her favorite North Face sweatshirt. Sitting on the side of her bed, she put on her indoor sneakers and laced them up.

Trudging down the stairs, Amelia heard laughter and forks hitting plates. She paused, out of view from the kitchen, and relished in the fact that she had a wonderful family and didn't need anything else. Daydreaming so intently, she'd let her guard down and Emmanuel caught her leaned against the wall with her eyes closed.

"Amelia!" Emmanuel only had one volume...loud. "Whatcha doin' out here?' Emmanuel grabbed her hand and dragged her into the kitchen. "Guys, Amelia's been listening. How'd you guys not see her? Geez."

She wished at that moment a large abyss would open on the kitchen floor, and she'd be sucked in, never to be seen again. Her eyes instantly found Quinton, but he wasn't looking at her. His focus appeared to be on Emmanuel holding her hand. *Does that bother him?* Hopefully not, but just in case she won't let him know that he does this on a daily basis. *Just ask him. You need to communicate.* Once again she heard words that didn't belong to her. This time, Jeff's advice about being open pushed through her worry.

"Hi!" Amelia lifted her hand briefly to greet her entire ranch family.

Emmanuel tapped on Amelia's arm, "Guess what?" Emmanuel waited for everyone to stop talking. He had confided in her that he couldn't talk when others were talking because it makes his brain swirl. Amelia had tried to get him to talk just to his intended audience by placing his hands over his ears and continue to talk to that person. While that worked once or twice, he hadn't responded to that method well.

A loud growl filled the room. Emmanuel scowled his brows and pierced his lips, knit tight together, as he crossed each of his arms over his chest. When Amelia tried to touch his shoulder he stepped back and kept that same disdainful look on his face. "I want everyone to listen," he mumbled to Amelia.

Amelia put her hand up when there was a break in the majority of conversations floating around the table. "Emmanuel would like to say something to all of us."

"Go ahead, Emmanuel," Amelia made a sweeping gesture with her hand to let him know everyone was listening.

Emmanuel loosened his arms and facial features to the point where someone might detect excitement on the little guy's face. "Homeschoolers get a snow day tomorrow? We should have moved here a long time ago."

"Yes, we should have," Quinton agreed as he stared at Amelia. She felt herself blush, as heat rose from her neck and settled in her cheeks.

Since Renee never canceled school, she felt the need to defend her decision to call school off for the following day. "There will be plenty of shoveling for the kids in place of school. It may not be a typical school day, but you'll be working. Everyone's pitching in on this storm, it's building to be doozy.

As a matter of fact, gear up. There's enough out there to do a first round of shoveling, tonight."

With Amelia and Quinton's gazes still locked on each other, Jeff spoke up, "Pull up a seat and eat." He knew the intense storm would wreak havoc with her emotions.

"No thanks, I'm going downstairs to work out." Amelia always resorted to working out whenever her anxiety ramped up.

Amelia noticed a twinkle in his eye. "You shouldn't be alone, Amelia." Everyone at the table verbally agreed with him and glanced at Quinton.

"Luckily for me I have got great company." Amelia held up her headphones and phone indicating that she'd be listening to music.

Sean spoke up supporting Jeff. "Amelia, there's nothing else anyone can do tonight. As for tomorrow, Raddix and I will take care of feeding the livestock, Damon's got his horses and you checked the greenhouse earlier, there aren't any other chores to do on a storm day and you know it." Sean pointed a finger toward Quinton and Amelia, "I know you two are the ones in charge, but sometimes the superiors have to listen to the peons, especially when they are thinking straight and those in charge have their heads in a fog."

Amelia's mouth dropped. Her uncle had rarely acknowledged people, yet here he was concerning himself with her welfare. Admiration filled her chest. It had taken many years for him to adapt after losing Aunt Sara in such a horrific way, but she loved that his playful, teasing side was returning, even if it was only to embarrass her.

Hopping up from his seat, Quinton picked up his plate and started toward the sink, "You don't have to tell me twice, "I'll go change."

Carolyn took his plate from him, and whispered, "Run quick, before she can argue."

"I heard that," Amelia shrieked amusingly.

Ten minutes later Quinton and Amelia were in the exercise room warming up. She chose the elliptical, while he ran next to her on the treadmill.

Amelia's breaths surged, leaving her breathless, as she watched Quinton increase his speed and push himself harder and harder. She knew her lack of oxygen had little to do with her own vigorous warm up on the elliptical and everything to do with the man next to her. It also didn't help when he'd taken his shirt off to wipe sweat off his face. She needed to distract herself with something other than sneaking glances at his ripped upper body.

Quinton's game of questions helped a little. "Favorite workout music?"

"A mixture of genres, but it has to have a beat, I consider energizing," Amelia answered. "Your turn."

"Quick movin' country."

"What does that even mean?" Amelia laughed.

"Nothing slow." Quinton clarified.

"Protein shake after the workout or no?" Amelia questioned.

"Preferred, yes, not always practiced. You?"

Amelia nodded her head. "Same."

After her ten minute warm up, Amelia sauntered over to the weights. She pulled a medium resistance band through her feet and placed it right above her knees. Her first circuit consisted of a swat with an overhead press. When Amelia lifted two fifteen pound weights off the rack, she heard Quinton cough.

Amelia drank him in as he strolled over to her in his gray athletic shorts using his white muscle shirt to wipe sweat dripping off the side of his face and down his arms.

"You wouldn't choose a weight too heavy for you just to impress me would you?" He asked with a cocky grin.

Amelia scoffed, "Get over yourself pretty boy. This is one of my normal routines."

"Good to know." Quinton smirked.

Amelia tossed a challenging look his way, "Oh, I'm sorry, I just realized, I'm probably showing you up and you'd rather have me use lighter weight to make you feel good, right?" Amelia couldn't contain her smile and she wagged her eyebrows at him.

"Oh you." Quinton put his hands just below her rear and lifted her off the ground with the weights still in her hands.

Amelia let out a beautiful laugh, one she hadn't remembered existed. Her mother had always said that God put people in our lives right when we needed them. Amelia couldn't help but marvel about the way Quinton showed up right when she'd needed a foreman. Perhaps God had even more plans for her and Quinton's lives.

"Put me down. I can't afford for you to get hurt lifting me." Amelia ordered.

Quinton hoisted her up higher. "Are you questioning my manhood?"

"It's a dig toward me, not you...trust me." Amelia's eyes traveled over his broad shoulders. She imagined how his strong shoulders would feel underneath her fingers. Thankfully she had weights to hold.

Once he settled her on the floor, he moved his hands to her waist, but didn't allow any room between them. "You use whatever you want. I love the way you carry your muscles." Quinton ran his hands up her back, over her shoulders, and down her arms. "Don't put yourself down. I think you are absolutely perfect."

*Go ahead, kiss me. I'm ready for it.* Amelia silently begged. *Maybe I should put the weights down first. Maybe I should warn him that he's going to be sadly disappointed.* Quinton had plenty of time to close the gap and kiss her, yet he didn't. In fact, he smirked.

"What?"

Quinton leaned forward and kissed her forehead. He took a step back, threw his shirt over the arm of the treadmill before returning to the free weights.

*Yup, he's trying to torture me.*

There wasn't a visible flaw on Quinton Richards! His back muscles were just as impressive as the front. As her eyes finally met his gaze, she hoped she didn't look like a scared deer trapped in headlights. She wanted to convey her readiness. Darn it. The amusement on Quinton's face let her know that she'd been caught gawking at him...again.

*Oh, give me strength Jesus.* She knew that Jesus was her rock and right now she was in between the proverbial rock and hard place.

Humor flooded his eyes, "Are you okay?"

"Yup." She lied. Amelia swallowed hard despite her dry mouth.

Feeling brave, Amelia moved over, so Quinton could have room on the mat. He kept moving closer and crowding me off the mat. "You know, if you play with fire, you're bound to get burned."

"If I can get just one little kiss, I'll take third degree burns." His voice filled with heat.

Amelia set her weights on the mat and pulled off the band. "Oh really?" She gently grabbed onto his biceps and lifted onto her tiptoes as Quinton dipped his head slowly toward her lips. Amelia's pulse raced faster than Duncan or Buttercup, her favorite race horse growing up. "Quin, "I have to tell you something." Amelia breathed against his lips, "I am a total amateur—"

"Hey Dad!" The door swung open and Emmanuel stood there red-cheeked and soaked head to toe.

Quinton's head dropped. Moving toward Emmanuel he gasped jokingly, "What happened to you? Did you forget to wear ski pants?"

Emmanuel started to speak so quickly and brush his fingers together in front of his body really quickly. As Emmanuel walked toward his dad, Amelia noticed that he walked on his tiptoes. Admittedly, she researched autistic tendencies early on to help understand Emmanuel better, and walking on tiptoes was one of the mannerisms that many autistic children expressed.

"You wanted slow, you'll get that with him around," Quinton joked as he looked back at Amelia.

Emmanuel huffed, "Dad, you interrupted me. That's disappropriate."

Amelia bit back a laugh at the little guy's attempt to correct his dad. Instead, he misused the English language. She gave Quinton a jokingly stern look reprimanding him for his action.

"I wanted to come with you guys so you don't have to talk alone."

Smirking at Amelia, Quinton spit out, "Oh, that would be awful."

Quickly, Amelia covered her mouth, so Emmanuel didn't think she was laughing at him.

Whenever Emmanuel got interrupted, or excited about his story, he started back over at the beginning part of a story multiple times before getting his first sentence out. This time wasn't any different. "Jeff threw me in the snow because... Jeff threw me... And you wanna hear this. Jeff threw me in the snow when I told him he was weak and old. Isn't that funny?"

Amelia smiled as Quinton ruffled his son's hair and laughed along.

"C'mon, Dad, will you come have hot chocolate with me? Amelia, you should come too." Quinton looked back at Amelia, but she couldn't quite read his eyes. Would he really tell his son no?

Amelia smiled and knelt in front of Emmanuel, "I really have to finish my workout to get out some pent up energy, but how about you pick out a game in the closet and we'll play when I'm done since you don't have school tomorrow."

Amelia held up her flat palm for Emmanuel to slap it five and he didn't disappoint. "Awesome. Let's play Apples to Apples? I love that game. I'm really good at that game except when I let people know which card is mine and then people don't want to play with me. I won't do that this time though." He scrunched up his face, making him look like one of the Lollipop Guild munchkins from the Wizard of Oz. "I can't really promise I won't cheat; it's just so hard. I have to win."

Amelia loved how quickly Emmanuel adjusted to her. At first he didn't talk to her, or it was in one or two word phrases. Now he rambles on, melting Amelia's heart.

"All right, Bud. Let Amelia get her pent up energy out." Quinton smirked and lifted his eyebrows up and down.

Amelia retrieved Quinton's shirt and tossed it at him playfully. He pulled it over his head covering up all his hard earned muscles. She thought that the way he leaned quickly toward her meant that he wanted to steal a quick kiss. Maybe he figured it was better than nothing.

Thankfully, Emmanuel grabbed his hand and pulled him toward the door. Amelia took a step back at the same time. His jaw dropped, "No way cowboy!  A quick little peck will not suffice." *If he only knew that she'd been waiting forever for this first kiss, he'd understand.*

Before the door closed, Amelia sent him on his way with a flirtatious wave. She returned to her weights to start her circuit, hoping to release the stress from her body. Now if she could just get through the storm, and talk to Quinton, she'd be good.

# Chapter 17

**Amelia**

Fortunately, the ranch still had power. Even if they hadn't, Raddix had said that the generator was ready to go if necessary. Though it wasn't big enough to run the whole house, it covered the fridge and freezer combination in the kitchen, along with the big freezer chest and fridge downstairs. The store and butcher shop had their own generator that Raddix also confirmed its working status.

Amelia finished her work out and took a shower. She threw on a pair of lounging pants and a fitted t-shirt. She pulled on her Bozeman Icedogs zip up sweatshirt. Though Montana doesn't have any professional sports, they have some of the greatest minor league teams. Hockey was her dad's favorite and whenever he could break away, he took Amelia to their games.

One thing about Montana weather is dress in layers. Even on the ranch. Amelia liked to keep the thermostat low and wear a sweatshirt. However, she knew that whenever anyone from the ranch arrived, the first thing they did was turn up the heat. That immediately brought her mind back to the workout room. Was it really so hot that Quinton had to take off his shirt? Thinking of Quinton without a shirt ignited a fire within her. Amelia rushed down stairs to avoid being alone with her thoughts of her hunky cowboy.

*Her* cowboy. Nah. He wasn't really hers. They had definitely made some gains, but could she really relax and just enjoy whatever this developed into? Amelia was always waiting for the other shoe to drop.

The storm continued to blaze. Everyone decided to congregate in the main house because the whiteout conditions even made foot travel between the cabins and the main house a challenge. Amelia heard a loud bang and bolted down the stairs. She dashed around the corner where everyone sat relatively unaffected by the noise.

"Is everyone okay?" Amelia blurted out, holding onto the wall."

Without answering her question, Raddix and Jeff immediately left their seats and moved to Amelia's side. Everyone else looked at Quinton, who appeared a little confused because everyone was perfectly fine.

Katy gestured for him to go to her, "I'll watch Emmanuel for however long it takes."

Quinton reached Amelia's side in just three quick strides. Jeff looked up at him with compassion in his eyes. Amelia knew he was trying to, for lack of better words, train Quinton on how to deal with her during storms.

She had prayed profusely that her body would stop reacting this way during storms, yet here the same reaction persisted. Amelia described it almost as an out of body experience. She couldn't stop it. Pain and angst radiated through her body as if she were watching herself in the mirror being branded like her cattle. Would Quinton still want her after tonight?

Breathing became visibly unbearable and labored as flashbacks flooded Amelia's mind. All of the kids had seen glimpses of this before. All of them except Emmanuel. He moved toward his dad and tapped his arm until his dad acknowledged him, "Is Amelia going to be okay? I like her. She's not going to leave me like mommy did is she?"

Quinton didn't even know how to respond since he had never seen this side of Amelia or Emmanuel before. He looked toward Jeff for answers, but before he could say anything, Amelia responded to him herself. "Have you ever had a nightmare, Buddy?" Amelia reached out her hand to see if he would take it and he did. "I relive a very bad event..." Amelia took a deep breath searching for air to continue her explanation, "...every time there is a storm." Amelia shook her head and whipped her hands to her ears. "...It's like a nightmare, but I'm awake."

Amelia closed her eyes, covered her ears and slid down the wall. Instead of singing she started screaming, "No, no. no."

Renee rushed in and escorted all the children downstairs to where they were sleeping for the night. Emmanuel put his hands over his ears, like Amelia taught him when he wanted to say something, and yelled at the top of his lungs, "I like you—me and dad."

Just as Jeff was getting ready to grab her shoulders and shake her out of this torment, Emmanuel's words broke through to Amelia. She opened her eyes, but didn't drop her hands yet. Based on the dropped mouths of every adult surrounding her, she must have heard the little guy right.

Amelia's hands slowly fell from her ears. Amelia crawled on her knees toward Emmanuel. She reached out to hug and thought better of it. "May I hug you, please?'"

Without answering, Emmanuel twisted his body placing the side of his arm into her chest and Amelia wrapped her arms around him landing on his other arm.

"You are definitely an angel sent from God." Amelia kissed him on the cheek and he pushed back from her embrace and wiped his cheek off as he waved a hand at her and made his munchkin face again.

As Amelia set back into her heels, Quinton jokingly scolded his son, "Hey, do you know how lucky you are to have her kiss you. Don't wipe it off."

Raddix gave Quinton a little shove, "Looks like your son got further with Amelia than you did."

Quinton growled while all the guys laughed, at the sad, but honest truth.

Jeff got serious real quick as he placed a hand on Amelia's back. That wasn't so bad this time, sweetheart. I think Emmanuel's your lucky charm around here. Are you okay?"

Amelia nodded her head, but didn't move. Another loud bang happened and ninja style Amelia hopped to her feet, but still in a crouched position, and wrapped her arms around her knees.

Raddix ran outside to check it out.

Quinton sat on the floor next to Amelia and lifted her onto his lap.

Amelia yelled, "Don't lift me, you'll hurt yourself," but it had already been done and Quinton cradled her head on his chest.

"Are you questioning my manliness again?" Quinton wrapped his arms around Amelia, cradling her head in the crook of his shoulder.

When Raddix reappeared he knelt down and touched Amelia's calf, "Em, it was just the lid to the dumpster. We forgot to secure it before the storm.

"See beautiful, you have nothing to worry about. Your past can't hurt you and there's a whole room full of people who will not let anything happen to you right now."

He leaned close to her ear and whispered, "Especially me."

The deafening silence of this small ranch burst into a monstrous storm, but Jeff was right; Amelia had a breakthrough thanks to Emmanuel. Could she have another breakthrough and realize that Quinton really cares about her?

# Chapter 18

## Quinton

Three days ago Quinton had witnessed first hand how storms tore Amelia down. He'd rocked her on the floor until she'd fallen asleep. Then he'd carried Amelia to her room and covered her up. Quinton had sat in a chair next to her for about thirty minutes just watching her sleep.

Despite the most recent storm, relatively warm weather started out nicely for the beginning of March. Meteorologists predicted that fifty-two degrees would top off the high for today. Quinton started in the barn right after breakfast. Damon had a group of five children ranging in age from six to twelve— all with either autism or down syndrome— coming to participate in the equine therapy program.

"Are you ready for today?" Quinton helped Damon gather the bridles and saddles.

Damon smiled, "Sure am. We had to stop our program due to COVID. Hopefully, we can get back on track. We helped a lot of children." Quinton heard pride oozing from every orifice in Damon's body.

"Ya know, Emmanuel would like to work with you and Duncan again." Quinton wrestled with his thoughts and words before continuing. "It's not that I'm against him riding...obviously. I worry that his gross motor skills are not where they need to be for riding. Seeing him hurt would destroy me."

Quinton had never been so transparent with another cowboy ever. Damon was easy to talk to. He listened and encouraged others like no one he'd ever met before. Perhaps that's why the kids like him so much.

"About that," Damon began, "he's a natural. You should seriously consider getting him his own horse. Those issues you worry about will disappear and he'll have a 'buddy' for a long time."

Quinton didn't say anything for a moment wondering if Damon might have a good point. Rose told him when Emmanuel turned three to get him on a horse, but that had never happened.

He believed that Amelia thought the same thing since every time she could, she slipped the suggestion of getting Emmanuel a horse into a conversation. Maybe Quinton should start listening.

"Why don't you start acting like a cowboy instead of a scared mom?" Damon razzed Quinton. "Go grab Emmanuel and let him join this group?"

Damon suggested. "What he lacks in motor skills, he makes up for with an intuitive sense of what the horse is feeling."

Quinton moved forward and shook Damon's hand while slapping him on the back with his free hand, "Thank you. That does mean a lot to me and Emmanuel will love it."

"You're every bit a cowboy, don't let Damon tell you any different." Quinton cringed at the sound of her voice.

Leaning back on his heels he slowly turned to face Selena. "Good morning Selena, what can I do for you?" Quinton didn't care for her coming in when she looked like she forgot the majority of her outfit at home—that did nothing for him—and he'd told her before, but she just didn't listen.

Today, she sauntered toward the men oblivious to the fact that she interrupted their conversation. Her too-high high heeled shoes caught on a floor board and she sprung forward. Quinton's knee-jerk reaction was to put out his arms and she fell right into them. Selena proceeded to squeeze his muscles then rub her fingers up and down his arms. It made his skin crawl; it didn't set him on fire like Amelia's touch.

At that moment Amelia walked into the barn and Quinton tossed Selena out of his arms and she stumbled to secure her footing. Then she noticed Amelia. "Oh Amelia, you might want to check the floor, my heel got caught and fortunately for me your new brawny foreman..." she squeezed his biceps again, "...caught me. I was just coming to discuss a date with him. I'm sure you can spare him some evening after work, can't you?"

"I'm—" Quinton was going to shut that request down fast.

"—Quinton is an employee here, he's not a prisoner, so he can use his free time how he wishes." Amelia reached the barn door quickly and slammed the door on the way out, leaving Quinton to wonder what she came into the barn to begin with.

*Now, I'm just an employee again. Great.*

"Perfect, when are you available to go out?"

Quinton stared at her with disbelief. She stood there smiling like a heartless idiot. Using the firmest tone he could without yelling, he laid into her. "I will never be available. I do not date women who throw themselves at men with their bodies."

"Urg." Selena looked back and forth between Quinton and the closed barn door. "You're kidding, right? Are you and Amelia dating?" She didn't wait for his response. "No one has ever chosen Amelia Lawrence before; especially when I'm the other choice"

'Well, never say never." Quinton stretched out his hand toward the door, "I'm sure you remember the way out."

Acting unfazed, Selena stopped at the barn door. "I'll check back in with you once you get through your outcast phase."

Quinton opened his mouth to speak, but Damon grabbed his arm, "It's not worth it."

"If you're good here, I'm going to go find Amelia." Quinton stated as he lifted his hat and ran his fingers through his hair.

Damon smirked as he watched Quinton exhibit nervous tendencies, as he mentioned Amelia's name. "I'm good, Boss. Send Emmanuel out here first, I can use his help."

"Thanks, I will."

"Hey, Boss." Quinton turned to look at him, "Next time, let her fall on the ground. Have fun," Damon wagged his eyebrows at him.

"You're lucky I don't have anything to throw at you."

As Quinton made his way to the greenhouse, he tried to plan what he would say to Amelia when he opened the door. He would just tell her what had happened after Selena left, she already knew what happened before, and that's why he's in the doghouse.

Could he distract her with laughter? He loved to make her giggle, but he doubted he'd hear that adorable sound out of her mouth.

His pre-planning efforts were deemed worthless when he opened the greenhouse door. Amelia's teal eyes locked on him until he turned to secure the door. His pulse raced as he strolled toward her. In jeans, rubber boots, and a solid blue sweatshirt, she dragged the hose to the next row of plants and sprayed them down, ignoring this presence.

"Hey sweetheart, how's your morning so far? I didn't see you at breakfast." He tried to build up to it since he quickly noticed that laughing would not do.

Amelia's face looked flush with red blotches. "I was working out."

"That early? How come?" Quinton enjoyed the natural back and forth conversation about everyday things.

"Couldn't sleep."

"How come?"

Amelia flicked her head in his direction, "Don't think for a minute it has anything to do with you, Cowboy!"

Quinton smiled, "Are you getting sassy with me." Excitement ran through his veins causing his pulse to race. He loved the way Amelia flirted and teased him.

Every time he looked at, or touched Amelia, his heart swelled, threatening to pop out of his chest. How could he get her to believe him that she was the one he wanted?

Because he wanted it, and he assumed she needed it, he held out his arms long and wide, welcoming her into his embrace. She glimpsed at him before she cranked the hose spray higher and turned it on him, drenching him head to foot. "Perhaps that will cool you off and you won't need to have any blondes in your arms again."

Amelia returned the hose to the appropriate setting for the plants and continued watering them.

Her smile melted Quinton's heart. Wet jeans weren't the greatest feeling in the world, but he'd endure it all the time just to see her face light up.

Quinton moved in behind Amelia, giving her a bear hug that lifted her off the ground, soaking the back of her shirt. She squealed, "Put me down."

He obeyed, but left his hands on her hips and rested his chin on her shoulder. "Talk to me."

"I'd love to say that Selena is my problem, but—"

"— I told Selena where to go today, as politely as I could. Ask Damon."

"Oh, really?"

"Yes, really. Please trust me. You're the one I want. How about you come spend some time with Emmanuel and I?" He smiled. "I promise I'll make him keep the video games, war, and Lego talk to a minimum."

# Chapter 19

**Quinton**

Amelia arrived at the cabin as Quinton finished popping popcorn. Quinton gave Emmanuel a bowl and the little guy scurried off to the living room. He passed a bowl full of popcorn to Amelia, and she politely declined.

"Who doesn't eat popcorn with a movie?"

"Me. Is there some kind of law that says I have to eat popcorn during a movie?" Amelia teased.

Quinton strutted toward her, stopping close enough that his chest grazed her shoulder. He leaned in real close and whispered into her hair, "I like to keep my mouth available for kissing during a movie too, but not with my son in the room." Quinton tossed a piece of popcorn in his mouth, as he winked at her and then placed his hand on the small of her back and led her toward the couch.

Settling next to Amelia, Quinton left a sliver of space between his thigh and hers. He appreciated his son's movie selection—Guardians of the Galaxy. The thrill of an action movie got his blood pumping. Likewise, the beauty to his right threatened to stop his heart.

"Come and get your, Lord, oh yeah. Come and get your Lord, oh yeah." Emmanuel quietly sang as Star Lord appeared on the screen, dancing.

Truly, Emmanuel was the cutest boy in the world. Quinton didn't care how biased his opinion was. "Buddy, it's 'come and get your love' not Lord. It sounds like you're singing for them to come get Star Lord." He and Amelia quietly chuckled.

Emmanuel shrugged one shoulder and continued singing it the way he wanted.

A simple brush of Amelia's arm on his biceps filled his arm with an electric current that jolted him. She filled his heart with a longing he hadn't felt in years.

In light of their current audience, Quinton couldn't steal the kiss he'd been working hard to gain for weeks. As a result, Quinton's nerves were on high alert. His leg shook up and down rapidly. Amelia gently placed her palm on his mid thigh, silently asking him to stop shaking. He sucked in a deep breath.

She must have known it affected him because she started to pull away, but he placed his left hand over hers, preventing her from taking it away.

He wrapped his closest arm around Amelia's shoulders. "Is this okay?" he whispered into her neck, getting a strong whiff of her coconut perfume.

Amelia leaned into him.

As the movie played, Emmanuel balanced on his weighted ball until he lost balance, caught himself, and repeated. "Star Lord is the best." Without taking his eyes from the TV, he continued, "Too bad his mom had to die."

"Are you okay, Buddy?" Quinton's voice held an extreme amount of caution.

Emmanuel started crying. Running to the couch, he hopped on Amelia's lap and buried his head in her shirt.

Quinton's chest tightened. Not only was his boy struggling with the loss of his mom, but he found comfort in Amelia. Focusing on Amelia and Emmanuel, Quinton coughed to prevent his own tears from falling.

Moments later, Emmanuel abandoned the current movie and turned on *Toy Story 2*, picking it up where he left off with the toys in Al's Toy Barn. As quick as Emmanuel hopped on Amelia's lap, he slid off just as swift and returned to his ball to balance. Quinton glanced at Amelia and met her glassed over eyes with concern. Before he turned completely, a tear slipped down her cheek. Amelia quickly wiped it away with the back of her hand. "What's wrong?" Quinton's head swirled. He couldn't take two people in his life crying . . . at the same time.

"Emmanuel is such a sweet boy." Amelia didn't say anything else, but stared aimlessly at the TV.

Quinton didn't want Amelia to pity him or his son, but he didn't see pity in her eyes...he saw kindness, compassion, and maybe even love.

As the movie played, Emmanuel kept asking, "What does that mean?" when the character's dialogue went over his head. Quinton kept pausing the movie to explain the meaning to his son. Quinton repeatedly apologized for the movie taking longer due to all the questions.

"Never apologize for anything that has to do with Emmanuel. If someone doesn't like having to stop a movie, so Emmanuel can understand something, that's not your problem, it's theirs." Amelia brushed a loose tendril that fell from her ponytail behind her ear. "I think you are an amazing father for making sure he understands, who else is going to teach him?"

Amelia's admission and smile turned Quinton's neck, ears and cheeks a light shade of red. "Flattery will get you everywhere." He wrapped his arm around her again, as they relaxed .

"What's that mean?" Emmanuel didn't understand why Mr. Potatohead looked away from Barbie and kept repeating, 'I'm a married spud, I'm a married spud.'"

Quinton explained, Spud is another name for a potato. He's married and after you get married, you can't look at other women.

Emmanuel's face revealed zero affect, but his words delivered a punch, "That's no fun—that's dumb!"

Quinton and Amelia roared. Amelia laughed so hard more tears fell. Quinton gently swiped the pad of his thumb over her cheek wiping away her tears. He stared into Amelia's eyes and realized at that moment that he didn't want to look at any other woman than Amelia.

"For his and his future wife's sake, I'll make sure he knows how fun it can be to have one woman that he's in love with."

He loved it when Amelia blushed. It satisfied him to break through all her tough exterior walls.

When the movie finished, Quinton asked Amelia to wait while he got Emmanuel settled in bed.

Amelia came out of the bathroom, as he was descending from the ladder. She turned and bumped into him, spilling the cup of water he held all over him.

"I'm so sorry about your shirt." Amelia's hand shot to her gaping mouth, but her eyes twinkled letting him know that she found this mishap funny.

"This is the second time you've soaked me today," his tone was playful. Putting the cup in the sink, he freed his hand to pull the drenched shirt from his well sculpted frame. Amelia sucked in breath making Quinton chuckle.

"Don't laugh at me."

Without thinking Quinton wrapped one arm under her thighs and swung her to his chest. She instinctively wrapped her arms around his shoulders.

Amelia squealed, but then got serious, "Put me down, Quinton."

Instead of listening he pressed her closer to his bare chest. "It's so much easier to kiss you from here."

"But you're making me self conscious."

Quinton scowled, as he put her down. "I'm sorry. I just like to keep you close."

Amelia frowned as she grabbed his hands and laced them together. "You shouldn't feel sorry. I should love that you do that because it's nice being close, but I don't know if I can ever be comfortable with that." Before Quinton could say anything Amelia continued, "There's one more thing."

"Lay it on me." *Could there be anything worse than having Amelia feel self conscious around me?*

"You've been married and had who knows how many other relationships prior to that. I've never had a relationship. I've never kissed anyone before, let alone made a child. I can't compete with your experience." Amelia blurted out too many words too quickly that Quinton stared at her like a deer in headlights.

Quinton chuckled, "Experience is a loose term. Yes, I was married for a short time where I helped make a child, but that doesn't mean I'm some expert. Prior to meeting Rose I had only kissed a handful of girls. My most memorable were Jenny Maxwell, a cute little blond when I was in kindergarten and Anny Wilson when I was at her thirteenth birthday party playing spin the bottle.

He squeezed their still connected hands and kissed her forehead. "You're the only one I want to kiss."

"See you've had practice; I haven't had any. Zero. Zilch. Nada."

"That's what you got from what I said?" Stepping his legs out into a V, so he could be eye level with her. He placed her hands on his bare shoulders, instantly sending heat down his arms. Then Quinton lowered his hands to her waist. "I've got a great idea to put this behind you," He knew his mischievous smile hit the mark when Amelia lifted her eyebrows in suspense waiting for him to finish his thought. "You can pretend I'm someone else and we can practice kissing until you feel like you're prepared to kiss me."

Amelia chortled and then quickly stifled her laugh hoping not to wake Emmanuel, "That sounds like an excuse to kiss me. Mr. Richards. Your thoughts are purely motivated by selfishness, not trying to help me."

"I tried. The reality is, I don't care. What's the worst that could happen? It's not rocket science, you'll figure it out." Quinton tried to joke about it, and Amelia rewarded him with a smile. He truly wanted her to be completely comfortable around him. "The other option. . ." He paused, filling Amelia with anticipation. "You could just let me lead."

Standing to his full six foot four inches, he gazed down into Amelia's ocean colored eyes. He cupped her face and she yet again rewarded him with a blanket of heat when she stepped forward and traced her arms over his trim waist and up his back.

Quinton closed his eyes and let out a low moan. "Amelia," he breathed inches from her face. "You drive me insane and there is nothing I want more than to kiss you right now."

"Suit yourself, but don't say I didn't warn you." Quinton would have laughed had she not said it in the most sultry voice he had ever heard directed at him. But before he could capture her lips a scream forced them apart.

"Dad, I need you." Emmanuel yelled from his room.

Quinton rested his forehead against hers, "To be continued."

"I really should be going. It's getting late." Amelia countered.

Quinton yelled up to his son. "I'll be right there, Bud"

"I'll let you take care of Emmanuel." Amelia stepped back dragging her palms down Quinton's back, sending lightning bolts through his body. "See you tomorrow."

Quinton watched from the porch until Amelia crossed the threshold of the main house. *Lord, please stop letting things interrupt us, so I can show Amelia that she is special.*

# Chapter 20

**Quinton**

Quinton hadn't slept well and he knew why. Every time he'd been close to kissing Amelia, Emmanuel interrupted them. He woke up early and greeted Carolyn and Cash in the main house as they finished up the breakfast preparations. Quinton asked if Carolyn minded going to sit with Emmanuel while he slept. Quinton had to get in a good, hard workout, or he would explode.

He had never had this much help with Emmanuel at the Ranch in Texas. Everyone had stayed to themselves and only interacted if they'd had to. Here, everyone pitched in and helped one another. He was so grateful that God gave him this opportunity.

A little over an hour later, Quinton had emerged from the basement where he found Cash alone in the kitchen. "I'm sorry I took Carolyn away for so long. I thought Emmanuel would have woken up by now."

"Don't apologize. Carolyn loves Emmanuel and this was something good for both of you. Carolyn needs to feel the joy of watching a child and you clearly needed to get something out."

Quinton chortled, as he wiped the sweat off his face. "Yeah definitely."

"We all love her. You just need to be patient with her. I can see it in the way you look at her...everyone can." Cash encouraged Quinton to continue his efforts with Amelia.

Quinton took long strides toward the counter where Cash was putting together some sort of dessert, "I think she's starting to see it, but Emmanuel keeps interrupting us."

Cash suggested, "Carolyn and I are happy to watch him if you want to go out alone."

"Thanks, Cash. I'll let you know. I'm going to get cleaned up for the day. I'll send Carolyn back over."

Throwing a sweatshirt on to face the mild March weather, Quinton ran across the yard to his cabin.

He found Carolyn sitting in a rocking chair scrolling on her phone. Given the stillness, he knew Emmanuel hadn't woken up yet. "Thank you Carolyn. Sorry I took so long."

"I got a little bit of time to read during the day, don't be sorry. I should be thanking you." Carolyn snickered.

As she walked toward the door, she turned back to face Quinton, "I'd be remiss if I didn't tell you how painfully obvious it is that you and Amelia like each other. It's cute to watch this budding relationship, but if one of you doesn't make a move soon, you're going to kill me."

Quinton roared, alleviating a little bit more of that pent up energy he hadn't released during the workout. Or maybe it'd reappeared with the mere mention of Amelia's name and the vision of her beautiful face swarming around in his head.

"Cash just told me to give her time and you're telling me to move now." Quinton stated for no particular reason.

Carolyn scoffed at Cash's advice, "Cash and I wouldn't have a relationship if it hadn't been for me. Trust me, you want to make the first move. Women really do like that. It will give you lots of points in the long run." Carolyn gave him a playful wink before she left.

Quinton had made plenty of first moves; second, third, and fourth moves too that hadn't gotten him anywhere. Today, he had to catch Amelia alone before Emmanuel got out of school. If anyone but Emmanuel interrupted them he could yell at them to get back to work. Yeah. Today is the day that he would kiss Amelia, but first he has to get Emmanuel ready for school and meet everyone for breakfast.

"Another great breakfast Cash and Carolyn, thank you." Jeff always boasted about the couple's fabulous cooking skills.

Quinton noticed that Amelia only ate her eggs, but she seemed okay. He particularly loved how she let her leg rest against his when she'd scooted closer, so Raddix could sit next to her. He couldn't get Carolyn's advice out of his mind though *"You want to make the first move. Women really do like that."*

After checking in with everyone, he found out that early this morning Damon asked Amelia to get the equipment ready for his therapy students today. Quinton wished Damon would have texted him and he could have figured it out, that's something he'd have to discuss with him at another time. For the time being he knew that Amelia would be in the barn by herself and he wasn't going to let anything stop him.

He'd sent everyone off to work. Giving himself a minute to compose himself, he helped Cash and Carolyn clean up.

Carolyn noticed little beads of sweat forming at Quinton's hairline, "Thinking about what we talked about?"

Quinton nodded, "My plan is in motion now. Once I put this last dish away, I'm out."

"In that case, give it here. Go." Carolyn ordered. "Wipe your forehead." Her last direction made Quinton smile before he left.

Quinton couldn't get to the barn fast enough. Hopefully Amelia was still there and alone. The entire way across the yard he coached himself. *Act, don't think. Kiss, don't talk. Show her how desirable she is. It's now or never.* Quinton pulled open the door, he thought about nailing the door shut, so no one would interrupt them this time.

# Chapter 21

**Amelia**

Amelia watched Quinton march toward her with shrewd brown eyes full of intent. Frozen in her spot, all she could do was stare at the hunky cowboy determined to reach her. With his final two strides, Quinton backed Amelia up against the barn wall then placed both hands on either side of her shoulders. He dipped his head and kissed her with passionate fury that books and movies depicted so well. Amelia's hands grabbed both sides of his open chamois shirt to keep her jelly legs from dropping her to the barn floor. Quinton pulled her from the wall and wrapped one arm tight around her waist and the other hand rested behind her head, threading his fingers through her hair.

Securely in Quinton's embrace, Amelia snaked her arms around his neck and let him continue to control the kiss. Hopefully she felt as good to him as he did to her. A little moan escaped from Amelia before she even knew it was coming.

Immediately, Quinton let out a long, deep growl that couldn't be mistaken for anything other than enjoyment, but Amelia instantly pulled back and asked, "Did I do okay?" Amelia couldn't believe that not only had she finally kissed a man, she had kissed one who knew how to express hunger and desire, but also tenderness that melted Amelia's heart.

"You did better than okay, sweetheart. My brain can't even think straight." Quinton stared at her so long she felt self-conscious and she ducked her head to avoid his gaze.

Breathing heavily, Quinton left a trail of gentle kisses from her jaw to the base of her neck, leaving one last kiss on her protruding collar bone. "I'm more concerned about you, How was your first kiss?"

With a twinkle in her eye she couldn't help, but tease him, "Since I don't have anything to compare it to, it was good, I guess."

"Good? You guess?" Quinton looked playfully offended.

Leaning so close that their breath intermingled, Amelia enticed him even more, "Maybe...I...need...a...bit...more...practice." She dropped a passionate peck in between each word.

Quinton didn't hesitate. He captured her lips again and she let out a soft sigh. He squeezed Amelia tighter against his chest yearning for more, but instead he pulled back desperately replenishing his oxygen supply.

Her breaths were short and shallow. "Electrifying," her voice full of admiration.

"Electrifying. Truly?" Quinton's smile drew her in more and she rested her head on his upper chest and inhaled his tantalizing cologne wreaking havoc with her entire body.

"Yes, truly." His kisses caused her body to explode with heat. It was as if a volcano erupted and her blood was the hot lava rushing throughout her body.

Lifting her head with a concerned look catching Quinton off guard, "Actually, if I'm being honest, I think I still need even more practice." Amelia winked at him, setting his heart at ease.

Quinton's one shoulder shrugged accompanied a sultry smirk. "If you think more practice is the best thing, I'm happy to oblige. Speaking from experience though," he returned the wink, "your lips are heavenly."

Amelia felt comfortable and safe in Quinton's arms. For the first time, she didn't worry about her body or lack of experience, she just enjoyed the moment and boy what a moment it was. This was definitely the happiest moment of her life.

Biting on her bottom lip, Amelia held on to his arm with one hand and started making small circles over his strong pectoral muscles with the other hand. Quinton let out a low growl, which kept the already burning inferno within her intensify.

Quinton traced his fingers up and down her arms and shoulders and then gently pulled Amelia back. He gently lifted her chin between his forefinger and thumb, forcing her to look into his eyes. "You turn my brain to mush. I can't think straight around you."

"Really?" This time, she only questioned his authenticity for a brief second because Amelia felt the same exact way.

Quinton got within an inch of her mouth and murmured, "Really." his lips covered hers in a gentle, loving way that Amelia relished in.

Beep, Beep, Beep. The alarm on her phone pulled them away from each other. "I have to take over for Katy in the store." Quinton stepped back after giving her one more quick kiss. Amelia's heart swelled. "I'll see you in a little while." Is this what her mom meant by true love? No. It was too early to be using *that* word.

"Hey," Quinton got her to turn back toward him, "Cash offered to watch Emmanuel, so I could take you out for an official date. Would you like to go out tomorrow?"

Amelia walked back backwards toward the door as he followed. When he reached her, she lifted on her tiptoes. She could feel his breath on her lips, "That sounds like a plan." Then she gave him a quick kiss. "See ya later, Cowboy."

# Chapter 22

**Quinton**

Amelia pranced out of the barn leaving Quinton staring hopelessly. *No experience, tsk. She knew exactly what she was doing.* Her warm, soft lips turned Quinton's body into a blazing forest fire. All he wanted to do was run after her and ask for a second round.

Quinton shook his head, still unable to think about anything other than that kiss. He'd have to let Carolyn know that she was right and tell Cash definitely needed to listen to his wife more.

"What's up with you?" Damon entered the barn without Quinton noticing.

"I just came to help you get set up for your adult equine therapy session. People will be here soon."

Damon smirked. "Yeah I know that, but you've never helped with that silly looking grin on your face before."

"I don't kiss and tell. Let's just get to work." Quinton hoisted a saddle from the wall.

"Alright. It's about time . . . that you don't kiss and tell." Damon lifted the corner of his mouth and fist bumped Quinton.

The rest of Quinton's day had gone similarly. The entire ranch knew by lunch time that Quinton and Amelia had finally kissed. Apparently Amelia shared her happiness with Renee. The first thing Rocco said to Quinton when they met in the field to nurse a calf's leg was, "Kiss anyone special today?" Quinton enjoyed Rocco's dry sense of humor. Even if he hadn't, nothing would upset him today.

At the end of lunch, Carolyn had shared with Quinton that she'd be putting together ice cream sundaes for the kids because they all reached their reading and math goals for the month. "Ice cream is Amelia's weakness." It took a minute for him to realize why she had told him this. Then he confirmed the time he would need to return.

Quinton had told Amelia at the morning meeting that he'd take care of the greenhouses today. He'd never done it by himself and it had definitely been more fun with Amelia around. Once he finished cultivating the soil and watering, it was time to surprise Amelia.

In the main kitchen, Carolyn had the toppings in bowls arranged neatly on the table. She finished scooping the ice cream into bowls and placed them in a straight line on the table. Clearly, this wasn't her first ice cream rodeo. "What can I do?"

She handed him a bowl of ice cream. "Prepare this for Amelia."

He had never done anything like this before, not even as a kid. He stared at the toppings aimlessly for a brief moment and then it hit him. Simple. Amelia didn't need grand gestures; she needed to know he cared.

When he finished, the kids came rushing to the kitchen. Carolyn led them to the ice cream and let them build their sundaes. Finally, Amelia came into the kitchen. Quinton strolled over to her with the ice cream bowl extended out. "I made this for you." He dropped a quick kiss on her cheek.

"Oh, Quinton, that's adorable. Are you giving me your heart?"

"Yes, with chocolate and peanut butter, your favorites."

Amelia's eyes instinctively shut when she took a spoon full of ice cream with peanut butter sauce and Reeses Pieces. "Mmm. That's delicious." When she opened her eyes, Amelia rewarded him with another kiss. "Thank you."

Once Emmanuel finished his ice cream, Quinton surprised him by leaving him with Damon to start his regular horse riding lessons.

"Will you watch me, Dad?" He'd always found it hard to say no to Emmanuel with his cute impish smile and sandy blonde skater hair, but this time he had to stay strong.

Quinton knelt down in front of his son. "Just for a few minutes, Buddy. Then, I have to finish my work. You're in good hands with Damon. He'll teach you everything you need to know in order to be safe."

Emmanuel seemed fine with his answer. Seeing the progress his son had made, warmed Quinton's heart. Just a few months ago, Emmanuel hadn't stayed with anyone if Quinton hadn't been present too.

After watching Emmanuel's first few trots around the corral, Rocco had caught Quinton's attention. He jogged over to help. "Let me get that. Are you supposed to be lifting things yet?" Last week Rocco had had a slight run-in with an ornate mama protecting her calf during immunizations leaving him bed-ridden for twenty-four hours.

"Thanks, man. You know, it's hard to ask for help, but I appreciate it." Rocco gingerly moved back toward one of the horse stalls. "I'm just trying to get the horses' annual exams finished. Spring is just about here and these beasts have been pent up enough this winter. They are ready to bust outta here and breed."

Quinton chortled. He realized most of his conversations with Rocco always led back to pro-creating. "Do you always bring everything back to...nevermind"

"Occupational hazard. Perhaps, someone has a little too much pent up energy of his own and is a little touchy. The breeding schedule of a horse is a pretty routine conversation on a ranch."

The sudden urge to escape quickly overwhelmed Quinton. He threw his hand over his head in a quick wave. "Glad you're feeling better."

The dreary afternoon weather hung over the ranch, but Quinton's spirits were high thanks to his extracurricular activity this morning. Kissing Amelia had been the best thing that had happened to him in who knows how long. He wondered if Emmanuel would object to him marrying Amelia. *Whoa. Too soon, Quinton.*

Carolyn and Cash prepared a fresh pot roast dinner with potatoes and carrots to welcome Axel and Allie back from her mom's. Quinton and Emmanuel arrived after everyone had already claimed spots at the table. Emmanuel ran over the kids table and joined his new friends.

Quinton relished in the fact that Emmanuel had friends. He thought about the situations that had occurred in Texas and he realized the major difference between Texas and their new home. The former had spoiled children who felt they were entitled to everything. Whereas the latter children were down-to-earth people who built a family ranch and focused on bringing up their family the right way.

"Anyone going to tell me who the hot new cowboy is." Allie blurted out.

Axel snapped his head toward her. "Hello, your husband is sitting right here."

Everyone laughed while Allie placed her hand on her husband's cheek, "You're the most handsome man in the world," She gently brushed his lips and then turned her attention back to Quinton. "So who's going to tell me?"

Amelia spoke up, " Allie, Axel, this is Quinton, the ranch foreman. I hired him in January. He's done a great job fitting into our ranch family."

Fake coughs from Damon, Raddix, and Jeff filled the room as Quinton walked around the table with an outreached hand to greet Axel, "Hey man, nice to meet you."

"You too, but this one is mine."

Before Quinton could do anything but smile, Damon piped up, "You don't need to worry about that."

Allie rested her elbows on the table and her chin in the palm of her hands. "This sounds juicy, do tell. What did I miss while I was gone?" Allie had always been a gossip. Amelia tried very hard to relate with the woman.

"Someone has the hots for his boss!" Damon laughed as Quinton strode back toward the empty seat near Amelia.

Allie looked at him confused and then softly repeated what Damon said. *Someone has the hots for his boss.*

By the look on Axel's face and the way his glare met Quinton's, the foreman knew Axel understood the statement. Quinton didn't much like the glare, cutting him in two like the swing of a lightsaber.

What Quinton deemed way too long after the statement, Allie started clapping her hands and bouncing in her seat, "Oh, Amelia; Amelia's his boss. This is great. Maybe we can go on a double date sometime."

Axel spoke up in all too serious of a tone, "Yeah right. If you think we're going on a double day with someone you just classified as the *hot new cowboy,* you're dead wrong."

Dinner hadn't started off well, but fortunately, the conversation shifted away from Quinton and Amelia and everyone ate amongst themselves. Quinton wanted to know what he had done to warrant this guy's 'warm' welcoming. Everything was unlike his former ranch in Texas, until Axel showed up.

Quinton reached for Amelia's hand under the table and gave it a little squeeze and was rewarded with a thousand watt smile warming him to the core.

Once dinner ended, Jeff marched his very adult, yet childish acting, son over to apologize. "I'm sorry about the way I acted regarding you and Amelia. Like Raddix, I'm pretty protective of Amelia, she's been through a lot and I don't want to see her hurt."

"I appreciate it, man. Like I told Raddix, I care deeply for Amelia, so your looks don't bother me. Also, I appreciate you looking after her, but that's my job now. So if you'll excuse me I'm going to see why she looks upset talking with *your* wife.

"Excuse me." Quinton pushed a chair into the table, so he could make it to Amelia. When he reached her, he rubbed both his hands up and down her arms. "Are you okay?"

"Yeah, same ol' stuff. Girl crushes on hot, cowboy out of her league, and girl gets destroyed."

Quinton pulled Amelia to his chest and kissed the top of her head. "Don't you dare listen to Allie. You've made great progress working on yourself. She doesn't know what she's talking about. Besides, You're out of my league, sweetheart, but I'll keep fighting to show you that we belong together."

She pulled back slightly. "Thank you."

"Do you want to come witness the bedtime battle and then we can talk?"

Amelia gave him a quizzical look. "Bedtime battle?" She nodded her head.

Quinton put his hand on the small of her back and let her lead the way through the kitchen with Emmanuel trailing behind them.

# Chapter 23

**Amelia**

There was less *battle* in what Quinton phrased *bedtime battle* than Amelia had expected. Instead Emmanuel let Quinton help him brush and floss his teeth with only a short battle over the use of toothpaste, which Quinton won. Then there was a series of routines done in the same order every night, she'd been told, that just took time. Emmanuel picked out his book; Quinton read it. Emmanuel had one last sip of water and then went to the bathroom. Before trudging back up the ladder for his dad to tuck him in, he addressed Amelia.

"Goodnight, Amelia. Will you be here in the morning?"

"Oh no, Buddy, but I'll see you at breakfast for sure." Amelia's face grew hot at the implication from the question. She saw Quinton watching the whole scene unfold from the loft. His smile told her that he enjoyed watching her be uncomfortable.

Emmanuel ran and slammed into Amelia, wrapping his arms around her waist. He almost knocked her over. "Whoa there, Buddy, you are strong."

Emmanuel didn't smile when he said good night to Amelia, but he rarely smiled at anything, so that didn't surprise her. However, the big hug and asking if she'd be here in the morning, spoke volumes of how Emmanuel had grown in general and how he felt about Amelia. The feeling was mutual.

Emmanuel fell asleep fast. Amelia watched Quinton stroll over to the couch with a smile on his face. He pulled her to her feet. Cupping her face, he gave her a tender kiss that she accepted. "Would you like to sit on the porch with me?"

"I might be a little cold. Can I borrow a sweatshirt?"

Quinton scoffed. "Sure, but I bet you won't need it." He dropped a few tender kisses on her soft lips.

When they reached the banister on the porch, Amelia leaned her pelvis into the wood before Quinton gently wrapped his arms around her, enveloping Amelia like a cocoon making good on his promise to keep her warm.

"Thank you for being such a patient man. I know Raddix and now Axel can be a bit much." He hadn't knocked anyone's teeth out here, recalling that he had to leave his ranch in Texas because his temper flared, but she didn't know what transpired.

"You bring out the best in me." Quinton crushed his lips to Amelia's. She could feel the passion that consumed him. He tilted her head, so he could deepen the kiss. When Quinton pulled away, Amelia slowly opened her eyes. He was staring at her lips. She put her fingertips to them. They felt puffy, revealing the effects of their desire for one another. "I still have to cash in on our little bet from the snowball fight."

"What do you want?" Amelia queried.

"I'm saving it for something big." Quinton grinned.

"Will you tell me your story from Texas?" Amelia held onto Quinton's back.

Quinton groaned, "It doesn't paint the best picture of me." Quinton ran his hand up and down her back.

He should have been excited that Amelia wanted to know everything about him. She wouldn't judge him, especially since it involved Emmanuel. Given her love for the little boy, she would have to work hard not to hurt anyone who had messed with him.

It didn't take long before Quinton started explaining. "Zane Gilman, I think he's Hitler's brother." Amelia smiled at his World War II reference. She wasn't sure if it was because Emmanuel probably speaks of the evil dictator and the name came quickly to his brain, or if because this guy really was evil. "He took over as foreman the last year we were on the ranch. The power blew up his already massive ego. As you can imagine, his son, Max, also had the same arrogant attitude. Zane spent a decade raising his son to be just like him."

"Did he have a wife?"

"Nah, she left him when Max turned one. She didn't act anything like Zane. Her loving devotion for Max soared, so when she declared she'd be leaving, I knew something transpired that wasn't kosher. Of course Zane told everyone, including Max that Becca didn't want to be a mother and left them. I never believed it for a moment."

"Poor woman." Amelia's heart ached for Becca. She couldn't imagine having to give up her child.

Quinton took in a breath. "Once Zane took over, Max became the ranch bully against the other kids. All the other parents felt the same way I did...we had many talks about it. Once we talked about being a united front to talk with Mr. Cromwell, who owned the ranch, but we decided against it when we saw how chummy the two men were."

"So, there wasn't one single incident that caused your temper to boil over?"

Quinton chortled, " Definitely not. On a daily basis, Max bullied one child, or another on the ranch. Seeing the relief on a child's face at the end of the day when they didn't have any interaction with Max that day broke my heart just as much as it did for the child who endured his abuse. I tried talking to Zane multiple times and he just deflected. He accused me of being jealous that he got the foreman job instead of me."

"That must have been so hard. It's just another example of how patient you are." Amelia wrapped her arms around his waist, giving him a brief hug before he led her to the bench to sit.

"Everyone needed their jobs, so no one wanted to rock the boat. The straw that broke the camel's back was the day Max picked up Emmanuel by the shirt and told him to shut up about his wars, Legos and video games. Emmanuel was holding his favorite game chip. Max smashed it to the ground and used the heel of his boot to grind it in the dirt. That's when Zane and I rode up from pushing cattle."

Amelia felt Quinton's body tensing more. "I'm sorry. You don't have to finish the story if you don't want to."

Quinton kissed the top of her head. "It's okay. I removed Max's grip from Emmanuel's shirt. Zane started running his mouth about me touching his kid and the irony of that statement struck me. So I laid into him about his hypocrisy, his tyrant disposition, and the authoritarian training of his son. Then he called Emmanuel a two bit retard who didn't know anything. I lost it. Five of the ranchers pulled me off Zane, but I was too fired up. I got in Max's face, with fire in my eyes, and told him that I'd teach Emmanuel to do the same thing to him if he bothered any of the kids again."

Quinton shrugged his shoulders. Amelia didn't blame him. She'd never resorted to violence herself. Instead, she'd developed into a coward by hiding from situations instead of dealing with them. "I'm at a loss for words." Shock filled Amelia with indignation. Why were people so mean to other people? "I don't know why people can't just be nice. How did Emmanuel deal with the situation?"

"Like he does with everything else. First he asked me what those names meant because he'd never heard them before. Then he said he was fine and started rambling on about one of his favorite topics."

Amelia stood in front of Quinton and rested her palms on his forearms. "I won't lie, that really bothers me. I hope he realizes that he is the smartest boy I've ever met."

Quinton pulled her up to a standing position. "I love you, Amelia." Her body immediately tensed up. She could tell Quinton was searching her face looking for a response. What could she say? Did he just say that because of Amelia's fondness for his son, or did he mean it? "Amelia... give me a sign, heck a slap will work at this moment. Give some type of reaction."

He started to loosen his grip on her waist and she caught his wrists and left them resting on her hips, "I feel it, I just...am scared to say it out loud." Amelia couldn't look at him. She knew that if she took one look into those dark chocolate brown eyes, she'd see the good-natured, loving man that she'd grown to trust and wanted in her life. *What's wrong with that?* Sadly, stupid doubt rang louder in her ears.

"You'll get there. I can tell you right now that you have nothing to worry about and every word I say is true, but until you believe it, you don't want to voice it; I get it. Stings the ego a bit, but knowing that you feel it is good enough for me...for now."

# Chapter 24

**Amelia**

At the sound of the rooster, Amelia's heavy eyelids opened. She'd spent too long at Quinton's last night and was paying for it now. She'd never complain though. There wasn't anything she loved more than being in Quinton's arms. Her mom had always told her that love would feel freeing and exciting. Just thinking about Quinton produced butterflies in her stomach. She knew she'd fallen for Quinton, so why couldn't she say it.

Despite the still cool temperatures, a lot of the snow had melted. Warm spring weather would appear in a couple of weeks. Amelia threw on a sweatshirt and some jeans. Out in the barn she greeted Duncan. "Good morning, Sweetie. Do you want to go for a ride?"

"I'd love to, beautiful." Amelia jumped at the sound of a deep, throaty response from a man she couldn't wait to see.

"Quinton! You scared me. What are you doing out here this early?"

"Uh, my job." Quinton chuckled. He pulled her in close to his chest and kissed her cheek. He strolled over to the saddle and hoisted it off the wall and onto Duncan.

After securing the seat, he stood shoulder to shoulder with Amelia, nudging her gently. "Penny for your thoughts."

Normally, Amelia had kept her thoughts to herself, but over the past week with Quinton, it had been different. She couldn't wait to see him, talk to him, and definitely kiss him. "Thanks for getting Duncan set up for me." She gave him a quick kiss to show her gratitude.

"Anything else you need? I like kisses for payment." He teased her.

"I'm sure I'll think of something for you to do."

Folding his arms across his solid chest making his biceps bulge even more than normal, Quinton leaned up against the barn wall. "Would you like to be alone on your ride, or could I join you?"

"Saddle up, Cowboy." Amelia winked.

The sun peeked through the trees, prompting Amelia to silently thank God for this beautiful earth, and all the blessings he bestowed on her including the brawny cowboy who sat ramrod straight on the back of a beautiful stallion.

They arrived at a rock wall that Amelia and Raddix used as a mural growing up. Quinton tied up Duncan and Rocky to a tree near the water for them to drink.

"What's this?" Quinton scoffed, looking at a heart with Raddix and Selena's names inside of it.

"He had it bad for her in high school. It destroyed him for a while after she used him." Amelia sighed.

Her relentless nemesis had shown up at the ranch again trying to persuade Quinton into taking her on a date. The muscles in her arms and stomach tensed every time Selena was around. She'd really thought her pushiness had been attractive. Thankfully for Amelia, Quinton didn't think so, but for how long? Would he ever give in to her persuasive techniques?

"Did you paint all these?" He pointed to a space scene with the solar system and then to an elaborate beach scene with a dolphin leaping out of the water.

Fortunately he pulled her from her negative thoughts. "Yeah. I love space and the water. When I long for it, I come here. Someday I'll get to the ocean, but right now I'm just focused on making sure I keep my family's legacy growing strong."

Quinton wrapped his arms around her waist from behind and kissed her cheek. "Will you let me be the one to take you to the ocean?"

Turning her head slightly to see Quinton's strong jaw, she kissed it. "I'd love that. Would we bring Emmanuel?"

"At some point, yes. I imagine he'd love the water too. Is that okay with you?"

"Definitely." Amelia turned to face Quinton. "You're a package deal that I'm blessed to be a part of; I love that little guy." She knew it was too early to say that she thought she was in love with him, but she could confidently tell Quinton how she felt about his son.

"Thank you. Emmanuel is very fond of you."

Amelia hugged Quinton around the waist. She never realized how much she needed the warm comfort of a man who really cared for her. A single tear slipped down her cheek that she quickly wiped away, but Quinton still noticed.

Holding her at arm's length. "What's wrong?"

"I never believed I'd have this. A gorgeous cowboy who really likes me and he has an adorable son who brightens my life." She couldn't believe how forward and blunt she'd become since Quinton had kissed her. Maybe everything was coming together for her and she was using all the wisdom from her parents and Jeff to make sure this relationship lasted.

Quinton interlaced his fingers with her and led her to a patch of wildflowers that recently pushed through the thawing ground.

"I'm not sure what this is, but it's beautiful, like you." He picked one and handed it to Amelia.

Sniffing it, Amelia squeezed her eyes shut. "Thank you. They're yellow bells." Quinton made her feel like a beautiful woman that he adored and she couldn't get enough of him.

"We're in this together. I know you're not going to be healed from all your self-destructive thoughts overnight, but I'm going to show you how much you mean to me."

Amelia knew this man was her future and that she needed to work on herself, so she didn't drive him away.

# Chapter 25

**Quinton**

The next week had passed by, sloth style. It'd seemed like everything on the ranch had needed Quinton's attention. At the end of the week, the trough system they use to keep the water moving for the animals had seized up, and he'd spent the early morning hours breaking the ice that'd built up. The setting sun and his aching arms revealed the harsh truth that he might not be able to fix this on his own.

"Hey, Cowboy!"

"Hey, yourself, beautiful." Quinton stood and wiped his hands on his jeans.

"Any luck with fixing that thing?" Amelia wrapped her arms around her midsection. Quinton wondered why she was still nervous around him.

Quinton smirked. "I'll get it fixed. Don't you worry." He dropped a kiss on her cheek. Not wanting to stop there, he dropped a gentle little peck on her jaw and then continued with more trailing down her neck.

Amelia's giggle was music to his ears. He'd grown accustomed to hearing her laugh and seeing her smile. Everyone knew that Quinton had fallen head over heels in love with Amelia, so he never wasted a moment to show her.

*You're a package deal.* Her words lingered in his brain. Emmanuel had told him that he would love to live with Amelia *"like she was my mom."* When Quinton explained that if he married Amelia, she'd be his stepmom. Emmanuel flapped his arms excitedly.

He pulled Amelia to his chest and let his lips roam over hers like it was their first kiss again. He deepened their kiss and was rewarded with a little sigh from Amelia.

Pulling back, Quinton rested his forehead against Amelia's and allowed himself to catch his breath. "How about we go out when I finish with this contraption?" Cash and Carolyn had agreed to watch Emmanuel.

"Are you cashing in your bet? Where are we going?"

"Depends. Do I have to cash in, or are you going willingly? Have you already eaten?" Quinton inquired.

"I'll go willingly. No, I was waiting to eat with you."

Quinton's heart ached for Amelia. So many times he'd worked late on the ranch and Rose ate with Emmanuel instead of eating with him. He didn't realize until right now how much that bothered him. "Let's get a bite to eat at the diner in town."

Amelia lifted on her toes and gave Quinton a kiss that lingered longer than Quinton had anticipated, but didn't complain. "I'd love to. How about you let me help you fix that?" Amelia tipped her head toward the water system. "I became a pro at helping my dad."

"What?!" Why didn't you tell me? "

"You said you could do it."  Amelia shrugged her shoulders playfully.

"I recant my statement." Quinton held his elbow out for Amelia to wrap her arm through. When her hand rested on his bicep, joy rushed through his body. "I can do anything with you by my side."

After they finished dinner, Quinton walked hand-in-hand with Amelia down the sidewalk staring into the front window of each of the small shops. "Why don't you come to town often?"

Like a bull in a China shop the bakery door flung open, almost smacking Amelia in the face before Quinton pulled her out of harm's way. Selena's devil-like smirk made Quinton's stomach sour, wishing he hadn't eaten all of his meal and the rest of Amelia's.

"Well, what have we here? You're slumming it this evening, Quinton." The door banged shut. "I thought you had better taste." She traced her slim, non calloused fingers up Quinton's shirt sleeve. He pulled away. *What is wrong with this woman?*

He felt Amelia's body tense and all he could think of was getting her away from this woman before she spewed any more venom out that would erase the progress Amelia's counselor helped her make. "Have a good night, Selena." Quinton swept by her with his hand holding Amelia's in place between the crook in his elbow. She tried to pull away, but he refused to let her.

When they reached his truck, she finally spoke. "That's why I never come to town."

As soon as he pulled the door open for Amelia, he cut off her entrance into the truck. He felt the intensity in his gaze. "That works for me. I can have you all to myself at the ranch." He pressed a haste kiss on her lips before he moved out of her way, let her settle in, and shut the door.

The ride back to the ranch started off quiet. He requested her hand by turning his palm up on the console between them. "How do you feel about marriage?"

Amelia brought her hand to her chest. "Me? I've never been married, so I only have my fantasy thoughts from childhood. How about you? You've actually been married. Would you consider remarrying?"

He kissed the back of her hand. "If you're going to be my wife, I'd remarry tonight."

Amazingly, four months had passed since Quinton had arrived at the ranch. He couldn't believe how much had happened during that time. He'd fallen in love with his boss and she'd developed feelings for him too. Emmanuel had made many friends, and so had Quinton. This ranch had become his family. One day he would make Amelia his wife.

# Chapter 26

**Quinton**

A pang of regret had pierced Quinton's chest the following Sunday morning when he had to miss church to help the ranch hands gather up run away cattle. It had been bad enough that he couldn't be with Amelia and Emmanuel, but they were going to stay later to discuss the carnival. Somehow Quinton needed to focus on his job at hand and stop dreaming of being at church with Amelia.

By lunch time all the cattle were securely returned to their pasture and the ranch hands were fixing up the broken fence the four-legged trouble-makers used for an exit. As Quinton walked toward the main house, Sean joined him. "Thanks for all your help this morning. Sorry you had to miss church."

"No worries. I've always stayed behind when the cows get out," Sean replied.

At that moment everyone returned from church. Quinton couldn't wait to see Emmanuel and Amelia.

Emmanuel came running into his arms and Quinton scooped him right up. "Guess what, Daddy? I get to help with the carnival and so do you.Y ou're going to love it.

"Sounds great," Quinton declared as he walked toward everyone else carrying Emmanuel in his left arm while Sean trailed slightly behind them.

Sean chortled behind him, "Tread lightly, son. The women are in charge of the planning, you could get in way over your head."

"Where's Amelia?" Quinton asked his son.

He pointed to the store.

"You head in with Sean and I'll go get Amelia. Is that okay with you, Sean?"

"Sure thing."

As soon as Quinton walked into the store, he felt the tension in the air. "Amelia, what's wrong?"

"You know small town gossip at church. Can you imagine that gossip at church? I can see why people have a problem with people who proclaim to be Christians."

Quinton didn't like the sound of this. After the encounter with Selena in town, he'd made it a point to love Amelia even more. He felt her slowly slipping away and he wasn't sure what he could do about it.

"I've got to take inventory to make sure we're ready for the carnival. You should head in and have lunch." Amelia brushed him off.

"Amelia, I'm not letting you push me away. I don't know what was said, but I wish you'd trust me and not what others say."

"I just want to be alone right now."

Quinton wanted to fix the problem, but he knew this was the process Amelia had to go through. He knew she'd eventually be secure enough and wouldn't care about what others said. Hopefully this happened soon before his heart shattered into a million pieces.

# Chapter 27

**Quinton**

Quinton shared the news with Jeff, Sean and Raddix when he returned since they wouldn't leave him alone until he did.

"Just give her time and space. Her insecurities will go away eventually," Jeff encouraged.

Quinton dragged his hand over his face. "I better not find out whoever it was that set her backwards."

Once all the lunch plates and mess were taken care of, Axel and Allie gathered the kids to play outside.

"Why do they get out of this?" Raddix's exasperation made Quinton wonder what they were in for.

Allie smiled. "I've already agreed to set up a fruit stand and be ready with some baked goods made with our fruits."

Axel wrapped his arm around his wife's waist and with a big cocky grin declared, "And I'm already married. Have fun boys."

Sean and Raddix looked at Quinton quizzically. Quinton was perturbed. Axel continued to rub him the wrong way with this cocky, arrogant attitude. It was hard to believe that Jeff was his father. They were polar opposites—Jeff was kind and enduring, whereas Axel thought he was better than everyone around him.

When the couple left the kitchen, they kept the door leading to the foyer open and within moments everyone in the kitchen cringed.

"Hey, Amelia." Allie's bubbly voice echoed through the foyer, into the kitchen. "I'm sorry again for upsetting you about Q—"

"—Nah, you were right, there's no way the old maid, overweight chick could get the...what did you call him—oh that's right—*the hot new cowboy.*"

Shaking her head, Allie said, "I didn't say that."

"Close enough. I heard you and Selena today, so don't deny it. You're just lucky I love your in-laws, or you wouldn't be here right now. I suggest you learn how to be part of this ranch family, or maybe you and Axel should consider working for another ranch. I'm sure Selena will find something for you." She paused briefly. "Doesn't matter anyway. You probably saved me years of heartache. Thanks, I guess."

Quinton rubbed his palm up and down his day old stubble and stood, but Jeff and Sean quickly intervened. "You can't fix this right now," Jeff said sympathetically. "Be patient, son."

*Allie again. She's been nothing but trouble since her and Axel came back. Too bad they wouldn't return to her mother's and stay there.*

Katy helped everyone move past the awkward moment, "So gentlemen as you know the carnival is only three months away. It will be July Fourth weekend—the fourth, fifth and sixth. We've decided to try some alternate activities this year. I am hoping you wonderful men will help."

Amelia walked in the room. His pulse picked up pace, as his eyes trailed her body. Though he'd seen her in less when they worked out together, the fitted t-shirt and jeans hugged every one of her curves. His eyes made their way to hers., causing his heart to gallop faster than his favorite chestnut in the barn when she held his gaze. But, all too quickly, she looked away to decline Carolyn's offer for lunch.

Quinton couldn't take his eyes off Amelia. She sat across from him and clasped her hands together before resting them on the table showing her professional side.

Katy didn't finish her earlier thought. Instead she rambled on about what everyone else at church agreed to do.

Quinton felt bad, but he really didn't care what they were going to do, he just wanted to help Amelia and if in the process Axel and Allie left, that would be a win too.

"Sure thing." Amelia's sweet voice sliced through his thoughts and he hated that he missed whatever she'd just agreed to, hopefully Katy would repeat it for him.

Looking at her list, Katy started checking things off. "Allie's set with the orchard booth, Renee has a kids craft booth and bounce house. Carolyn and Cash are set with the food truck. Amelia has the dance as usual, and I've set up the rides, Jeff, Axel, Rocco, and some other married ranchers in the area have agreed to be in a dunk tank and that just leaves our single gentlemen."

This didn't sound good. Katy wouldn't even spit it out, she had to drag on about how the first day would consist strictly of the rides, food, and fireworks at night. Then on the second day they would repeat everything except for the fireworks. Instead they would have a dance that apparently Amelia had planned for the past ten or so years and new this year...

Katy smiled at Quinton, Raddix, Damon, and Sean. There are about eight other bachelors at church who have already agreed to the new idea..." another brief pause. "...since we get a lot of traffic for this event, families and singles from hundreds of miles away come for our carnival, it provides great revenue for our church and we hope this will bring in more, so we can help out more families..."

"Please just spit it out," Quinton guffawed trying to seem friendly, but the anticipation was getting on his nerves. Being so close to Amelia and not being able to hold her or talk with her probably contributed to his short nerves, more than anything He wanted this to be done.

"A bachelor auction." Katy spit it out like requested, and now Quinton wanted her to take it back.

All at once all four men began protesting, "Not going to happen,." "No way!" "Never!" "Why can't the women be up there?"

It wasn't clear which man stated which comment, but it was certain they were all in agreement...a bachelor auction was a bad idea.

Jeff stood up and wrapped his arm around his wife's shoulders to guard her from anything the men might say. Not that they were being mean, but Jeff protected his wife to the tenth degree. Very honorable.

"Let her finish the details, you don't even know what the event entails." Jeff sat back down. "Go ahead."

"Thank you, honey." Katy's eyes landed on each of the men, "It's pretty simple, the women pay five dollars for a paddle. They will use that paddle to bid and the highest bidder wins a date with you." Each male will get one hundred dollars from our profits to use on the date, so the only thing you have to invest is your time."

A pin dropping in the silent room would have pierced their ears. No one knew what to say, but Quinton knew what he was thinking. *Will Amelia bid on me?* Quinton didn't want to go on a date with anyone, but Amelia.

He couldn't believe the words that came out of his mouth next. So much for listening to Sean, or Jeff about not being able to fix it. So much for giving Amelia space to heal herself. He couldn't agree to going on a date with anyone other than Amelia.

"Would you bid on me? I don't want to go on a date with anyone, but you." Quinton's low, deep voice got her attention. He saw it. He saw the pain and confusion in her eyes and that crushed him.

Amelia pushed back from the table, "I'm going to workout. If you need anything else from me, Katy, let me know; otherwise, I'll have the dance ready, like always."

Then she was gone. Quinton heard her bound down the stairs and he felt the house rumble when he heard a door slam moments later.

"I guess not." Quinton hung his head.

Raddix piped up, "I think we need to define: *give her time and space* because you clearly don't get it."

Quinton glared at Raddix. This was the best place he had ever worked. He knew how protective Raddix was of Amelia, but she was his to protect now.

Thankfully Damon thought along the same lines at Quinton. "Raddix, you don't have a clue. You've never been married, or had a committed relationship and then just had to let her go. You're looking at two men..." pointing to himself and Sean "...who have, and now Quinton is in the process of dealing with it. Maybe his situation will work out better than things appear right now,, but if not, he's going to have a long road ahead of him. It's not all about Amelia."

Damon nodded at Quinton, which he returned gratefully.

Sean spoke sternly to his son, "Raddix, your overprotectiveness is part of the problem. If Amelia would have dealt with the pain back in high school, she wouldn't be going through this right now. You need to let her hurt. She will reach rock bottom and then she'll build herself back up. That's the only way it will work."

Raddix nodded in agreement.

"So you two…" gesturing toward Raddix and Quinton "…get on the same page to help Amelia, and play nice," Sean ordered.

# Chapter 28

**Amelia**

Amelia sat at her desk in front of her laptop waiting for her counselor to appear. She was tired of living with this insecurity. She'd stilted things between her and Quinton... again. But this time she knew it wasn't him and let him know it. That didn't stop him from looking sad whenever their eyes met.

Within seconds, Dr. Bethany arrived on the screen. Like the other sessions, she expected Amelia to give her a recap of her life since their last visit. Fortunately, she saw her doctor twice a week, so there wasn't much to recap.

"I don't like being insecure, but how am I supposed to trust that Quinton is really picking me over other beautiful women? How am I supposed to ignore hateful things I hear?"

"You have to believe you're beautiful at the very least." Dr. Bethany encouraged. "Tell me about your interaction with Quinton."

Amelia took a deep breath. "It's not just one interaction. First, he says so much with his steamy eyes —I'm here for you, I love you. It's the way he bumps his shoulder into mine when we're out taking care of Duncan, or the way he flirts and teases when we're winding down for the evening after Emmanuel's gone to sleep ... it's everything."

"Is that right?" Dr. Bethany's singsong voice wasn't lost on Amelia.

The side of Amelia's mouth rose slightly as she'd relished in the memory of the hug and long-lasting kiss on the cheek Quinton had rewarded her with when she'd finished the barn chores. That day Raddix and Sean had helped Rocco welcome nine baby calves into the world, so it had been all-hands-on-deck.

Thankfully, Amelia had found placements for every calf; growing her goal of building her dad's legacy.

"I'm going to ask you a question, Amelia and you need to answer within three seconds of me asking —just blurt out whatever comes to your mind instantly. Ready?"

A frown pulled at one corner of her mouth. "Fine."

"If Quinton asked you out right now, to do whatever you wanted, what would you say."

Dr. Bethany counted, "One, one thousand...."

"I'd say yes." Amelia's high tone sounded irritated. "Quinton has never been the issue. It's always been me, so what did that prove? I'm tired of being insecure. I do fine, and then wham! a beautiful woman appears or a snarky comment is made and I'm done."

In her very professional tone, Dr. Bethany explained, "The first time I asked you that same question, you said, 'no' just as quickly as you just said yes."

Amelia shrugged her shoulders remembering that first session months ago. She knew her feelings had changed for Quinton. The biggest fear she had now was losing him due to her own insecurities.

"You have the ability to trust Quinton or not. Has he proved himself untrustworthy?"

"No." Amelia rested her head on her hand.

Dr. Bethany leaned forward, into the camera, "He's told you that he isn't interested in Selena, yet you're choosing to not believe him. You need to believe him until he tells you differently."

"I want to. I'll try."

"That's all anyone can ask. How's Emmanuel doing? Dr. Bethany asked, as she jotted down notes.

The sound of kids in the front corral distracted her. She grabbed her laptop with both hands and carried it like a school lunch tray to the window allowing her the best visual. "In addition to being crazy smart, and a natural at riding horses, he's great."

Just then, her phone vibrated. Quinton's profile picture appeared—the selfie of him and her in front of the barn doors—filled the screen. "Dr. Bethany, our time is almost up, Quinton's texting in need of help. Is it okay to stop here and I'll see you on Tuesday?"

Once Dr. Bethany wished her well, Amelia swiped up on her screen. She read each word closely and slowly like she always did, relishing in this communication with Quinton.

**QUINTON:** THERE ARE A LOT OF SPRING APPLES TO HARVEST, WOULD YOU BE ABLE TO COME HELP ME?

A smile lit up Amelia's face. The thought of being close to Quinton made her happy. Maybe that's what her counselor meant when she said, "You'll know when to let Quinton into your life completely."

Amelia debated with herself for a few minutes and then she just texted him back without thinking about it anymore.

**AMELIA:** SURE. I'LL BE THERE IN A LITTLE BIT.

Three dots instantly appeared like he'd been waiting for her reply.

**QUINTON: THANKS.**

Amelia sent him a thumbs up reaction and then ran to her room to change.

# Chapter 29

**Quinton**

Quinton could have finished the harvesting on his own, but truth be told, he wanted Amelia by his side.

For the last six weeks he had shown her many facets of his personality. He'd enjoyed flirting with her, and taking care of her like the morning he had plated her food and covered it for later since she hadn't arrived for breakfast on time. Amelia didn't even get mad when he picked her up and tossed her in the water trough. Of course, he helped her out too. He couldn't wait for her to stop guarding her heart and give it freely to him.

Oh, how he yearned to kiss her when they sliced bacon together for Jeff —he'd shown improvement since the first time— and again after they made up from a significant disagreement regarding using the tractor, so the ranch hands didn't have to work as hard.

This afternoon when school got out, Emmanuel had given him a note that he and *Miss Amelia* created in writing class.

*Dear Quinton*

*You're amanzing and I like you. I'm sory!*

*Love,*

*Miss Amelia*

Quinton smiled at his son after reading the letter that Amelia definitely didn't know anything about. The penmanship was the first indication, but he also knew that Amelia would not let a letter go out with spelling and punctuation mistakes. Knowing his son's distaste for writing, made it all the more special. He blinked his eyes a couple times. This had given him the courage to ask Amelia to pick the first batch of apples with him.

Fortunately, he'd convinced Axel and Allie to take care of other crops, leaving him and Amelia alone. He hadn't enjoyed being anywhere near Allie, so even if Amelia hadn't agreed to come, he would have requested to work alone. How dare she join forces with Selena to hurt Amelia. Jeff had expressed his embarrassment, so Quinton knew he hadn't been alone in his thinking.

Quinton placed the most recent apple he picked in a basket and when he stood, his heart threatened to pound out of his chest. Amelia was jogging toward him. Why wouldn't she bring a four wheeler out? Obviously he had one with him, but wasn't the other one parked and ready to go?

The black and white bicycle type shorts didn't fit snug to her body like they used to. Her racerback tank top sagged a little too, unlike a couple months ago in the workout room when it hugged every curve she had.

Quinton had noticed that she'd lost weight, but she clearly hid how much with jeans and bulky sweatshirts. She still made his body feel like liquid fire, so it's not like the weight change made his desire for her.

When Amelia reached him, she was barely out of breath. "Where do you want me to start?"

She glanced his way. He just wanted to swoop her up in his arms and kiss her or at least hug her.

"I'd like you to help me with this tree. There's a lot on it." Quinton's gentle voice brought her eyes to meet him.

Her mesmerizing teal eyes captured his entire being, making his blood run hot. She walked to the back of the tree and started twisting apples free from branches. That just wouldn't do for Quinton. He picked up an empty basket and brought it over to her and then proceeded to twist apples right next to her.

Quinton intentionally brushed her arm, and he heard Amelia sigh. When he turned to face her, Amelia's body seemed to turn into stone. She squeezed her eyes shut and her hand froze still attached to an apple hanging from the tree.

"Em," Quinton grabbed her arms and turned her body to face him. "...look at me, please." Quinton used the softest tone he possibly could; he just wanted her to hear him out.

Without opening her eyes, Amelia acknowledged his request, "I need you to put a shirt on before I can open my eyes and have this conversation."

He leaned forward and kissed her temple.

Amelia pushed at his shoulder, but he didn't move. "I can feel your smirk."

Grinning and cocky, Quinton chuckled. "Is my bare chest distracting you?" He whispered into her neck and got an instant reward when his fingers felt goosebumps on her arms.  He didn't even wait for her to respond, "Sorry, Sweetheart, I left my shirt somewhere hours ago."

"It's just me. Em, please open your eyes."

His pulse raced when her eyes first raced over his chest before resting in sync with his. That pleased him.

"How was your session today?" He wanted to add, *do you see yourself through my eyes yet?* But he refrained.

Quinton caressed her shoulders and up her neck until he cupped her face. Slowly, he leaned toward her and kissed her forehead. She leaned into his hand. Just being in her presence made him feel alive.

Amelia finger-combed her ponytail that rested on her shoulder. "Dr. Bethany said that she thinks I'm making great progress."

*Yes!* Quinton wrapped his arms around her waist and pulled her toward him. She latched onto his arms, feeling the muscles in his upper arm and shoulders. Strands from Amelia's ponytail instantly tickled Quinton's chest.

When Amelia backed up slightly, he had a bit of relief from the molten lava running through his entire nervous system. That was until Amelia stood on her tiptoes and leaned closer. Quinton was sure their lips would meet. His heart started pounding faster and faster, but she didn't come anywhere near his lips. Instead, she pressed her soft lips against the veins pulsing in his neck and Quinton let out a deep moan.

Quinton didn't even think, he couldn't. He lifted Amelia to his chest and kissed her with over six weeks of hunger and passion. He hoped he was sending her the message that he loved her something fierce. Just to make sure, he slowed his movement and gently trailed her jaw with kisses. "Can we please get past this?"

At this point, Quinton wasn't too proud to beg. He'd spent the last month focusing on ranch work, raising Emmanuel, and capturing as many moments with Amelia that he could.

With gentle hands, Quinton lowered Amelia to the ground with him. "I've been miserable. I know this is a process, but are you in a spot where we can go through this journey together?"

Amelia blushed and ducked her head, but Quinton gently tugged her chin back toward him, "I'm not trying to embarrass you. I just want you to know that I want you in my life."

"I want you in my life too. I'm sorry I'm like this."

"Don't apologize. This is who you are. Look, you got over your self-consciousness about your lack of experience once I gave you some practice." He wagged his eyebrows at Amelia, hoping to get more practice right now. "Now, you need to realize that you are the only woman for me and no matter what woman tries to come on to me, I'm going to choose you every time."

"You have women gawking at you everywhere you go—you're gorgeous. You can't promise me that."

Quinton repositioned himself on the ground with his back up against a fence post. He gently pulled Amelia down with him. He planted her in between his legs and leaned her back on his chest. "I can promise you that. Amelia, love isn't just a feeling. More often than not, it's a choice, and I choose to love you.

"Love?"

"Yes, sweetheart. I love you." He'd told her that before, why did she seem so surprised by it now?

"Listen, if I kept dismissing your compliments about me, what would you say? How would you feel?"

"I'd think you were an idiot. Have you seen yourself?"

Quinton's chest and abdomen rumbled from laughter. "That's how I feel when you won't accept my compliments. Not everyone is going to find a single person beautiful. You have to let your guard down and believe that I find you exquisite, lovely, ravishing, riveting, gorgeous, dazzling, enticing, delectable—"

"—Alright, enough of the synonyms." Amelia howled through her smile. "How do you even know so many synonyms for describing a beautiful person?" She shifted her body and gently kissed his cheek, while he shrugged and winked at her.

"So does this mean you'll be mine?" he murmured against her lips.

Responding breathlessly, "If you'll have me, but I can't promise I won't get insecure and jealous ever again.

Quinton dropped his forehead. "Just talk to me."

"Okay, as long as you promise to let me know whenever I need to make improvements." Amelia's voice sounded vulnerable, but she kissed the pulsing vein on his neck for a second time.

Quinton pushed her back gently, "I think you've figured out already how to make me lose my mind all by yourself—you don't need any improvements." Quinton loved the way Amelia's shy smile and blushed face looked at that exact moment. "In fact, no more kissing unless we're standing." He chuckled

"Come on. Let's get these apples." Quinton lifted Amelia to her feet, then stood himself. If it took him the rest of his life, he'd show this woman that she was perfect, to him and that's all that mattered.

# Chapter 30

**Amelia**

Amelia found herself in the barn brushing Duncan. Emmanuel and Damon had just finished Emmanuel's riding lesson and after the little guy swiped three strokes down the stallion, Amelia told him that she would finish up since Carolyn had a treat for all the kids inside.

"Thanks, Amelia." He took off for the main house.

A sense of peace filled Amelia to the brim as she brushed the nut colored horse. Lost in her thoughts, she missed that Quinton entered the barn until he wrapped his arms around her from behind and rested his chin on her shoulder. The intense smell of fresh cut hay mixed with his rosewood cologne made Amelia's body tingle from head to toe.

"We just unloaded the new horse for Damon to break. I think this one will be a doozy, even for him."

Turning her head, Amelia kissed Quinton on the cheek, "Thank you."

"For what," Quinton asked earnestly.

Amelia continued to brush her horse. "For everything. You work hard, you're patient, kind, and loving with me. I think you complete me."

Electricity swishing through the air of the barn. Amelia spoke with her counselor earlier in the day. She'd admitted that she definitely loved Quinton. Dr. Bethany had convinced Amelia that she'd made great progress with the trust exercises they'd done and now it was up to her to show Quinton how she felt and trust that he'd be honest with her.

Being wrapped in his arms felt right. She briefly thought about telling Quinton that she had fallen in love with him, but she hesitated too long and the moment passed.

"Hey, why are you brushing the horse down and not Emmanuel?" asked, standing erect.

A smile spread across Amelia's face. "He started to and then I sent him in with the other kids to get the snack that Carolyn made for them." She brushed a few more strokes down Duncan's mane. "I really enjoy brushing the horses," Amelia admitted.

Quinton kissed her cheek, "Alright, but don't make a habit of it because he has to learn hard work."

Amelia sidestepped. Fortunately Quinton loosened his grip, so she could turn and face him. She stood tall, slapping her feet together like an obedient soldier. Simultaneously, she brought her outstretched, straight as a board, fingers just above her right eye to salute Quinton. "Yes, Sir. Is there anything else, Sir."

"Funny, real funny!" Quinton threw Amelia over his shoulder and her body stiffened. Her head was in direct alignment with his backside.

"Quinton Richards, put me down right this minute." Amelia shrieked.

"And what if I don't?" Quinton teased. The commotion caused the horses to snort.

A laugh burst from her throat, but she refrained from answering his question because she didn't know anything she could say that would scare Quinton into submission, "You're causing the horses too much anxiety, you should put me down, or they'll come to my rescue."

"Is that so? I could march you outside and just drop you in the trough again and see how the horses help you then." Quinton playfully strutted toward the door.

Amelia tried another tactic. "Q honey, could you set me down please, so the blood stops rushing to my head?"

Quinton set her down and wrapped his arms around her waist, "You're a manipulator, you know that right?"

Shock set in on her face and she set a hand over her heart, "Me, a manipulator, I think you are sadly mistaken. I just prefer looking at your handsome face instead of your rear." She didn't need to keep reminding him how self-conscious she was about him lifting her. Amelia rested one hand on his cheek and with the other hand she gripped his bicep to steady herself on her tiptoes as she gently touched her lips to Quinton's.

He pulled Amelia closer to his chest and deepened the kiss. She snaked both her arms around his neck and ran her fingers through the hair at the nape of his neck. A low growl escaped him. He trailed kisses down her jawline, as he stepped back breathing heavily. "All right, that's enough."

"What's wrong? We're standing up." A sly smile and soft chuckle escaped her.

"You're full of jokes today, aren't you?"

With that same smile, Amelia just shrugged her shoulders and tossed her hands toward the ceiling with her palms up.

"I have to finish planning the dance for the carnival. Can you believe we're a month away?" Amelia tried not to think about the carnival because that meant that the bachelor auction wasn't far off. She obviously would bid on Quinton, but her dad had always told her not to underestimate opponents. Amelia had heard of bachelor auctions before and the men sold for astronomical amounts, Knowing Selena, she'd come prepared to win.

"You know, you never did answer me..." Amelia tilted her head and knit her eyebrows together, urging him to remind her of his question. "...are you going to bid on me at the auction?"

Amelia let out a soft laugh. "Wouldn't you like to know?" Quinton crossed his arms over his chest and every delicious muscle flexed, causing Amelia to catch her breath, "Are you trying to give me a reason to bid on you?"

"Maybe."

Tapping him on his bicep as she stepped past him, "You keep that up and I don't know how I could resist bidding on you." She winked as she put the brush back and continued toward the door.

"I've got a little more to do, Em. See you at dinner." Quinton kept his arms over his chest, as he turned to face her.

"See you inside Q." Amelia blew him a kiss before she left the barn.

Back in her office Amelia wrapped up the day's paperwork and sent a quick text to Damon.

**AMELIA:** IS EVERYTHING GOING TO BE READY FOR THE SURPRISE?

Before she could put her phone back on the desk, three dots appeared.

**DAMON:** THIS ONE HAS BEEN A LITTLE

TROUBLE, BUT GIVE ME ANOTHER

WEEK OR TWO AND I'LL BE ALL SET.

A smile reached Amelia's eyes, hoping the surprise would be well received.

**AMELIA:** THANKS FOR ALL YOU DO, DAMON!

He responded with a thumbs up reaction.

Amelia couldn't believe how far Damon had come since arriving at the ranch. She'd never imagined a mom wanting to leave her four beautiful children, period. Yet, when Damon's ex-wife had announced that she was leaving the ranch and leaving the kids with Damon, Amelia hadn't been surprised. She had only ever seen Damon treat his ex with respect, love, and kindness, but Roxanne never seemed to 'fit in' with ranch life. When he asked to expand his services to include riding lessons, Amelia fully supported his endeavor, hoping it took his mind off his ex. When she had come up with the equine therapy suggestion, Damon worked with Amelia to build the children's and adults program from the ground up.

Before Amelia put her phone down, another text came through.

**Carolyn:** DINNER'S READY.

     **Amelia:** THANKS, BE THERE SOON—DON'T WAIT ON ME.

Everyone had started eating by the time Amelia arrived. Quinton stood to greet her with a kiss on the cheek. Carolyn had already dished her out a plate, covered it with a napkin, and set it next to Quinton. Amelia sat in her seat as she thanked Carolyn for the extra care.

While everyone engaged in their conversations, Quinton leaned his chiseled jaw close to Amelia and whispered, "Would you like to go for a walk after dinner is over? Carolyn already said she'd watch Emmanuel for me." His hot breath on her neck sent shivers down her spine. She gently squeezed his leg under the table when he chuckled in her ear at the effect he had on her.

"Yeah, that sounds great."

Everyone finished dinner and cleaned up the room. The kids scurried off to the basement while Amelia and Quinton slipped out the front door hand in hand. The way Quinton's large calloused hands wrapped around her smaller, slightly calloused one, kept her warm and flooded her heart with joy.

As they reached the orchard, Amelia had been walking with an extra bounce in her step and Quinton took notice. He stopped and rested his hands on her hips, "What made you so happy today, besides being out here with me?" Even his smug look made Amelia all warm inside.

"Cocky much?" Amelia guffawed. He shook his head playfully. She, however, couldn't keep her secret any longer. "Ok, don't get mad,"

Quinton dropped his hands, "Why do women do that? They tell men not to get mad before they even tell us anything. If you suspected I'd be mad, why'd you do it in the first place?"

"Good point. I'll think about that next time." Amelia was pleased when Quinton let out a soft chuckle. "I've been working with Damon on a surprise for you and Emmanuel." At this point her nerves took over and she began to ramble. "Technically, it's just a surprise for Emmanuel and maybe I should wait until another time and then talk to you about it and pretend that this conversation never happened—"

Quinton kissed her lips gently. She believed it was just to stop her from talking, nonetheless she liked it. "Please just tell me."

"Okay. So, I've been watching Emmanuel in his riding lessons and Damon agreed that he is doing amazing. He's truly a natural. I got him his own horse. Damon's been breaking her. He only needs two more weeks and then Emmanuel will have a horse of his own." Amelia spoke so quickly and the faster she spoke the more her shoulders lifted to her ears and by the time she finished her eyes were squeezed shut waiting for his response.

Silence.

Her right eye opened, taking a quick glimpse at Quinton's face. Unreadable. Both eyes studied him for a moment. A loud sigh escaped as her shoulders dropped. Amelia couldn't take the silence anymore. Are you mad at me?

# Chapter 31

**Quinton**

"You're such a jerk!" Amelia had attempted to shove Quinton, but he hadn't budged. Two months had passed since Amelia had given Emmanuel a brown American Paint with white patches he'd named Yoshi. Quinton would never forget that day when she'd told him about the horse. He'd attempted to act mad, but the minute Amelia tried to shove him, unsuccessfully, and had called him a jerk, he'd let out a boisterous laugh. He'd also never forgotten the moment that followed. He'd run gentle kisses first under her earlobe and then down the length of her neck before his lips had met hers. He'd continued to kiss her, until she'd parted her lips, allowing him to deepen the kiss. The strawberry flavor he'd tasted on her lips still lived in his memory. She'd said so much without saying a word. He'd known her resolve had been slipping; she'd finally started to trust him. That realization alone had sent a dose of adrenaline pounding through his veins.

Damon had chosen this horse for Emmanuel because they are known to be good with children and they build a deep bond with their rider. It hadn't taken long for Emmanuel and Yoshi to become one. Emmanuel took care of Yoshi every day alongside his dad, or Damon and the ranch hands.

Emmanuel even joined in with the other men who hadn't stopped razzing Quinton about Amelia gifting the horse, saying it was the step right before marriage. "When are you asking Miss Amelia to marry you?"

"When the time is right." Quinton replied.

In the last four weeks since the kids had gotten out of school they'd been expected to work on the ranch with their parents for one hour a day before they were free to be kids. They'd swam, played on the playground, and ran through the fields, but this morning was the first morning of the carnival, so the parents took care of the chores before the kids had even woken up.

Amelia's phone vibrated in her pocket. Retrieving it from the front of her jeans, she read Quinton's name in the banner at the bottom. She smiled as she read his morning message. Good Morning, Sweetheart. Are you free right now? Emmanuel and I could use some help in the cabin, real quick.

Amelia tapped out a fast response, Sure. Be right there.

"Come in," A faint voice replied after Amelia knocked on the door. When she entered, Amelia couldn't find Quinton, or Emmanuel. She noticed the place seemed untidy. She wasn't judging, but Amelia had never seen Quinton's living space like this before, so it struck her as odd. The couch cushions seemed strategically placed on the floor. Some of Emmanuel's stuffed animals were scattered throughout the downstairs.

She spied four nerf guns placed carefully throughout as well. One behind the Keurig machine, one on each end table on either side of the couch and Emmanuel's Luigi stuffy had one positioned in his hand like he was protecting his bunker behind one of the couch cushions.

"Hello." Amelia heard the trepidation in her own voice. "Where are you guys?" Amelia wasn't nervous. In fact, it was painfully obvious they planned to ambush her. The bathroom door was shut, so she expected them to come storming out any second. "I thought they were in here." Amelia decided to play along. She picked up the nerf gun that rested behind the coffee machine. "They must have meant the main house."

Amelia opened and shut the door quickly before silently darting behind the island in the middle of the kitchen floor, where she could now ambush them. Immediately, Amelia heard, "Dad she left."

"No she didn't. She just wants you to think that...trust me."

"How do you know?"

"Shh. I'll explain later."

Amelia bit her lip really hard to prevent herself from laughing. Now the waiting game began. Who had more restraint, Quinton or herself? Almost eight fifteen. Quinton knew they could get into the carnival at nine, not that she cared about getting there on time, but Emmanuel knew too, and he definitely wanted to be one of the first people there.

"Come out now, Amelia and we'll call it a truce." Quinton hollered from his hiding place.

She refused to speak.

*A truce. Is he crazy? There hadn't been one bullet shot.* Amelia knew that Quinton's determination ran deep.

Amelia heard rustling upstairs. Now she knew they were in the loft. They had a sniper nest and she was a sitting duck if they stood over the railing.

Still crouched behind the counter, she hoped they attempted to come down the ladder, then she could sneak attack. Wait. The bathroom door creaked open. *Who is in there?*

"Psst. Quinton," a familiar voice hissed.

*Is that Raddix?* Amelia couldn't believe Raddix was in on this. *He'll regret going against Amelia.* "She's gone, let's go find her."

"Are you sure she's not hiding somewhere?"

"She can't stay quiet this long." Raddix declared.

*He thought he knew her so well.* Amelia silently laughed. *"Can't stay quiet this long."* Raddix will get the first bullet right in the chest for that comment.

Amelia had never liked losing, so she'd put her heart into every challenge. This was the biggest competition she'd faced in a long while. She'd planned the battle in her head: Raddix goes out first, then Emmanuel, and lastly, Quinton.

Footsteps. Whispers. Amelia calculated the timing in her head. She leaned around the counter and spied Raddix keeping watch. Amelia aimed, pulled the trigger, and whipped back around concealing herself again completely behind the counter.

"Ow!" Raddix jumped.

Instantly, Amelia pulled the yellow level to reset the trigger and shot Emmanuel in the leg as he came down the ladder.

"Dad!"

Amelia repeated the same process again. The bullet bounced off Quinton's back. All three of her opponents snapped their heads toward her hideout. She heard footsteps coming toward her from both sides of the counter. What to do? If she waited, they would definitely take her out. If she ran for it, they would most definitely catch her. Amelia didn't think, she just ran.

Amelia popped up and dashed to her left. Raddix met her half way between the counter, and her initial spot. She shot him again and escaped into the living room.

"Dad, let's get her." Emmanuel and Quinton ran after Amelia who remained quiet behind in the hall closet. The father and son duo tiptoed past the closet door. A few moments later, she heard another set of footsteps shuffle past her too. Raddix. Amelia waited for his footsteps to go further into the house.

Amelia slowly opened the closet door and strategically checked the first room. Clear. She moved on to the bathroom. She creaked open the closet door. Clear. She whipped back the shower curtain. Clear. Where could they be? One more room. That's Quinton's room. Should she go in there? All's fair in love and war and this was war. Amelia checked under the bed. Clear. She tried the walk-in closet. Amelia used her free hand to push back his clothes. Her breath caught momentarily at the faint smell of his rosewood cologne. *That's cheating. Using the sexy smell of a great man to distract me...that's all Raddix. He's always played dirty. Not this time boys. I'm going to find you.*

One last place. The master bathroom. She tiptoed to the closet door and tossed it open. Clear. There wasn't anywhere else to hide. The transparency of the glass shower doors eliminated a place to check. The soaking tub revealed empty space. Where are they?

Amelia's heart pounded erratically in her ears. Now she expected someone to jump out from somewhere and shoot her, but where from? Gliding out of Quinton's room, she started back toward the living room, but didn't see anyone there either. At that moment Amelia's patience gave out. She slapped her free hand against her thigh in frustration.

Bang, Bang, Bang. All three guys shot multiple nerf bullets at Amelia. She tried to take cover, but they rained nerf bullets down on her like confetti on New Year's Eve. Amelia put both forearms in front of her face as she backed up toward the bedroom. "Ow! Ow! Stop. You won!."

The firing ceased. "We won, Daddy!" Amelia smiled as she watched Emmanuel and Quinton high five each other. "You're not mad at us, are you, Amelia?"

"Definitely not, little guy. That was fun." Amelia gave Quinton an alluring look and placed her hand on her hip. "You, however, are in big trouble.

"It's not my fault you're a bad aim," Quinton said, winking at Amelia.

Amelia's mouth dropped before she retorted. "Bad aim. First of all, I had gotten all three of you before you'd known what hit any of you. Second, three of you and one of me—that says it all—and third it's a nerf gun. Give me a target and a nine millimeter and I'll out shoot you any day."

"Oh really?"Quinton walked toward Amelia with determination to take on her challenge . . . and win.

Raddix stepped up, "You don't want to take that bet, trust me." Quinton paused and stared at Raddix. "You've heard of Annie Oakley, right? Meet the modern day Annie Oakley with a G4 Glock nineteen. You won't win."

Amelia let him off the hook. "Yeah, you can have some time to think that challenge over." Crouching down to Emmanuel's height, "Would you like to go to the carnival now?"

"Yeah. Can we leave, Daddy?" Emmanuel jumped up, forcing Amelia to stand quickly next to Quinton.

Quinton wrapped his arm around Amelia's shoulder and kissed her temple. "Are you ready, Sweetheart?"

"Let's go." As they left Quinton's cabin, Amelia directed her attention to Raddix. "Did your dad already leave for the carnival? I was supposed to catch a ride with him because Quinton won't be going until later."

"Yup. My truck is loaded. I'm heading out right now too. You can come with me."

Emmanuel complained, "I want to go right now."

Amelia mouthed to Quinton, "He can come with us if you want."

"If I let you go with Amelia, will you listen to her until I arrive?"

Emmanuel hugged his dad, "Of course I will. Thank you, Daddy."

# Chapter 32

**Amelia**

When they arrived at the carnival, Raddix parked behind their stations to check in with his dad. As the two men unloaded Raddix's truck, Amelia walked Emmanuel around to the different booths. A delicious pizza aroma slapped them in the face. Unfortunately, it came from the Whittaker's booth. Emmanuel all but begged for a slice. Amelia had come to realize that Emmanuel had a strict schedule regarding his pizza. For the last five years he'd had pizza every Friday and she hadn't wanted to be the reason his schedule got messed up, so she bought him a slice and headed back toward Jeff and Katy's booth. Thankfully, she hadn't had to interact with Selena. Not that she expected to. In all the years she'd known Selena, she hadn't lifted a finger to help anyone at any time unless it had benefited her.

All of the parishioners had helped to put a fresh coat of paint on each booth to make them look lively and fresh. By the time Amelia and Emmanuel reached the ranch's booth, Carolyn had already sold half of their baked goods and it was only lunch time. Jeff and Axel were slaving at the grill while Katy continued to take orders and shifted the customers to another line to wait for their order.

"Katy, do you need some help?" Amelia inquired.

"Yes, Please."

"I'll go drop Emmanuel off with Renee and be back."

Renee operated the bounce house for the kids. After letting her know that Emmanuel had to stay with her at the bounce house until either she or Quinton came to get him, she agreed to watch over the little guy. Amelia appreciated Renee's help.

The lunch rush lasted until almost three o'clock. Amelia had fired up a third grill and had helped cook the orders. Amelia wondered what was taking Quinton so long at the ranch. She had texted him when she dropped Emmanuel off with Renee, but he still hadn't responded.

Katy, Jeff, and Raddix all collapsed in a folding chair for a few minutes once the rush ceased. They thanked Amelia for help and she left to find Emmanuel. The carnival filled the football sized field behind the church. As she strolled toward Renee, a commotion to her right caught her eye. Selena was waving her hands and yelling at some poor young boy inside her family's booth. "Always a drama queen." Amelia prayed aloud. "Please be with that young boy, Lord."

Amelia's mind had drifted to thoughts of Selena flirting with Quinton. It had seemed odd to her that Selena had given up on pursuing him. Selena had never given up until she had gotten what she wanted. Watching Selena scream at that poor boy left a sour taste in Amelia's mouth.

"Hey Renee, has Quinton showed up?" Amelia saw Emmanuel jumping in the bounce house with Dominic and Darlene.

"Not yet." Renee took tickets from the next three children in line. She instructed them to put their shoes inside a cubby box. Then she told Dominic, Darlene, and Emmanuel that their time was over for now.

The trio decided to use the church swing set, while Amelia called Quinton. When he hadn't answered, she started to worry. Should she go home to check on him? How would she get Emmanuel to go with her? She couldn't leave him with anyone else, but what if she brought him home and found his dad in a bad situation?

Ten minutes later her phone vibrated in her pocket. Her anticipation at seeing Quinton's name across the screen had fallen flat when Renee's name filled the banner at the bottom of her phone.

**RENEE:** THE BOUNCE HOUSE IS EMPTY IF THE KIDS WANT TO COME BACK.

The kids scream with excitement letting Amelia know the swings had lost their appeal.

**AMELIA:** BE RIGHT THERE.

As an unknown man approached the swings. "Hey pretty lady."

Emmanuel grabbed Amelia's hand and stepped so close to Amelia that he grazed her toes. The kids took off running toward Renee and the free bounce house to avoid any interaction with this stranger. As they turned back around Amelia smiled at Emmanuel. "Thank you, Buddy." Something about that stranger unsettled her stomach.

The kids quickly threw off their shoes and returned to jumping. When Amelia looked back, the man had disappeared. That seemed odd to Amelia. There was a lot of ground for him to cover walking in his nonchalant slow pace. Instead of worrying about it, she returned her focus to the kids.

Amelia joined Renee at the side of the bounce house. "How's Rocco doing?" Amelia hadn't checked on her friend since he'd told her that he'd healed fine and to stop fretting over him.

"He's still got some nasty bruising, but he's healed really well." Renee hugged Amelia thanking her for being not only a great boss, but a wonderful friend to her and Rocco. Amelia saw worry on her friend's face.

"What's wrong?" Amelia could almost imagine the anxious thoughts going through Renee's head. She had been married to the man for only six or seven years, so the thought of almost losing him so early into their marriage must be wreaking havoc with her emotions. Amelia and Quinton had only known each other a few months and she'd spent her whole day worrying about him and why he hadn't texted her back.

"The kids and I are always worried that it'll happen again." Renee wrapped her arms around her stomach. Based on the way Amelia is currently worried about Quinton, she assumed Renee felt nauseous.

Amelia gave Renee a hug to comfort her. "It very well may happen again, but if there's one thing I know about Rocco, it's that he learns from his mistakes." Amelia's counselor kept telling her that mistakes are everywhere and the successful people are the ones who learn from them. "Keep praying and giving your anxiousness to God because he cares for you." She hoped the reference to First Peter gave Renee peace.

Their peaceful conversation ceased quickly when the kids stormed out of the bounce house toward them. "Mommy, Emmanuel keeps doing this," Darlene put her hand on the small of Renee's back to show her mom.

He did it again and Darlene arched her back. Amelia hoped Quinton would arrive to handle this, but no such luck. Someone had to teach Emmanuel a little social cue. "Emmanuel, when a girl arches her back like that, it means she doesn't want you to touch her."

Quinton showed up before Amelia could say anything else. "What's going on?"

Amelia jumped up and hugged Quinton when she realized that he was okay. She liked the way he instantly wrapped his arms around her waist. She ran one hand through his slightly damp hair. He smelled clean with a hint of rosewood. Amelia closed her eyes and inhaled his scent before releasing her arms from around his neck. She gently swatted him on the bicep, "Where have you been? I've texted and called...nothing."

Quinton smiled. His amused eyes told Amelia he liked that she worried about him, or maybe the smile was because she smelled him. "You are the proud new owner of three baby calves. Rocco, Bill, and I have been busy men while you ladies get to soak up the fun at the carnival. Both Renee and

Amelia swatted him—one on each bicep. "Kidding, kidding," Quinton said, stepping away from them.

Amelia couldn't remember Emmanuel's question. He'd hung his head and crossed his arms over his chest—the sign to show when he was upset that people weren't listening to him. "Please continue, Emmanuel. Sorry, I was so happy to see your Daddy since I hadn't heard from him…anyway; please continue with your side of the story."

"…but I like to touch her. She's pretty. My Daddy touches your back like that and you don't do that thing with your back." Emmanuel's innocent face made Amelia smile—he was so adorable.

Amelia's face got really hot and she knew she must be at least three shades of red. Renee's snickering from above and Quinton's beaming smile wasn't helping matters.

"Well, buddy, everyone's different. If I were you, I would wait at least another ten years before you do anything your daddy does."

Darlene shared, "Dean said that he was going to deck 'em if he didn't keep his hands off me."

"Go get your brother and come back here please." Amelia knew first hand that Renee had never condoned violence. She had seen Renee talk adult men out of fighting, so she wasn't concerned with Dean learning this from his parents. She assumed he innately felt the need to protect his sister and she admired that. It reminded her of Raddix protecting her during her school years.

Looking at Amelia, Emmanuel asked, "What's that mean…deck 'em?"

"It's another way to say hit," Amelia explained.

Quinton knelt down to meet his son and Amelia backed away, "Hey, Buddy, you know how I tell everyone to keep their hands off you unless you say it's okay?" Emmanuel nodded to show he understood. "This is the same thing. You get upset when people touch you, so you have to respect when others don't want to be touched."

"Darlene could touch me and I wouldn't get mad. Besides Dad, she didn't tell me not to." Emmanuel declared. Frustration, at his own inadequacy to explain this, crept up in Quinton's voice, though he also felt upset for his son.

Quinton gave his son a sympathetic smile, "I get it bud, but you need to keep your hands off her.

When Darlene and Dean arrived, Renee helped talk through the situation with the three kids. Dean shared, "I like Emmanuel, but she's my sister, and she didn't want to be touched."

Renee's face flooded with pride. "I love that you protect your sister. You need to remember that Emmanuel is your ranch family too. He doesn't always understand things the way we do, so instead of waiting until you're so mad that you want to hurt him, get help from one of us right away. We can help all of you fix the situation."

"Okay, can we go play now? Dean asked.

After Renee determined that all three kids were settled and happy, she looked to Quinton to see if he had anything to add and when he didn't, she sent them away to play.

"Thank you so much for the way you guys handled that." Quinton's voice rang with appreciation.

Before he could say more, Renee swatted at him a second time, "What are you teaching that boy?"

Quinton looked at Amelia's red face and could feel his own neck heat up. He placed his strong, working hand on her lower back, "See it doesn't affect her." Quinton couldn't help but laugh.

"Oh it affects me alright." Amelia fanned her shirt to get air. Even though this July started off being hotter than any other July in the last ten years, she knew that the extremely handsome man touching her with such care was, in fact, what spiked her body heat.

How would she get through this evening?

# Chapter 33

**Quinton**

Quinton put the truck in park when he pulled in near the main house. The sun had set a long while ago, and Emmanuel had fallen dead to the world on a blanket shortly after the fireworks had started. He'd put his noise canceling headphones on before they'd started, but even still Quinton had wondered how his son had fallen asleep, and had stayed asleep with loud explosives filling the air. The little guy had worn himself out running around the field playing with the other kids, but mainly that bounce house had become his safe haven.

Quinton had appreciated the way Renee had spoken with Dean about how to help Emmanuel understand something that might seem obvious to everyone around him. He looked at the main house longingly. It pleased him that their new ranch family wanted to help Emmanuel and not make fun of him, or make him feel bad for thinking differently.

Raddix immediately popped into his head, so did Jeff, and Sean. He knew he would have to have a conversation with these men very soon. Quinton hadn't lied when he told Amelia that he'd assisted Rocco with delivering three new baby calves, but he'd left out the part about taking a trip out of town to get the ring he currently stored in his pocket. He'd known if he shopped at the only jewelry store in town, Amelia would have heard about it before he arrived at the carnival yesterday.  Now, if he could only be sure that Amelia would say 'yes' to his proposal.

"Let me get it." Quinton stopped Amelia from getting out of the truck. Instead he briskly rounded the front of the truck and opened her door. He extended his hand gently tugging her out of the truck. Her smaller hand fit perfectly inside of his. He pulled her to his chest and wrapped his arms around her waist. "Sorry I worried you earlier." Before she could respond, Quinton descended on her lips, capturing them slowly and gently hoping to show her he would treat her with respect, the way a gentleman should.

Quinton rested his forehead on hers, "Em," he groaned. "Thank you for taking such good care of Emmanuel today. It'd been a while since he'd declared his love to Amelia. Without a doubt she would be the best wife for him and the best mother for Emmanuel. *When will she be ready to tell me that she loves me?* He hoped it would be very soon. He pulled her closer. The feel of Amelia's hands sliding over his sides and up his back sent a trail of warm sensations in their wake.

"Thank you for trusting me with Emmanuel. I'd do anything to protect him. I love—" Amelia stopped herself. Quinton thought she might have been about to say that she loved Emmanuel, or maybe him. He hoped she'd say it about both of them. "—I'd love to help you get him settled, if you don't mind."

Quinton kissed her forehead and led her away from the truck, so he could shut the door. Amelia grabbed Emmanuel's stuffed animals he'd brought along for the ride while Quinton carried Emmanuel into the cabin.

Amelia brushed Emmanuel's skater hair away from his cheek with her soft fingers and gently kissed the young boy's face. The simple gesture pulled at Quinton's heart strings. Instead of climbing him up the ladder, Quinton had placed him on an air mattress in Quinton's room. Emmanuel used that sometimes when he had bad dreams.

Instead of letting the night end, Quinton laced his fingers with Amelia's. "Want to check the stars out for a little bit?" Amelia nodded as she wrapped her free hand around his bicep and rested her head against his shoulder.

Quinton and Amelia stood silently gazing at the stars. The hot, July day surrendered to the soft gentle breeze, as the bright stars lit up the night sky. All around them the faint flickers of lighting bugs shone throughout the tall grass. Crickets rubbed their wings together creating that loud chirping sound that was peaceful unless it was inside your home. Here in God's country, the calming noise brought out a tranquility like he had never known before coming here.

"Did you have fun today?" Quinton rested his back against the railing and stared into Amelia's eyes as he interlaced their fingers on both hands.

Quinton recognized the twinkle in her eye. *Here comes her sass.* "Once I stopped worrying about whether or not you were okay, I had a great time."

Quinton's heart constricted. She really did care. Emotion overtook him and with all the passion he had for her, Quinton kissed her hard and strong showing how much he loved her. He'd told himself he wouldn't say it again until she was ready. Not because he was being immature, but because he hadn't wanted to pressure her into saying something before she was ready.

"Are you ready for the dance tomorrow night?" Amelia smiled at him coyly.

No! It's not that Quinton couldn't dance, he just hadn't had anyone to dance with for a long time. "You know I don't dance, so probably not."

A gentle breeze forced the wisps of hair at both sides of Amelia's temple to wave in her face. With the tips of his fingers, Quinton caressed Amelia's forehead as he looped the hair around her ears. "How about you?"

"The dance is my favorite part of the whole event. That's why I always plan it." Amelia pinched her eyebrows together questioning Quinton's astonished look. "Something I said shocked you."

"I figured with all of the time you spend working, you wouldn't have much time for dancing." He placed his free hand around her waist, tugging her a little closer to him.

Her palms on Quinton's chest stopped her from getting too close. "Just because people in high school deemed me an outcast and I chose to stay on the ranch all the time doesn't mean I didn't learn to dance." Amelia kept her voice neutral. "My mom and dad danced all the time, so they taught me and as I got older Raddix always wanted to impress the ladies. He needed a dance partner to practice with, so I helped out."

Thinking of Raddix dancing with Amelia to impress the ladies seemed weird to him. "Raddix, really? That seems a little inappropriate." Quinton joked.

"Ew, gross! It wasn't like that and you know it." Amelia swatted him again.

With her palms rested on his chest, Amelia pushed up on her tiptoes. When her lips were within an inch of his mouth, she breathed, "You're the only one I want to dance with."

Quinton let out a low growl and tilted her head slightly while capturing her lips with a force that he knew revealed how crazy she made him. She matched him kiss for kiss. Quinton forced himself to stop. Breathless, he reached for Amelia's hand to walk her to the main house.

"You're sending me home?" Amelia teased. It only took a brief second of looking at her face for Quinton to know that Amelia realized that Quinton had reached his breaking point. "Sorry, a man can only take so much."

Quinton stopped outside her door. His self-control even impressed himself, but more importantly, he hoped it touched Amelia and let her know how special she was to him. He gave Amelia a peck on the cheek and wished her a good night.

At that moment, the rest of the gang arrived back from the carnival. It had been a long day. Everyone trudged from their vehicles. Quinton felt bad asking Sean, Jeff, and Raddix to hang back for a few moments, but he'd felt the need to get their approval before proceeding forward.

Once the door shut and the ladies were inside, Quinton shifted from one foot to the other while he talked. "I have to talk to you guys about something really important." Jeff smiled like the bad version of the grinch, but

Quinton knew there wasn't a bad bone in that man's body. He obviously knew what Quinton wanted to talk about. Sean smirked and Raddix had a neutral look on his face, so he figured they probably guessed too.

"I'm going to ask Amelia to marry me." He blurted out and waited for a response from any of them. All the men were quiet for so long that Quinton didn't think he'd get an answer. He continued, "I am asking you guys because you all have an important role in Amelia's life, and I don't want to disrespect any of you." Even though Raddix was younger than him, he still respected the way he'd watched out for Amelia since they were young.

Sean and Jeff shared a look with each other that Quinton wondered about. But before either of them could say anything, Raddix said his piece. "It's no secret that I didn't trust you when you first got here, but you've grown on me. I like the way you make Amelia smile and I might actually be able to focus on a love life of my own with you taking care of her." Quinton gave him a quizzical look. "I always felt guilty about dating."

Quinton's slight look of understanding must have appeased Raddix because he continued on, "It will be great to have you in the family." Raddix stuck out his hand. Quinton grabbed it and pulled the smaller man toward him and gave him a one arm hug while they shook hands.

"How about you two?" Quinton's plastered smile faltered slightly when Jeff began to talk. "What are your intentions with our Amelia?"

Hearing Jeff's "dad" voice spiked Quinton's anxiety all over again. He'd become great friends with Jeff, but asking for his surrogate daughter's hand in marriage seemed to bring out a different man, as it should. "I am going to love her with every ounce of my being. She'll let me know when I'm a bonehead because that's going to happen and I'll beg for her forgiveness, when I have to."

Jeff and Sean shared another concerned look which kept Quinton on pins and needles. "That's fine and dandy, but there is a bigger problem that I can see." Quinton's eyes opened so wide that his eyebrows naturally rose questioning what the problem could possibly be if he'd promised to love Amelia with all of him. "Which one of us gets to walk her down the aisle?"

Quinton let out a breath he didn't realize he was holding when Sean slapped him on the back. "I don't care if all three of you walk her down the aisle—whatever she wants." His laughter traveled into the night air.

At that point, Amelia's silhouette in the upstairs window caught his attention. He waved. Three heads turned toward the house, and there stood Amelia watching the men converse. Jeff turned back around and hushed the men before he whispered, "These windows aren't sound proof, and you know women—they hear everything." Jeff gathered the men in like a true football huddle, "When do you plan on asking her?"

"The ring's in my pocket. The moment will come to me. I was hoping she'd tell me she loved me first."

Raddix rolled his eyes. "Seriously man." He started to stand up, but the other men pulled him back into the huddle. Raddix shook his head and guffawed. "She hasn't told you that she loves you yet?"

Quinton shook his head showing his disappointment, but recovered quickly, "She said she feels it, but can't say it yet."

Jeff assured him, "She will in time. Do you trust that she loves you? Does she show it?" Quinton shook his head. "That's all that matters, actions are better than words—Katy taught me that."

Quinton snuck a peek at Amelia's window again. He didn't know when she had walked away, but she had. The huddle dispersed and the men went their separate ways. Quinton loved that they all gave their blessing. Now the bigger question—when would he ask her?

# Chapter 34

**Amelia**

Wake up.

Repeat.

Amelia felt like that movie *Groundhog's Day*. Everyone started their day out just as they had yesterday —preparing more food, stuffing trucks full, loading up the animals and heading to the carnival. The only thing that wouldn't repeat was the fun nerf gun fight she had with Quinton, Emmanuel, and Raddix. Quinton, being gone the majority of the day, was another thing she hoped would not repeat either.

Amelia looked forward to dancing with Quinton later that evening. She secretly hoped that Selena would be there to see her and Quinton dancing. Watching the men huddled together underneath her window last night had brought out the detective in her. Sadly she knew the best way to get any information would be to grill Emmanuel. He would surely know what his dad was up to, right?

Today, Amelia promised to help Raddix move the herd to the next paddocks while Sean manned the horse corral with Damon at the carnival. Unfortunately, her cousin loved to procrastinate. Amelia had some time, so she joined Emmanuel on the swings. "How ya' doing, Buddy?"

"I'm bored. All my friends have already left and I'm stuck here waiting for Dad." Emmanuel always struggled with not being first. He didn't need a good reason for wanting to be first either...he just wanted to be first. Having to wait for Quinton, started his day off poorly. Amelia felt sad for the little guy, so instead of gathering the information she wanted, she challenged him to a swing race.

Emmanuel didn't take the bait. His frustration ran deep this morning, but at least he didn't bolt away like he'd done when she first met him. Once Quinton exited the barn and told Emmanuel to hop in the truck, so they could leave, that put a smile on Emmanuel's face. He jumped off the swing and ran to the truck.

Amelia smiled as Quinton held out his hand to her. This never got old. Quinton's gentleman qualities touched her soul. Her heart started to beat faster and faster. The instant her hand touched his palm, he pulled her into his chest and wrapped his arms around her waist. "Trying to pick up where you left off last night cowboy?" Amelia winked at him to let him know that she didn't mind at all.

"This might be our only time semi-alone, but I'd take you in my arms any time of day." Quinton's deep, low voice combined with the musky cologne and fresh hay started a fire in Amelia's stomach. The man is killing it. His rugged good looks coupled with his heavenly scent intensified Amelia's desire to be near him.

Holding onto his biceps, Amelia pulled herself onto her tiptoes and gently covered his lips with hers. Quinton quickly took the lead and kissed her with fervor that she matched him kiss for kiss. A soft moan escaped from her and Quinton instantly tightened his hold on her with one hand while the other hand ran up and down her back sending jolts throughout her entire spine.

Amelia rested her palms on Quinton's chest as she pulled back from the most intimate kiss he had ever given her, so she could catch her breath. At the same time Emmanuel yelled to his dad to hurry up.

"We'll be there as soon as we can. The music starts playing around one. You'll save a dance for me, right?" Amelia inquired, as she ran her fingertips from the tops of his shoulders to his elbows.

"Not giving up on the dance, huh?" Quinton smiled at Amelia, who shook her head. "I'm saving every dance for you." Quinton kissed her already numb, puffy lips, with a gentleness that left her yearning for more.

Emmanuel yelled one more time to his dad, so Amelia nudged him toward the truck, "See you soon. Have fun with Emmanuel."

Once Amelia couldn't see Quinton's tail lights any longer, she whipped her phone from her pocket and pulled up Raddix's name under her texting app.

**AMELIA:** WHERE ARE YOU?

**RADDIX:** I'LL BE RIGHT OUT, SORRY.

Raddix's immediate reply satisfied her.

**AMELIA:** OKAY. MEET YOU IN THE BARN.

Amelia rushed there to saddle up the horses. Raddix appeared a short time later looking like death warmed over. The dark circles under his eyes let Amelia know that he hadn't slept well last night. Amelia had only seen Raddix like this one other time in his life. For about a week after Selena gutted him from the inside out, he walked around like a zombie. Amelia prayed that Raddix didn't get back into her clutches. The Wicked Witch of the West didn't have a thing on Selena.

"Whoa, you alright?" Amelia tried to stay lighthearted, but she had a gnawing feeling that Raddix was in for another heartache.

Raddix mumbled something that Amelia couldn't decipher as he met Amelia at the saddle rack. "What happened to you from the time you were outside my window with Quinton to right now?"

"Selena."

That woman's name burned Amelia's ears like nails on an old fashioned chalkboard. Amelia never disliked someone as much as she did Selena. "Want to talk about it?"

He tried to remove a saddle, but Amelia placed her hand on his forearm encouraging him to stop avoiding the discussion. "She lied again," Raddix spat out. His arm dropped to his side and spun around on his heels. He started pacing a short distance in the barn. "Yesterday she and I were talking about the dance and the auction. She told me how much she missed me and how we never should have broken up." Raddix raked a hand through his already messy hair.

"She said she wanted to get back together. We'd go to the dance together and she'd bid on me at the auction." Raddix shook his head. "I wasn't sure if I really wanted it, but I considered it." Happy little reunions are never possible with Selena. She was a manipulator through and through.

"After seeing her flirt with a group of men the minute I turned my back, I knew she was just using me again to get whatever she wanted. Obviously it was to get their attention."

Amelia's heart ached for Raddix. How could this same person continue to tear his heart apart? Amelia definitely wasn't a confrontational person, but her devotion to Raddix compelled her to do something. What though? Nothing seemed to bother Selena. She seemed to always get whatever she wanted and when she finished with whatever that desire was—be it human or materialistic—she tossed it aside like trash.

Raddix hadn't said anything for a few beats. "What happened after you settled in for the night?" Amelia knew there was more to this.

"She texted me about an hour after I got home and told me that she just got wrapped up in old thoughts, and we couldn't be together." Amelia moved quickly to his side and he rested his head on her shoulder. Seconds later, she felt wet tears seeping into her bare skin below her tank-top strap.

"She's not worth it. Look for someone else to dance with tonight. Did you see the number of out-of-towners yesterday? I predict there will be more tonight." Amelia rubbed Raddix's back to comfort him. "You're a handsome man; any woman will be blessed to dance with you."

"Thanks." Raddix lifted his head and wiped his eyes. Amelia had only seen Raddix cry twice in his life—when his mom died and when Selena played with him the first time. She hated seeing her cousin feel badly about himself. "She said that she has her eye on someone that she didn't realize would be at the dance or the auction, so basically it was good riddens again."

Amelia smiled. "I won't wish bad things to happen to her; that's not right. I will pray that God helps you see that you are worthy of someone else's love and attention. You need to stop thinking about her, so I pray God help you do that."

Raddix squeezed Amelia tight. "Thanks Cuz. Let's get this herd moved so we can get to the carnival ourselves. Sorry I made it so late."

The stubborn cattle delayed them most of the day. Of course. It took almost more hours than she'd hoped to move every last one to the next paddock, shower, and arrive at the carnival. Quinton had texted a few pictures to show he and Emmanuel were having a blast dancing after lunch.

Late afternoon and finally Amelia and Raddix pulled into the parking lot for those operating booths. Amelia checked on how the people from Big L' Ranch were making out. Fortunately, a couple of Katy's friends from church helped at her booth, as they were once again jam packed with customers.

Axel and Allie were almost sold out of baked goods again today. They already had their supply for tomorrow, the final day, packaged and ready to transport. Joy filled Amelia's heart thinking about how much the church will be able to serve others with the success of this carnival.

When she checked on Damon, he had fifteen kids in line. He informed her that the line hadn't stopped since they openeding. Fortunately, Quinton helped him out at lunch time, so he could get something to eat. Raddix offered to give him a break, but he declined because Sean already offered to take over for him shortly.

"Wanna go dance?" Amelia slid her arm into the crook of Raddix's arm. "Hopefully Quinton and Emmanuel are still there."

The smile on Amelia's face dropped and she stopped dead in her tracks. Quinton and Emmanuel were definitely still dancing. Emmanuel danced in a little circle with all the other kids from the ranch, though he certainly moved a little closer to Darlene. He kept his hands to himself though.

Quinton also danced in a circle, yet it didn't look as cute and innocent as Emmanuel's circle. Amelia counted at least five girls dancing around Quinton. Most of them must have been day trippers because she had never seen them before. Her stomach turned then she saw Selena front and center shaking every fake part she had right in front of Quinton.

Raddix must have seen it too because his jaw dropped. "That ... witch. She's going after Quinton. The conniving monster was going to use me to get to him."

It felt like an eternity that Amelia stood there, but it must have only been seconds. Amelia turned around and walked away. Crushed. She wasn't mad, just hurt. Maybe mad would come later when this played in her mind over and over again, but right now, she just couldn't believe Quinton could tell her that he loved her and then do this.

Raddix ran in front of her to stop her. "You're not going to let her get away with this are you?"

Amelia bit the inside of her cheek to prevent herself from crying. She would not cry anymore over people who pulled the wool over her eyes. She knew that most women were more beautiful and feminine than her, but she yet again believed the wolf in sheep's clothing. Amelia didn't like Selena because of her nasty disposition, but Amelia learned that she can't be angry with the woman because others fall prey to her; that's on them. She thought of one of her favorite songs *Devil is a Liar*. The lyrics ran through her head. *They say image is everything makin' it hard to think that you're enough...* Amelia refused to feel bad about herself. Not this time. If Quinton wanted someone like that, so be it.

Hopefully Amelia could get Raddix to feel the same way. He didn't need Selena making him feel bad about himself. Amelia had never heard of him being anything except a perfect gentleman, so he could find a lovely woman whenever he wanted. Her, on the other hand, she was clearly defective.

At that moment Amelia turned back toward the dance floor when she heard her name being called. Emmanuel darted toward her. She dropped to one knee with her arms open to the little boy with extended arms. He turned his body to the side leaving, so Amelia hugged him around the shoulders. "I'm so glad you got here. I'm trying to dance with my daddy, but I keep getting pushed out of the way."

Emmanuel's sad face ripped Amelia's heart further apart. The little boy grabbed Amelia's hand. With her free hand, she grabbed onto Raddix's arm. "Come on. Obviously stay away from those women who are pushing this handsome little fella out of the way, but dance with some of the other beautiful women." Raddix's smile was contagious. Amelia couldn't believe she was smiling at a time like this, but fortunately, she'd grown a lot in the last few months.

Amelia, Raddix, and Emmanuel started dancing with the other kids. A sweet-looking blonde woman in cut off jeans shorts and a striped tank top sat at a table nearby. Pulling Raddix's shoulder down toward her, Amelia whispered, "That woman has been staring at you since you hit the dance floor. Go ask her to dance." He'd lost some more of his self-confidence last night, but Amelia gently shoved him in the woman's direction. Moments later, they were dancing.

If only things could be that easy for Amelia. She wasn't as beautiful as Raddix was handsome. He truly could have any woman, while she knew it would take a special man to truly love her. Amelia thought she'd found that in Quinton. Amelia let herself enjoy the time with Emmanuel.

Amelia didn't think the fling with Selena would be anything too long. She did know that she couldn't trust him, so it probably wouldn't work out with him as an employee either.

A slow song came through the speakers. Amelia spied Raddix extending his hand to the new blonde. She smiled and stepped easily into Raddix's arms. *Lord, please be with Raddix. He deserves to be happy. Let his woman be a blessing for him.*

Amelia turned to walk away and a hand grabbed hers. "Amelia, aren't you going to dance with my Daddy?" Emmanuel looked so innocent and sweet.

"I don't think so, Buddy. I think he has a lot of dancers to choose from." Amelia forced a fake smile for the little boy she'd grown so fond of over the last few months. Where had Quinton gone? How could he leave Emmanuel unattended? Granted Renee and Rocco were watching all the ranch kids, but it just rubbed Amelia the wrong way that he wouldn't check in with his son before leaving the dance floor.

Amelia left Emmanuel with Renee to check in with the event DJ to make sure the playlist would last the next five hours. She didn't know if she'd stay that long. Dawn comes early and staying here late tonight wouldn't be as fun as she initially thought. Dancing in Quinton's arms. Stealing kisses as often as the songs changed....*Stop!* Obviously that wouldn't be happening now. The man she thought loved her couldn't be found.

# Chapter 35

**Quinton**

Morning came too quickly for Quinton. He hoped to find Amelia first thing to find out why she'd never showed up yesterday. Amelia hadn't responded his texts or calls. Selena and a group of her cronies surrounded Quinton on the dance floor. When the first slow song of the night had started playing, Selena tried to snake her arms around his neck. Quinton escaped. He'd told the women he needed to help Jeff with the grill and thankfully Jeff had backed him up.

Emmanuel continued to jump on Quinton's bed not phased by his dad's lack of desire to move. Quinton grabbed his son by the waist and wrestled him to the bed. "Please stop jumping, so I can call Amelia and find out why she didn't show up yesterday."

"But Dad…"

Quinton interrupted, "One second, Son."

"I was talking," Emmanuel protested to no avail. Amelia didn't pick up and Quinton's head filled with worry. He couldn't imagine what would make Amelia avoid him. Why wouldn't she even speak to him? He'd prayed so hard yesterday that Amelia would show up and he could dance with her. The blonde vultures that surrounded him hadn't taken no for an answer.

Maybe Amelia really didn't love him if she wouldn't respond to him. Would she show up for the auction later this afternoon, or would he be forced to go on a date with the highest bidder? Even if a nice, sweet girl won him in the auction, he didn't want to be on a date with anyone except Amelia.

Quinton threw off the covers and quickly dressed. He'd forgotten that Emmanuel had something to say and the little guy refused to speak up about it again. Quinton hurried through brushing his teeth and washing his face. When he came out of the bathroom, he told Emmanuel to get ready because once he finished his chores on the ranch and showered they'd leave for the auction. Katy decided it would make the most sense to hold the auction early in the day, so the date could happen this evening since many of the attendees would most likely head back home right after the carnival shut down at five o' clock this evening.

"Have you seen Amelia?" Quinton asked Raddix who was mucking out the stalls early this morning with a smile on his face, which Quinton found odd. He'd never seen Raddix this elated before.

That smile faltered though at the sight of Quinton. Raddix stuck his pitch fork in a brick of hay nearby and got within an inch of Quinton's body. "You need to stay away from Amelia." Raddix's eyes darken. Quinton saw anger that seemed to be directed at him.

"What's your problem?" Quinton didn't budge. He'd thought Raddix supported his relationship with Amelia. Unrest filled Quinton. Something had definitely happened yesterday that turned Amelia away from him. He needed to get to the bottom of this if he had any chance of Amelia bidding on him in the auction, let alone marrying him.

Toe to Toe, Raddix continued to burn a hole through Quinton. "You lied to Amelia, and broke her heart. At Least your son was smart enough to dance with Amelia yesterday."

Quinton's expression softened. "What do you mean? Amelia didn't show up yesterday." Confusion plastered across Quinton's face.

Raddix cackled. "I brought her, I know she showed up." At this point Quinton took a step back. He'd never seen Amelia. What did she see, or think she saw? Raddix worked his way back to the stall that still needed tending, "Hopefully your dances with Selena and her friends were worth it."

"Dang." Quinton mumbled.

Quinton needed to find Amelia right away. He whipped out his phone and texted her.

**Quinton:** RADDIX TOLD ME YOU WERE AT THE CARNIVAL YESTERDAY. IT'S NOT WHAT YOU THINK. I LOVE YOU. PLEASE LET ME EXPLAIN.

Quinton didn't believe she would respond since she hadn't yet, but he could hope.

Emmanuel appeared in the driveway ready to go. Being the last day, he had promised to let the little guy jump in the bounce house all morning and once the auction started, they would figure out the next plan.

Just then, the front door of the main house creaked open; Amelia walked out. As soon as she saw Quinton, she turned back around. Quinton hated himself for hurting her. Obviously Amelia wanted to avoid him. *Not on my watch.* "Amelia, wait!" Quinton's no nonsense tone got her to stop, but it also caused Emmanuel to jump and put his hands over her ears.

Pointing to Emmanuel he soothed his voice. "Go in the house Buddy. Everything's fine, I just needed to get Amelia's attention." Once Emmanuel ran into the house, Quinton closed the gap between him and Amelia. He reached for her hand, but she quickly whipped her arms around her waist.

"Will you please look at me?" Amelia didn't attempt to turn toward him, nor did she respond verbally. He wanted her to yell at him. He deserved it. "It's okay that you don't want to look at me, but please listen to me. I am sorry I hurt you." Quinton raked a hand through his hair. "Emmanuel, the kids and I were dancing with Rocco and Renee. Then a lot of people crowded the dance floor and soon Selena and her friends were surrounding me. Once the first slow song came on, I high tailed it out of there and stayed with Jeff the rest of the night helping him cook."

Quinton didn't say anything hoping Amelia would do something, but she didn't. She stood their stone cold. Her calm breathing barely showed in the up and down movement of her shoulders. "Look, I didn't even go back for Emmanuel. I texted Rocco and asked him to bring Emmanuel to me."

Still nothing. How was he supposed to fix this if she didn't talk to him? "Amelia, please talk to me. Can't you see this was a misunderstanding?"

Just above a whisper, Amelia sputtered out, "Sure. No worries. Enjoy your time today."

"That's it?"

Amelia took a step toward the door and stopped. "Emmanuel told me you'd let him bounce in the bounce house all day today. I hope you don't let him down. In fact, you should be going."

"What is that supposed to mean?" Quinton barked. "Why would I let my son down?"

Amelia chuckled, "Selena is a master manipulator she can get men to do anything she wants. It's not her fault though, it's the man's fault for falling for it. It would break my heart even more to see Emmanuel get hurt."

Taking quick steps toward the door, Amelia tried to escape. Quinton's quick step beat her. He planted his feet in front of her and stared longing at her. His heart ached seeing the hurt in her red lined, puffy eyes. "I love you, please forgive me for hurting you. I seem to recall a beautiful woman telling me that everyone on the ranch loves one another so much that they forgive and start over. Apparently that doesn't apply to me."

"You're forgiven, may I pass now, please?" Amelia didn't even attempt to look at him. Her steady, unaffectionate tone ripped at Quinton's gut.

Quinton tipped her chin up forcing her eyes to meet his. "I know Selena is a manipulator and I am not affected by her, or any of those other women—"

"—I might believe that if I hadn't danced with Emmanuel within five feet of you and you didn't even notice my presence. Sorry if I don't believe that you weren't affected by multiple women; beautiful women surrounding you, rubbing their hands up and down your arms and who knows what else."

"Amelia." Emmanuel's little voice grabbed her attention. She spun toward him and crouched down directly in front of him.

Quinton knew that she didn't think too highly of *him*, but the smile on her face for Emmanuel was priceless. "Yes, Sweetie."

Holding tight to his little Mario stuffed animal, Emmanuel sweet voice shook gently. "Please forgive my daddy and come with us today. The plan for tonight won't work without you."

Amelia jerked her head toward Quinton and then back to Emmanuel. He hoped she hadn't see him moving his hand rapidly left to right inches from his throat trying to get his son to stop talking before he spoiled the plan.

"What's that mean Dad?" Emmanuel mimicked his Dad's hand motion. So much for that. Amelia certainly saw it now. He could only see the back of Amelia's head, but he imagined the full beam on her face as she studied Emmanuel's. The cute little face grimaced he made as he lifted his shoulders up was charming. Quinton knew that Amelia couldn't resist that face.

"It means, stop talking and don't reveal our plan." Quinton smiled at his son, so Emmanuel didn't think he was upset with him. Quinton shrugged his shoulders. "It's okay, Buddy."

Amelia reached for Emmanuel's hand. "I have to get some chores done. Then I'll see you at the carnival in a little while.

"You're still going to buy my daddy right?" Emmanuel leaned forward and cupped his hand over one side of his mouth like he was going to whisper, yet he didn't know how to talk quietly. "Please don't let any of those people from yesterday buy him, they didn't like me."

Amelia instantly pulled Emmanuel toward her and hugged him. She felt bad that she hadn't asked him first. Fortunately, Emmanuel didn't get upset. He did back up pretty quickly though. "Anyone who doesn't like you is not human and anyone who would subject you to that needs their head checked."

*Ouch*. Quinton knew that Amelia definitely intended that slam to hit him hard. It did. He'd let it slide knowing that he hurt her deeply.

"You are the best little guy I know and I like you more than all those girls put together." Amelia stood. She braved a glance at Quinton. "I'm going to work. I'll see you later."

Quinton couldn't drop this issue. He told Emmanuel to wait for him in the truck, so he could talk to Amelia.

"Please wait." Quinton jogged toward her and when she didn't turn around he stepped in front of her. "Em. Those women mean nothing to me. I ran to Jeff to get away from them. Please believe me." He reached for her hands and this time she didn't pull away. "I am fully committed to you; so is Emmanuel."

Amelia pulled Quinton to her and kissed him on the cheek before she whispered, "Q, I hear you, but your actions didn't show love for me. It showed the opposite. You already knew how difficult it is for me to trust men in this type of situation, so, yeah, I'm hurt. Let me be, right now."

"I wasn't thinking like that."

"Clearly." Amelia took her hands back and wrapped them around her midsection.

Quinton raked his hand through his hair. "What I mean is that I was wondering where you were, so you and I could dance."

"Funny, that's what I thought about all day too, yet it never happened. I had the perfect song ready for later in the evening. I planned it perfectly in my head. I'd be pressed tightly against your chest, dancing with my head resting on your shoulder and when the song ended, I'd whisper, 'I love you' in your ear and we could have a replay of Friday night watching the stars light up the sky while you held me." Amelia tsked, "Looks like I'm just a fool for thinking that." Amelia sidestepped Quinton avoiding any contact. "Please get Emmanuel to the carnival. I'll see you later."

Quinton didn't go after her this time knowing that Emmanuel's patience was most likely faltering. "I love you too, Amelia. We'll get through this. I only want you!"

Hearing Amelia say she loved him made his heart skip a beat. He knew they could get past this. He would ask her to marry him tonight and show her that she is the only woman for him. He and Emmanuel would make up a new plan on the way to the carnival.

# Chapter 36

**Amelia**

Pride filled Amelia. She'd told Quinton that she loved him, passively, but she'd still told him. Keeping it to herself hadn't stopped the barrage of pain she'd felt since seeing those women surrounding him, so she'd figured he should know. As she walked to the barn lost in her thoughts, she tripped over nothing. She screamed as she met the ground with a thud. Her hands and knees were scraped and blood started to seep out of different parts of the scrapes. It stung. Whenever she had scraped a layer or two of skin, it had always stung worse than a gash.

Raddix came rushing out of the barn, but Amelia was already wiping the dirt off her clothes and knees. "Are you okay?"

"Sure am. I don't even know what I tripped on." Amelia looked on the ground hoping something would pop out at her, but it became evident that she'd tripped over her own feet. "Let's get these chores done, so we can leave. Are you meeting your girl from yesterday?"

Raddix's smile reached his ears. "Yes, Lily is going to be there for the auction." He returned to mucking out the final stall.

"Is she going to bid on you?" Amelia felt excited and happy for him. It reminded her that she had a choice to be happy with Quinton, if she could trust him and move on. Could she do that?

"If I'm lucky." Raddix grinned.

"True that."

Raddix's lips pierced, "No, I asked her to and she said, 'If you're lucky.'" He pinched the front of his shirt and pulled it slightly out away from his body. "I'm lucky, right?"

"You might have met your match—a girl who likes to flirt. If you treat her like she's the only woman in the world for you, you'll be lucky." Amelia's voice trailed off, her eyes glazing over.

Raddix didn't waste any time. He hugged Amelia so fiercely that her feet left the ground. "If it's any consolation, I believe Quinton loves you and thinks you're the only woman in the world."

One comment from Raddix and the floodgates burst opened again. Amelia didn't think she had any tears left to cry. She'd successfully fought hard to keep tears from falling when Quinton's dreamy eyes had looked into hers. She didn't mind soaking Raddix's shirt because she knew he would shower and change before meeting his new lady.

"I've always told you, us men do things to upset women all the time because we don't think like women." Raddix just let her cry.

She let that sink in for a moment. Perhaps Quinton really did love Amelia. He'd told her that he'd retreated to Jeff in order to avoid those women. Surely, Amelia didn't have any reason not to believe him. She should truly accept his apology and move on. Isn't that what love does? Love keeps no record of wrong. Amelia loved First Corinthians chapter 13—the love chapter. It was time for her to follow God's advice. He's going to make more mistakes, and if she loved him, shouldn't she forgive him? She imagined that Quinton would forgive her for her mistakes, couldn't she do the same for him?

"Looks like you're finished here?" Amelia's smile reached her ears. Her watch told her that they only had two hours until the auction started. "Let's go tell Bill we're done and get ready."

Amelia loved Quinton with all her heart. She did believe his side of the story. It was about time she stopped being so insecure and trust him. This must have been what her counselor was talking about—knowing when she'd had enough of her lack of self-confidence. Her pain had led her to act immature; hopefully Quinton would understand and they could move on.

# Chapter 37

**Amelia**

Within thirty minutes, she and Raddix were on their way to the auction. Katy had texted her as soon as they'd gotten in Raddix's truck.

**KATY:** WHERE ARE YOU AND RADDIX? THE AUCTION IS GOING TO BEGIN IN TWENTY-FIVE MINUTES.

Amelia felt bad for making Katy stress out.

**AMELIA:** BE THERE IN TWENTY, SORRY.

Amelia hoped the heart emoji would remind Katy how much she loved Amelia, and wouldn't be too upset with her that they were cutting it really close.

**KATY:** I'VE LEFT RADDIX AND QUINTON FOR THE END, SO IT SHOULD ALL WORK OUT FINE.

"The end?" Raddix did not like that message. He expressed concern with being at the end, which were all reasons Amelia didn't understand. If his new woman couldn't wait to bid on him then she clearly wasn't the right woman for him. He claimed that rushing in five minutes before the auction started would not give him enough time to settle himself down. Amelia convinced him that waiting was the better option.

True to her word, Raddix got them there with five minutes to spare. Knowing that the entire town wanted to view the first ever bachelor auction, the committee set the makeshift stage near the rides. Everyone who wanted to see the event could. Also, one of the parishioners wired the majority of the field with speakers, so people could at least hear the proceedings.

Amelia saw Katy, Jeff, and Emmanuel near the front of the stage. When she approached them, Katy whisked Raddix to the back where the other eleven men waited. Amelia searched for Quinton, but couldn't find him. "Where's your daddy, Emmanuel?"

The little guy shrugged his shoulders and gave Jeff a funny look. His silence let Amelia know that she was out of the loop about something, but she didn't push him.

"Hey, shame on you Amelia." Jeff playfully scolded her. "Don't you dare put Emmanuel in that position." Jeff gave Emmanuel a fist bump and a nod showing that he did well keeping the secret quiet.

Utterly confused, Amelia shook her head. Moments later, she could smell Quinton before she saw him. His chest pressed up against her back, heat fluttering through her core. He extended his arm around her shoulders, as he presented a bunch of hand picked daisies to her. She let herself close her eyes and get lost in the fresh smell of both her favorite fauna and her favorite man.

When Amelia opened her eyes, she knew what she had to do. Turning into Quinton's chest, her voice strong, but quiet. "Q, I'm so sorry—"

"You? For what?"

"I should have forgiven you more easily because I do love you." Amelia loved the smile on Quinton's face. "My insecurity came through and I avoided you because I was hurt." He tried to interrupt her again, but instead, she placed a finger on his lips and continued talking. "I believe everything happened the way you said."

Wrapping his hand around hers, he moved it away from his lips. "Can I talk now?" His smile warmed Amelia's heart. She nodded. "I will make more mistakes, unintentionally of course. I just need to know that you'll be right by my side to kiss and make up." Quinton pumped his eyebrows. "I'll do everything in my power to make you the happiest woman in the world."

Before Amelia could respond, Katy shooed Quinton away to wait with Raddix and the other bachelors. "Let's go. The auction is starting. Go find your seat, Amelia."

"I need a bidding paddle." Amelia looked around as if one would magically appear in her sight.

Amelia spied Selena approaching out of the corner of her eye. "Aw, that's too bad that all the paddles are gone. Looks like I will get the man again. I kind of feel bad for you this time. You really seemed into Quinton. Too bad he'll be on a date with me this evening and as you know, I always get what I want. At this moment, he looks like a fun project."

Selena walked off and Amelia let her go. Amelia asked for forgiveness when her mind instantly thought of multiple ways to inflict pain on Selena. *Sorry Lord, I know you love her, but she is the devil.* That quick conversation with God made Amelia think about the devil fleeing in Jesus' name.

"Hey, Selena," Amelia yelled. The woman had only gotten three steps. What could she expect when she wore a tight, black, leather, mini skirt and three inch heels to a field? "I just want you to know that Jesus loves you despite everything you do and say." Selena blew out a snarky breath, rolled her eyes, and continued to make her way back to her table with the women Amelia recognized from last night.

"You don't need a paddle...trust me." Katy gave her an assured smile. In fact, Katy's smile held excitement and secrecy. *Why wouldn't I need a paddle?*

By the time Amelia reached Jeff and Emmanuel, two of the bachelors from church had already been auctioned off. One had brought in two hundred dollars. A woman from out-of-town had paid three hundred dollars for a date with the other bachelor. Amelia hoped those prices continued. The church would be able to spread so much love with the success from this three day event.

There were a lot of women bidding on these men. Most of them were from out of town, so they didn't know these men at all. Amelia noticed one of the women sitting with Selena attempted to vote for the next bachelor, but Selena ripped her paddle away from her. Something seemed off to Amelia. She wondered what trick Selena had up her sleeve. *Lord, please let Katy be right that I don't need a paddle."*

The next five bachelors auctioned off quickly. The highest bid out of those five men went to Phil, a young man who'd moved into town last year. Amelia spoke with him a couple of times at church and appreciated his love and knowledge for the Lord. Emely, another newcomer—she'd been coming to the church for about eight months—purchased him for five hundred dollars. Amelia hoped the date would blossom into something more for them.

"He looks petrified." Jeff laughed as he pointed toward Sean standing front and center, looking at the sea of women who would bid on him. Over the years, Sean had turned down numerous women in the area. He'd never desired to be with a woman since his wife died thirty years ago. The bidding started at fifty dollars and increased by increments of fifty. Within seconds, Sean's bid reached four hundred dollars and continued to rise. Shortly after the bidding ceased, Sean had left the stage, promised to Violet Kenny, the lady who owned the flower shop in town. She had always asked about Sean whenever anyone from the ranch saw her out and about.

Damon took his place on stage. The emcee for the event, another volunteer parishioner, made Damon flex his muscles for the ladies to ramp up the bidding. Damon begrudgingly did as asked and all the women screamed. Damon's kids didn't care for their dad being up there, but they knew it was for a good cause.

"You know there's a bet going for who gets the highest bid, right?" Jeff asked Amelia.

Laughter jutted from her gut. "Who's expected to win?" Amelia's cheeks hurt from laughing.

"Raddix. They have him as the overall winner, but they have a side bet too." Jeff didn't share that information with her because the bidding began and spread faster than a wildfire in California.

"Eight hundred dollars. Do I hear eight fifty? Eight hundred going once, twice, sold to number twenty-seven." The emcee smiled at Damon thanking him for participating.

"Wow, that will be hard to beat. I can see a brawl at the ranch tomorrow morning." Jeff crossed his arms over his chest, but his grin spoke volumes about how much he was enjoying this.

Amelia spotted Lily and quickly approached her before the bidding began again. "Hi, Lily?" The girl perked up. "I'm Amelia, Raddix's cousin."

"He told me so much about you. It's nice to meet you." Lily's angelic face made Amelia smile. Her white flowy summer dress revealed a fun, carefree person. She needed to help Lily win Raddix, especially since a woman at Selena's table proclaimed how much she wanted a date with him. Selena told the woman not to waste her time.

Amelia ushered Lily over to the table she shared with Jeff and Emmanuel. "The table of women behind you are all vultures, so stay over here with us."

"Thanks. I'm new in town. I just rented the apartment above Violet's flower shop." Lily explained.

Amelia made introductions. Both Jeff and Emmanuel were perfect gentlemen introducing themselves and welcoming her to town. As Raddix took the stage, Amelia explained that Lily and Raddix met yesterday. A twinkle in Jeff's eye let Amelia know that she didn't need to say anything else.

Lily bid on Raddix right out of the gate. In addition to one of Selena's cronies, Lily had four other competitors bidding against her. Amelia noticed the Cheshire Cat grin on Raddix's face. She predicted he had multiple reasons for that grin. He hoped to win the bet going on with the men at the ranch for the highest bid, though beating Damon's would be a challenge. It must have felt good that so many women wanted to go on a date with him.

The blonde with Selena stood in the aisle and declared her intention of winning Raddix. "Twenty-five hundred dollars." Everyone in the audience gasped, especially Selena.

She heard Selena loudly berate the woman as she tried to pull her back to the table. "That's not part of the plan." She successfully dragged the girl back to her seat.

Lily looked defeated. "I can't beat that."

"I'll cover the rest for you, go for three thousand.

Lily quickly followed Amelia's instruction. Just to see the smile on Raddix's face when Lily bid on him was worth every penny for Amelia.

"Three thousand going once, going twice, sold to number thirty-eight." From the stage, Raddix blew a kiss to Lily and mouthed *Thank you* to Amelia.

Lily took Amelia's hand. "Thank you so much. I'll pay you back in a couple of weeks." Amelia wasn't worried about the money. She just wanted to see Raddix happy. Based on what she'd just learned about Lily, she thought they would be a great couple. Lily, a licensed social worker, had just received her Masters in Psychology before moving here. She already had an established list of clients, whom she mostly saw online. She had seen people in her office before she moved to Montana, and would continue to see people in person if anyone nearby requested that. Right now being available online helped her expand her business counseling people all across the country.

Amelia's hands started to sweat as Quinton took the stage. Selena glared at Amelia as if she were daring Amelia to bid on Quinton.

"If looks could kill..." Jeff let his sentence die.

"She's trash." Emmanuel said matter of factly, eliciting shock and bursts of laughter from the adults at the table.

Selena stood in the middle aisle getting the emcee to silence everyone. "I'll make this easy on everyone, so we can get on with our dates. I'm bidding ten thousand dollars."

Amelia spied Katy at the corner of the stage. She smiled back at Amelia and mouthed, "It's okay." The entire crowd hushed. Quinton walked to the emcee and took the microphone. He put up a hand to settle the crowd down.

"I'm very sorry for this last minute change, but I don't think I'm qualified to be in this auction." Amelia saw Raddix and Sean join Katy on stage and

Jeff was grinning from ear to ear. "Emmanuel, could you come up here please?"

Emmanuel shook his head and ducked it into Amelia's arm. "I'm scared."

"Amelia, you will walk Emmanuel up here?" Quinton asked into the microphone. She'd do anything for her favorite little boy. When Emmanuel looked at her with asking eyes, Amelia grabbed his hand and led him to the stage.

Quinton met Emmanuel and Amelia in front of the stage. "Thanks, Buddy." He held the microphone in front of Emmanuel's mouth, but he didn't say anything and the silence became a little awkward. "You got this."

"Amelia, will you be my mom?" He handed her a fresh bouquet of flowers that Katy just placed in his hands. She loved the little guy and would love to be his mom. That would mean that Quinton and her would need to be married.

Instantly, Quinton dropped to one knee and held out an open red velvet box with a stone larger than she would have picked for herself, but the sparkle in the diamond made her smile. He knew her so well. The diamond set flush with the band "I love you so much Em. I'll never be perfect, but I'll love you perfectly. Would you do me the honor of being my wife?"

Amelia smiled at Emmanuel and responded, "I'd love to be your mom. Please have patience with me. I will do everything to love and protect you." She bent down and asked him for a hug. He gave her a side hug, which she knew was hard for him, and that softened her heart.

Then, Amelia focused her attention on Quinton. She grabbed his hand and gently tugged, forcing him to stand. She wrapped her arms around his neck and pulled him toward her. With her lips inches from his, adrenaline burst through her body. She couldn't believe he loved her enough to marry her. "I love you so much. Thank you for loving me and for fighting for me." Amelia gently brushed her lips against Quinton's.

"I'll always fight for you." He gave her another firm kiss. "As much as I love your kisses and love hearing you tell me that you love me, you never answered my question." Quinton firmly pressed his lips against Amelia's.

"Yes!" Amelia pecked his lips. "Of course—" another peck. "I'll—" a third peck. "Marry you!" Amelia melted in his Quinton's arms. The crowd erupted in cheers, hoots and hollers. The couple wrapped Emmanuel up in their arms.

"No, wait." Selena stormed the stage. He can't just drop out of the auction. I came to bid on a date with Quinton. I'm supposed to be going on a date with him right now."

Quinton smiled. "That's not going to happen. Since I'm not a bachelor, I am not able to participate. The only person I want to date is Amelia."

Selena stomped away like a teenager having a temper tantrum. She gathered up the ladies at her table and they all stormed off. Good riddance! Amelia felt bad for her nemesis, but knowing that Quinton chose her over any of the pretty, made up, blondes at that table boosted her confidence.

Katy walked toward Quinton and captured the microphone. "Thank you so much for attending our first bachelor auction. We hope you enjoyed yourself. If you won the bid for any of these handsome bachelors, please come see me and we can get you on your way.

Quinton lifted Emmanuel with his left arm while he snuggled Amelia with his right. They strolled back toward the table. Amelia replayed the proposal through her head, but still couldn't grasp the idea that she and Quinton, the most handsome man in the world, were one step closer to getting married.

Lily and Jeff met the trio in the middle. Amelia left the warm embrace of Quinton's arms to quickly hug them. The longing became too much to bear, so Amelia snuggled back up with Quinton. "Have fun with Raddix, Lily."

"Thank you so much. This wouldn't be happening without your help." Lily's bright smile revealed her interest in getting to know Raddix. That was all the payment Amelia would need. Lily briskly move toward the stage. Amelia noticed that the beautiful girl had a little skip in her step. Her feet just wouldn't move fast enough to get to Raddix.

Amelia giggled, pulling Quinton's attention away from Jeff who had shaken his hand and given him a man hug and a slap on the back to congratulate him.

"What's up beautiful lady?" Quinton asked, as he wrapped his arms around Amelia.

Amelia blushed. "I just wanted to be in your arms." She prayed Quinton never got complacent. Amelia loved the way he spoke to her, making her feel like a true princess.

# Epilogue

"**I** don't want a long engagement." Amelia snuggled into the crook of Quinton's arm, as they sat on his couch after Emmanuel fell asleep.

"Me either. Let's elope." They were both committed to each other. Quinton wanted to reap all the benefits of married life as soon as possible.

"Nah. Katy and I already got my dress." They'd found an elegant evening gown at the boutique in town. Amelia couldn't see spending hundreds or thousands of dollars for a wedding dress that she'd wear for maybe thirty minutes. At least with the evening gown, it could be used for formal outings, if she and Quinton ever desired to attend such events. As far as flowers, she didn't want to spend money on those either since the property had the most exquisite flowers. She'd have the kids cut her fresh flowers the morning of the wedding.

"Well, let's get married this weekend then." Quinton let Amelia plan any-thing she wanted, as long as he could be by her side every step of the way.

"It's only been three weeks since you proposed." Amelia turned into Quin-ton's side even more and rested her hand on his upper abs.

"I guess it's a good thing I already asked Carolyn and Cash if they'd have the food ready for Saturday."

"Really? What about your sister, is she able to make it? I've never even met her." Quinton pulled Amelia onto his lap and let his lips descend on hers. Not in a rushed, I can't wait to marry you for the benefits type of way, but loving. Quinton pinned her lips slowly and firmly, like he was trying to memorize everything about them. Hot currents ran through Amelia's body, settling in her chest where her heart turned into a pool of emotion. Heaven had shown her that she was worthy of being loved. *Thank you, Lord, for sending me Quinton. It took long enough, but everything in your time, I know.*

"She can't make it, but I'm not waiting for her. We got her blessing." Quinton stated matter of factly.

"Ok. Let's get married this weekend." Amelia squealed.

The sun sparkled down on the ranch Saturday afternoon. Quinton and Emmanuel both had on midnight blue jeans, white button down shirts and light blue suit jackets. Jeff agreed to officiate the wedding. Raddix helped him get his license online. It meant a lot to Amelia and Quinton to have Jeff marry them. Jeff had been there for Amelia even before either of her parents had died, but the way he'd helped her dad stay sane after losing Amelia's mom, she would be forever grateful. Then, once her dad had died, Jeff stepped right into the fatherly role for Amelia.

The couple said their vows on the back of the property by the river. Afterward they celebrated with their ranch family, swimming, dancing, and eating quite the spread that Carolyn and Cash prepared. As the newlyweds danced to *God Gave me You*—the Dave Barnes version, Quinton snuggled close to her neck and whispered, "I finally got my dance."

"Best dance ever," Amelia whispered back before kissing her husband on the cheek. Amelia wrapped her arms around his shoulders, pressing herself closer to his chest. "I love you."

Quinton pulled her back, so he could look into her eyes, "I love you more than I could ever tell you. I am going to live my life to make you happy every day. Well, let's be real, I'll try real hard. You realize this is the first time I've seen you dressed up? You are ravishing."

Katy had tried to keep Emmanuel at bay, but he ran to the couple and wrapped his arms around each of their legs. Quinton never let go of Amelia, but he pulled Emmanuel up with with them. "Are you guys going to leave me with Katy and Jeff, so you can be alone. What would you want to be alone for?"

Quinton smirked at Amelia. "Planning for this day was a lot of exhausting work. The husband and wife have to recoup, take lots of naps."

"Naps. No way. I don't take naps anymore. See ya." Emmanuel wiggled out of Quinton's arm and ran back toward Katy. They heard him reporting,

"Can you believe that those two are going to take a lot of naps when they go off without me?"

Every adult listening to Emmanuel laughed. Staring at the newlyweds dancing, Jeff gave them a thumbs up and winked at them.

"We'll never hear the end of that." Amelia laughed. Not that she cared. Despite her anxiousness about her wedding night, she couldn't wait to take *naps* with her husband. But as she thought about it, Amelia's smile faltered, and let her nerves take over. She prayed so much the last few days that she wouldn't worry. *Thank you God for this wonderful man. Shower me with comfort and calmness, so I can fulfill your will.*

It had taken a couple of days to prepare ranch matters. Then Quinton and Amelia were off on their honeymoon. He came through with his promise to take her to the ocean. Quinton had expected her to pick a tropical island in the Caribbean, or maybe Cancun; perhaps, Cozumel. Nope. Amelia chose California.

After arriving in Santa Barbara, they worked with José from the concierge desk to book the experiences Amelia wanted. They purchased tickets for the following day to attend the Santa Barbara Zoo. José planned for them to rent bikes and travel the Cabrillo Bike Path to Butterfly Beach where they would watch the sunset and bike back.

The day after their bike ride, Quinton brought Amelia to her surprise excursion. "What are we doing here?" Dread filled Amelia's voice.

"I'm cashing in on my bet. I know you aren't a fan of heights, but the best way to get over that is to meet it head on."

Amelia tsked. "Highly unlikely."

Quinton wrapped his arm around her shoulders. "We're going to parasail. I'll hold your hand the whole time." He dragged her gently by the air onto the awaiting boat.

Looking a little green, Amelia let the instructor wrap the strap under her upper thighs. When they were set, the instructor pushed a button on the back of the boat and Quinton and Amelia soared backward. "Aaaahhhhh. Quinton, I might have to hurt you."

"Here give me your hand."

Her white-knuckled fingers had a death-grip on her ropes. "Not going to happen, Cowboy." The bird's eye view wasn't as scary as she thought it would be. In fact, the invaluable view made her smile.

The instructor reeled them in when the flight ended. To make it up to her, Quinton brought Amelia to the first ice cream stand he found.

Quinton definitely planned on taking more vacations with Amelia alone, but also with Emmanuel. He would have loved the beaches. He probably would have loved parasailing too. Amelia found it kind of fun once she got over the initial fear.

Even Amelia admitted that she hadn't realized how stressed she had been trying to operate the ranch until she had an opportunity to have fun offsite. Quinton found out how athletic and competitive his new bride was when they engaged in a pick-up beach volleyball game at the end of Stearns Wharf one afternoon. "You could have played professionally."

"Nah. It's just fun," Amelia blushed.

Afterwards, they strolled around hand-in-hand. "Look at those mountains. They remind me of home, just with a lot more people." Amelia enjoyed the different scenery, but after a week, she was ready to be back at the ranch.

Strangely enough, Amelia was excited to see what married life looked and felt like on a daily basis. Of course they had fun alone, without responsibilities to weigh them down. Amelia hoped she'd be the wife God expected, the one that Quinton deserved, on a daily basis.

For their final dinner, they had originally wanted to find a seafood place—something they couldn't get back home, but then she'd decided she wanted to eat in the room. Amelia realized that she didn't enjoy eating in restaurants. She quickly appreciated the freshness of their food coming right from the ranch to the table. Additionally, she'd been spoiled for so many years by Carolyn and Cash's gourmet cooking that other dining experiences couldn't compare.

"Works for me. We can order room service and stay in." He pumped his eyebrows at Amelia. Quinton wrapped his arms around his wife's waist and pulled her tightly into his chest. "It's been a very long day. I think I'm in need of a *"nap."* Even though the dinner plans benefitted him as much as they did her, Quinton would have done anything to make his new wife happy.

Amelia smiled and reached up on her tiptoes to show her husband that a "*nap*" sounded like a great idea. Quinton's lips met Amelia's and matched her kiss for kiss before he took control. Quinton claimed to have self control, but room service turned into a distant memory once Amelia had kissed him. She wasn't complaining.

Tomorrow they'd be back on the ranch surrounded by a lot of people, so she relished in this alone time with Quinton. They planned to live in the main house, which would free the cabin up if they decided to hire more help for the ranch. When Quinton talked to Emmanuel earlier in the week, he'd seemed excited to move into the main house. That would be the first order of business when they got home.

Amelia knew it wouldn't be easy going from single woman to wife and instant momma, but it was also something she'd never thought she'd have. As she laid on Quinton's chest, her heart burst with joy that this exquisite man chose her. She propped her elbow on the pillows next to his head. Love filled her voice as she gazed into his chocolatey brown eyes, "Thank you for choosing to love me. Mr. Richards, I love you so much."

***Thank you for reading Amelia and Quinton's story. I hope you enjoyed their ups and downs as much as I enjoyed getting them through their troubles. Want to see who's falling in love next at Big L' Ranch? Read the unedited chapter from The Perfect Cowboy.***

# Unedited Chapter 1: The Perfect Cowboy

**Raddix**

Raddix Lawrence stormed through his cabin door. He told Lily he'd pick her up in an hour for their date. Date. Raddix hadn't been on a true date in years. Now, he had a date with the most gorgeous woman he'd ever seen. Long blonde hair, straight as a board that draped over her tan, toned shoulder. Blue eyes with green speckles were the first thing he had noticed last night when they danced at the carnival. Her soft petite fingers fit securely inside his rough, calloused hands. Raddix's heart skipped at the recollection. *What the heck was that? Am I having a heart attack?*

Gel filled hands weaved through Raddix's thick black hair. He left it on the longer side because he hated asking Amelia to cut it. Since he wore a cowboy hat most of the time, length didn't matter. Tonight he thought he'd try something new. Hopefully Lily still liked him without his cowboy hat.

"Howdy. Are you here, Raddix?"

"I'm in the bathroom, Amelia. Come on in. I'll be right out." Raddix hollered from beyond the open door.

"Quinton's with me." Amelia warned her cousin.

Sticking his head out the door, Raddix asked, "What is this a family affair?"

Raddix and Amelia were like brother and sister. They'd grown up together on the ranch since their father's were brothers, who'd lived at Big L' Ranch all their lives. Their great-great grandfather erected the main house in the eighteen hundreds.

Dressed in black jeans and a form-fitted tee shirt, Raddix stepped from the bathroom.

"Whooo-eee!" Amelia whistled. "Lily isn't going to know what hit her."

Adrenaline ran through Raddix. "Don't make me more nervous than I already am."

No doubt Raddix and Lily had chemistry between them. This would be the first of many dates to come ... if he didn't screw it up.

Raddix had only had one serious relationship in his life, lasting about three months. At the end of ninety days, he found out the relationship was a farce. Selena Whittaker, who lived on a ranch a few minutes past the

Lawrence's, had used him to get close to the quarterback on the football team in high school.

Admittedly, Selena destroyed Raddix in high school. She tried to use him again at the carnival to get close to Quinton. Fortunately Raddix didn't fall for it. Neither did Quinton. Instead, Quinton proposed to Amelia, leaving Selena alone, as she should be. Raddix wouldn't wish Selena on his worst enemy.

"Are you really nervous?" Quinton queried.

Raddix wiped the sweat from his brow and flung it to the floor. "I'd say so."

Amelia chuckled. "Don't do that on the date ... for sure it will be your last ... with Lily."

Raddix glared at Quinton then Amelia. "Are you two here to help me or harass me?"

Amelia's face lit up. "I think you and Lily will make a great couple, so I'm here to help. What do you need?"

"I have to pick her up in thirty minutes and I don't even know where we're going." Raddix admitted with a sigh.

Quinton suggested, "Show up with flowers and let her decide."

Raddix smiled like he'd take the idea, not having a better one of his own.

"That won't work. Lily is a psychologist. She'll see you as a weak, or indecisive man who can't make decisions. You don't want that. A woman wants a man who's strong in mind, body and soul."

"That's what she loves about me." Quinton winked at her, as he wrapped an arm around her waist.

Amelia gently elbowed him in the ribs. "This is about Raddix right now." Her smile let him know that she was teasing him.

"You need to eat. Pick a place to eat. Either a restaurant, or be creative and pack a picnic. I'm sure Carolyn could get something whipped together for you, if that's what you decide."

Raddix let that sink in for a moment. "Okay. What do I do after?"

"Do I have to plan the whole thing?" Amelia cried. "Didn't you learn anything about her last night when two were dancing, or did you just stare at her?"

"Stare." Quinton and Raddix said in unison.

"He probably wasn't breathing either." Quinton laughed.

"True story." Raddix wiped his palms on his jeans.

Amelia shooed him back into the bathroom. Go wash your hands. How do you plan on holding Lily's hand if you're sweating like a pig?"

He turned away from his cousin, as he retreated to the bathroom. Staring at himself in the mirror, Raddix gave himself a pep talk. "You are funny, kind, and handsome. Any woman would be happy to go out with you.'

"That's right." Amelia yelled from the living room. "Now get out here and stop worrying. I texted Carolyn. She's preparing a picnic for you. "

"Thank you." It's not that he thought badly of himself. In fact, women in the tri area always sought him out for dates, but he'd always refused.

Whether it was his previously shattered heart or long hours working on the ranch, he wasn't sure, but he'd never wanted to date, until now.

"Okay. It's a picnic and then…" Raddix let the sentence die hoping either Amelia or Quinton would fill in the blank. Most likely it would be Quinton since Amelia didn't have any prior experience dating. Luckily for her, God led Quinton right to her doorstep. Maybe He was doing the same for him by bringing Lily here.

"Is she athletic? Does she like to watch movies… though going to the movies is a bad first date because you don't learn anything about the other person." Amelia waved her hand widely scratching the last idea off the list.

"I've got it. Take her to do the thing you love the most. That way you can see if she's receptive to it, or not." Amelia smiled wide, impressed with her suggestion.

"Maybe you should go out with her, Em. You seem more excited than I do." Raddix joked.

"It's not a bad idea, but it could backfire too," Quinton offered his opinion.

"In what way?" Amelia asked, sincerely.

Quinton moved across the room and draped his arm around his fiancé. "If Lily isn't all that interested in whatever Raddix loves, but she pretends that could be trouble later."

"Lily seems like the kind of woman that will tell you straight out if she likes something or not," Amelia pointed out.

Amelia's phone chimed. She pulled her phone out and swiped up. After reading the text, she reported, "Carolyn's all done with the food." her thumbs flew wildly over her phone. "Thank you, Carolyn. He's on his way." Amelia dictated while she texted.

Raddix released a breath he didn't even know he held in. "Alright, you sure I look good enough?"

"Handsome!" Amelia assured him. "Roll the window down a little on your way to get her, so some of that cologne will wear off." She waved her hands in front of her face.

"You've always liked my cologne," he cried.

"Yup, I like salt on my fries too, but I don't pour the whole shaker on one batch." Amelia's voice, sarcastic.

Raddix didn't dignify her with a response. He knew he splashed on a little too much, but there wasn't anything he could do about it now.

Amelia and Quinton wished him luck and were on their way. Watching them stroll away with their arms wrapped around each other, Raddix realized how much he wanted a good woman by his side. He wished his mom were here to help him with this kind of thing. Man, how he missed her, especially at important crossroads in his life like this one. As he traipsed to his truck, Raddix prayed. *Lord, thank you for this opportunity to go on a date with Lily. Help me to be a gentleman. Don't let me scare her away. Please make her trustworthy. I can't handle another heartache.*

**Do you want to know when Raddix and Lily's love story will be released? Sign up for my newsletter at  and never miss an update.**

# How About a Review?

Your feedback is valuable, so please consider sharing your thoughts. This will help other readers discover this book and my other works.

Thank you from the bottom of my heart for reading and reviewing my book(s).

Amazon

Goodreads

Bookbub

# Acknowledgements

Many hands make light work! Without the love and support of all these people, *The Perfect Kiss* would have only been a dream of mine. My wonderful husband and children encouraged, helped with music for marketing reels, and accepted the fact that I tote my laptop with me everywhere. God blessed me with an amazing family!

Thank you to AstroLab for creating my website where *The Perfect Kiss* was introduced to the public. There, my subscribers provided feedback and insight, for that I am grateful. Additionally, thank you to my IG followers who have supported and encouraged me along the way. Linda, I appreciate our late night messaging about Atticus!

I'm honored to have an amazing ARC team who dedicated themselves to reading this piece and providing honest reviews. Thanks for helping promote this piece.

I'd also like to thank Pete and Deidre Cutter for dedicating their time to pose for the cover. To the amazing Jillian Cutter — thank you for capturing the feel of the book in your photography. One day, I know your name will be among the top photographers worldwide.

Last, but not least, I am grateful for all of you — my readers! Thank you for choosing this story out of the endless options you have. I love writing Christian, contemporary romance books and I hope to provide you with a plethora of stories to read in the near future.

# About the Author

Karen Tucci, a public school teacher by profession, now tutors writing students online and homeschools her two children.

A native of Maine, she has trekked miles of the Pine Tree State and visited countless others. It is through her life experiences that the basis for her romance stories develop. One of her favorite things to say when out adventuring is, "...that is definitely going in my next book!"

Fun fact: Karen had only read and wrote non-fiction growing up. It wasn't until her late twenties that she embraced the joy brought forth by doing both — reading and writing — within the different romance tropes. Now she reads at least fifteen fiction novels a month and writes daily!

## **Connect with Karen:**

Facebook Reader's Group.

To find out about special deals, giveaways, and new releases, join her newsletter:

https://www.trueheartromance.com

Instagram

Goodreads

Bookbub

Amazon